FIRESONG

FIRESONG

A

BRIGHTSTORM
TWINS ADVENTURE

UASHTI HARDY

Illustrated by George Ermos

NORTON YOUNG READERS
*An Imprint of W.W. Norton & Company
Independent Publishers Since 1923*

Copyright © 2022 by Vashti Hardy
Illustration copyright © 2022 by George Ermos
Map illustrations by Jamie Gregory
First American Edition 2022

First published by Scholastic Children's Books.

For information about permission to reproduce selections from this book, write to Permissions, W. W. Norton & Company, Inc., 500 Fifth Avenue, New York, NY 10110

For information about special discounts for bulk purchases, please contact W. W. Norton Special Sales at specialsales@wwnorton.com or 800-233-4830

Manufacturing by Lake Book Manufacturing
Production manager: Beth Steidle

ISBN 978-1-324-03045-4

W. W. Norton & Company, Inc., 500 Fifth Avenue, New York, N.Y. 10110
www.wwnorton.com

W. W. Norton & Company Ltd., 15 Carlisle Street, London W1D 3BS

1 2 3 4 5 6 7 8 9 0

For Kate and Linas

In the huge, wide-open, sleeping eye of the mountain
The bear is the gleam in the pupil
Ready to awake
And instantly focus.

—TED HUGHES,

FROM "THE BEAR"

LONTOWN
VORNATANIA

SKY-SHIP WEST DOCKS

THE GEOGRAPHICAL SOCIETY

THE LONTOWN CHRONICLE

THE SLUMPS

VAGUE STREET

MONTGOLFIERE PARADE

N

W

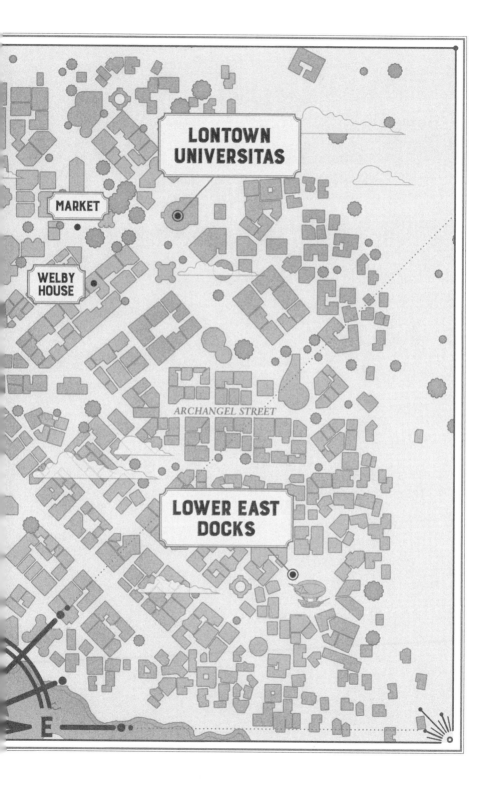

HYRRHOLM

SNAE STROND

JORDAUGA
The Eye of the Wide

THE SKARR ISLANDS

SAELL FJORD
TOFTVICK

THE VOLCANIC NORTH

FELLSANDUR

LIDA

DREKI HYGGR
(THE DRAGON'S BACKBONE)

Aor

THE HAWK ISLES

Northern Marshes

ISLES OF CARRICKMURGUS

VORNATANIA

Lontown

Pitch Mines

Chesterford

Dort

Popplewick

THE GULLDAM SEA

Dueldor

EAST INSULAE

NADVAARYN

Sand Dunes

The Citadel

The Last Post

THE SILENT SEA

The Everlasting Forest

THE ICE CONTINENT

The Great Ice Lake

South Polaris

THE GREAT WIDE

UNKNOWN

Ephemeral Isle

ERYTHEA

Tempestra

THE
DARKWHISPERS

STELLA
OCEANUS

N

W   E

S

UNKNOWN

THE VOLCANIC NORTH

Hyrrholm

Snae Strond

Jordauga –
The Eye of the Wide

THE
SKARR ISLANDS

Saell-Fjord

Toftvik

Fellsandur

Lida

DREKI HYGGR
(THE DRAGON'S BACKBONE)

Aor

N
W · E
S

THE HAWK
ISLES

CHAPTER I

EBBA MEYER

MANY DAYS' WALK from the city of Lontown, out where the busy streets, bustling markets, and dome of the esteemed Geographical Society were a distant glimmer of light, up beyond the thick oak forests, embedded in the nape of the frost-topped mountains, there was an incongruous cluster of gray buildings.

The structures were unlike the majestic curves and towers of the great Vornatanian city in the distance below, and different from the cozy cottages of Bifflewick or Chesterford; they were composed of stern angles, thick, opaque glass, and wide cementa walls, a material the architect had hoped would take off in the Wide. It was practical, cheap to make, and represented the strength of Lontown well. And it would turn a healthy profit.

The underground rooms, and most of the upper layer, were empty at the moment, but in several of the east wing labs, a handful of scientists busied themselves with samples and specimens, working from sunrise to twilight, into dusk, and on into the night. Ebba Meyer didn't want to work there; far too many questions went unanswered and the ethics were problematic, but the pay was good and she had a family to look after. And who was she to stand in the way of progress? Besides, the HAC did make some good points about the threat of misplaced intelligence.

She walked along the row of sapient creatures in their steel cages. The way they watched unnerved her sometimes: there was certainly heightened intelligence there, but sapients couldn't talk, so how could you ever really know what was going on behind their eyes? Ebba's shoulders lifted in a silent chuckle; as if an animal would be able to talk like a human! Of course, those Brightstorm children had said they'd heard wolves talk in their minds . . . But how convenient that only they had been able to hear them. Attention-seeking nobodies, trying to be like the heritage explorer families. Ebba sometimes thought that if she hadn't been a scientist, she would have been an explorer, but it had never been an option: the Meyers were from the west of Vornatania and not from an esteemed family. It wasn't how things were done.

The lab door swung open as a frenetic-looking man hurried into the room. "He's on his way," said Thomas Northwood, who was working the shift in the lab with her that evening.

Ebba glanced at the clock above the cages. "Aren't you supposed to be on your break? And who's on their way?"

"The boss, of course! He's inspecting Lab One already. He flew in from Lontown, not a word of warning."

Ebba beckoned him to help her. "Quick, help me get the sapients their meds; you know he hates it when they stare."

They hurried along the enclosures hastily putting the bowls of specially prepared food through the shutters.

A small terrier whom Ebba liked to call Frank stared at her with big brown eyes. Frank, she knew, was different from the others here; he was normal.

He had been found in a village north of Lontown and had become a local celebrity on account of the fact that he apparently liked to read the newspaper. Ebba suspected he had been mimicking the actions of humans and hadn't actually taken anything in, but when word had gone out to report any animals behaving curiously, for a small bag of sovereigns, news of the stray dog had been passed on to them and Ebba had been sent to retrieve him.

"Here you are, Frank." Ebba patted the dog on the head.

"Don't get attached to them," said Thomas.

"I won't," said Ebba, although she'd wondered if when they would eventually prove that Frank wasn't a sapient, she might be allowed to keep him as a pet.

Frank didn't want to eat the food. It was bitter and made him forgetful and sleepy. He just wanted to go back to the village and catch up with the *Lontown Chronicle* crossword. But it was all they were offered, once a day, and he would starve without it, so he lapped it up quickly so as not to taste it. When he'd finished, he looked at the human with his wide-innocent-eye look, knowing it was his best chance of getting out of this place.

"As if you could read a newspaper with those soppy eyes," Ebba said as though talking to a baby, tickling him under the chin.

Footsteps echoed along the corridor. Swiftly, Ebba straightened her lab coat.

Frank whimpered, then fell asleep.

Back in Lontown, the deep velvet-blue of midnight covered the slumbering city. The moon showed no bias, dusting the crooked, misshapen buildings of the Slumps and the elegant shapes of Uptown with equal beauty. The air was uncommonly still over the continent, and all was quiet.

The inhabitants of number four Archangel Street slept peacefully:

Harriet Culpepper in her office-cum-bedroom, surrounded by neat piles of paper, books, and instruments, her flying goggles on her bedside table.

In the room at the end of the hall, a glint of silver shone from beneath a pillow: the handle of Felicity Wiggety's lucky spoon. She muttered softly in her sleep about a new recipe, curls billowing from her nightcap and her large feet protruding from the end of the bed—her greatest asset, she said, on account of how she was certain they could detect anything from a change in the weather to a bad omen.

Between, in one of the central rooms, Maudie Brightstorm lay beneath a blanket drawn over her like a tent amid a litter of tools and gadgets, one hook of her overalls unclasped from when she'd begun to get ready for bed. But she had been struck with a sudden revelation about designing the valve that would be the answer to a more efficient energy transfer in the sky-ak engine, so she'd fallen asleep slumped over, on top of her notebook, with Valiant the sapient water-bear curled like a furry pillow at her feet, snuffling softly.

In the room next door, Arthur Brightstorm slept on his back beneath the open window. He liked to breathe the cold air of night because it reminded him of days in flight, when the extraordinary house invention that was number four Archangel Street had transformed itself into a sky-ship and they had spent weeks away on an expedition. Waning moonlight glinted off his iron arm on the bedside table to one side, and on the other, his hand lolled toward the floor, where a book by P. Acquafreeda titled *Into the Depths* lay beneath, splayed on the boards.

It had taken a while for everyone to fall back into the rhythm of Lontown life after the expedition to Erythea and the loss of the crew's beloved second-in-command, Welby. But there had been a lot to occupy them all with the conversion of the twins' former family home, Brightstorm House, into a home for orphaned children that they'd renamed Welby House in his honor. With the heavy emotional toll of the past two expeditions, there hadn't been any talk of another trip yet. Yes, it was true that Arthur was itching to take flight once more and be back with his hand at the wheel, feeling the wind in his hair and the promise of new horizons, but he didn't feel it was right to press Harriet on the possibility just yet. Besides, funds would need to be replenished. Above, the pale-feathered hawk Parthena perched sentry on the windowsill, looking out on the Lontown night and keeping watch.

Arthur's dream had him back in Brightstorm House with Maudie. They were young, four or five, and his father and mother were there, which was strange because his mother, Violetta, had died when they were born, so he only knew her from the few photographs he'd seen. His father's russet beard was wild, and he was suntanned and freckled as though he'd been away exploring for a while. Violetta was much like the picture he had of her, with a warm smile and an adventurous glint in her eyes. His parents were singing to them, and it filled Arthur with the kind of warmth that comes from belonging, as though his heart were made of sunshine. The soothing voices melded in harmony so that the depths of his father's earthy tones and his mother's shining, light notes were one in a hypnotic melody:

The beat of the earth is strong, strong,
Forged from the roars of time.
Slow, slow. Thrumming high.

Arthur's eyelids flickered in his sleep.

Parthena flew down from the open window. She nudged Arthur's cheek.

"Parthena?" he asked dreamily, trying to bury himself back in the arms of his dream. He didn't want to leave it; it felt so beguiling. His parents sang on:

It calls, we call, the voices.

Parthena nudged him again.

Rubbing his eyes blearily, Arthur looked at Parthena. "Whatever's the matter with you?" He glanced to the window. "It's the middle of the night." Half asleep, Arthur yawned and pushed himself up to peer outside. He knew something about strange characters sneaking around Lontown at night, so he thought it best to check, in case Parthena was alerting him to something. But all was still and silent.

The beat of the earth is strong, strong.

The echoes of the song drifted through him.

Perhaps she had sensed Arthur's dream of his parents. Parthena was a sapient animal, uncommonly understanding of human language and feelings, even though she couldn't communicate back through speech. Before Ernest Brightstorm's death at South Polaris, Parthena had been the loyal companion and sapient friend to Arthur and Maudie's father; Ernest and Parthena had discovered each other when he was young, on one of his expeditions into the north, and they'd formed a lifelong bond. Now Parthena stayed close to Arthur, although she sometimes chose to be with Maudie, and was even partial to spending time with Harriet's sapient cat, Queenie.

"You still miss him, don't you?" Arthur said, sitting back on his bed and stroking her silken white feathers. Her eyes seemed to say more; he wished he could hear her mind, like he had understood the thought-wolves speaking to him in the far south. His heart felt suddenly constricted, as memories of his parents, then Welby, entered his mind, followed by Tuyok, the leader of the thought-wolves, who was alive but so very far away.

Arthur thought about going next door to wake Maudie. They only recently decided to have their own rooms: Maudie's tools and various inventions overran their old room, and she complained that she would always trip over his piles of books, so they decided it was time. But at moments like this, he missed being able to get her thoughts by calling out in a whisper across the room. The dream had felt so real, almost as though his parents were in his room standing beside him.

But that was impossible.

Arthur drifted back to sleep, and although he willed the dream to return, it didn't.

CHAPTER 2

THE CATALOGUE

WHEN ARTHUR WOKE again, morning was well underway, so he hurried to wash and dress before heading to breakfast. He wanted to tell Maudie about the dream and the song, and how clearly he'd seen their parents, but Harriet and Maudie were already in excited conversation at the table.

"Ah, there you are. The sleepy bunny awakes!" Felicity ruffled his hair as he sat at the table. She poured tea and placed a platter overflowing with delicious-looking pastries before them. "My nephew Bartie went full nocturnal when he was a teenager. It's a time of change and no mistaking."

Felicity was right. He was broader in his shoulders lately, and his trousers seemed suddenly three inches too short. Maudie glanced up from behind a pile of post and grinned. She was taller too, not far off Harriet now.

"What are you two talking about?" asked Arthur.

"We've just had an order for twenty sky-aks for the Lontown postal service. That should keep Welby House secure for a while!"

Harriet pushed a document across the table toward him. "And we've received the patent for the water technology."

For several years, Harriet's sky-ship, the *Aurora*, had been the only clean engine in the continent of Vornatania. The others ran on pitch, a dirty fuel that Lontonians relied on, not only for their explorer and trade sky-ships, which left gray trails in the air behind them, but also for pitch lamps for the streets and homes at night. Harriet said that supplies of pitch had mostly been exhausted in Vornatania and mines now extended to the east and north of the continent, but it wasn't something the pitch companies liked to publicize because the islands of the north and east were independent and the mining was controversial.

Arthur glanced at the patent. It was assigned "To the people of Lontown." "You've given the water engine technology to the people?" He was always impressed by Harriet's tendency to go against the flow of what was expected in Lontown. Many were driven by heritage and wealth, protecting their hoards like honeybees, but Harriet always took a wider view.

She nodded. "It's a small way to try to address the imbalances within the city, and a first step to proving to the Erytheans that Lontonians aren't all about exploitation, and that we can all learn from each other."

Although the rest of Lontown was still unaware of the existence of another continent far to the east, there were Erythean agents living all over the Wide, keeping tabs on the rest of the world. Harriet herself had discovered her own Erythean heritage on the last expedition, and if they were to get to a stage of trust with the continents opening up to each other, Harriet was surely the person to set the wheels in motion. Nevertheless, it was a huge sacrifice to give her invention away for free. Arthur knew from the numerous offer letters that Harriet burned in Felicity's stove before she'd even finished reading them that the technology could have made her many thousands of sovereigns, no doubt.

But Harriet, being Harriet, simply took back the water engine patent of the people from Arthur and flashed him a confident grin and nod of certainty. Placing the document to the side, Harriet opened another large envelope. Inside was a black booklet tied with gold ribbon stating: *Dunstable's Fine Art and Luxury Antiques*. "Curious they should send me this. I don't believe I ever asked for a catalogue."

Felicity poured Arthur a tea, then paused and wiggled her toes. "I've a sudden strange fizzling. Something is afoot, I'm certain of it."

"There's an accompanying letter."

Not able to decide between Felicity's special merry-berry pastry and her Erythean-inspired water-wing biscuits, Arthur grabbed both and alternated bites.

"Arty, stop being such a hog!" Maudie admonished, adding another pastry to her own plate.

Arthur noticed that Harriet's eyebrows rose as she read the catalogue.

Maudie followed his gaze. "What is it?"

"It appears a rather significant auction is to take place."

Arthur yawned. "Auctions of old paintings sound a little . . ."

"Boring," Maudie finished.

Arthur thought back to how they'd once visited the Geographical Society gallery hoping to see paintings depicting different parts of the Wide, but instead it had been filled with stuffy portraits of members of the most esteemed explorer families dressed in their finery.

Felicity chuckled. "Now, you two, there are merits in the arts. It's not all stuffy portraits and sculptures of the likes of Blarthingtons, Hilburys, and, sorry for saying, the Vanes!"

The twins had discovered they were related to the infamous Vanes on their first expedition with Harriet to South Polaris. It wasn't welcome news: Eudora Vane, their aunt, had sabotaged their father's expedition to South Polaris, from which he never returned.

Harriet frowned. "It's not going to be just any auction. It's a sale of rare explorer artifacts. It appears they've been gathering notable objects for a while and are billing this as 'the auction of a lifetime.'" Harriet looked between the twins.

Curiosity ignited within Arthur. "Explorer artifacts? What sort?"

"All kinds. The index lists over one hundred lots. They must have had a big campaign to solicit the objects while we were away."

Scooting his chair closer to Harriet, Arthur peered at the brochure as she flicked through: Isadore Aldermyster's two-hundred-year-old water flask; Hector Hilbury's left hiking boot from when he reached the highest peak in Vornatania (the other was said to be buried at the bottom of a ravine when he almost fell to his death, but he miraculously made it back with one boot); Early Bafflewiffle's four-hundred-year-old diamond-encrusted compass; the Nithercott original celestial clockwork globe.

"The Nithercotts must be on hard times if they've put that forward; I thought it was held in their family vault." Harriet frowned. "There are certainly pieces of historical significance and sentimentality here . . ." She frowned in thought. "I can't help but think they would be best placed at the Geographical Society Museum, where everybody could enjoy them, rather than going to the highest bidder and being stashed in someone's private cabinets."

But that wasn't how much of Lontown operated these days. Centuries ago, Lontown had been a trading hub made up of many smaller towns at the center of the continent, a place where people from villages across the land, and the smaller surrounding islands, converged to exchange goods. Arthur remembered reading in one of Welby's books that the name "Lontown" had come from an old word for "pool" because it was a place where people of all backgrounds came together. When pitch was discovered and sky-ships were invented, the First Age of Exploration was born, and the families who were first to discover riches in faraway lands, such as the Vanes, thrived in the new way. The rest found themselves drifting in the wake of those hungry for power and esteem. There were some, like Harriet Culpepper and Ernest Brightstorm (as a new-blood explorer), who strove to redress the balance and share their discoveries more equally. But despite these efforts, Lontown had become divided, and the most prominent families ruled everything.

"Is that the famous Fontaine helmet? The one that saved Fortune Fontaine from the Rockfall of Dort?" asked Arthur, leaning close and squinting to make out the details of the image.

"That's how she got her name," said Felicity. "She was buried under one of the worst landslides in history and somehow survived! I've always wondered if my lucky spoon might be made of the same material," she added with a giggle.

Harriet smiled and flicked over to another page.

"Look!" Maudie jabbed a finger at the paper. A wooden box was featured, with an aged grain and rusty hinges. The lid was decorated with a huge ornamental moth, its black wings emblazoned with a jagged red pattern. "It's Mum's box!"

✳   ✳   ✳

On the day of the Dunstable auction, at ten chimes, Harriet and the twins left home and stepped into the sunny streets of Lontown with one mission on their mind: to win the bid for the Brightstorm box. Arthur and Maudie hadn't seen the box since it had been taken from them what felt like ages ago. Brightstorm House and all their possessions had been sold off after their father's false conviction for breaking the Explorer's Code. They didn't get any of those objects back after the conviction was overturned, and even though they had very few things of their mother's, they agreed with Harriet's view that explorer artifacts would be best placed in a museum, somewhere everyone could view them and learn from them—famous families and Welby House children alike. And somewhere that they knew would be safe, and that they could visit whenever they wanted.

The estimated guide price for their mother's box was high, but just within reach. Maudie had managed to secure several more orders for her sky-ak in order to raise additional funds. Arthur had worked every day with Felicity making marsh cakes that she sold in the market, and Harriet put forward every spare sovereign she could afford.

The catalogue didn't give much information about where the box had been all this time, but after some research Harriet discovered that when Arthur and Maudie lost Brightstorm House, the box had been bought by Merril Linwood, a small antiques dealer from the south of the city, for a mere sovereign. The dealer had left it in a storage cupboard at the back of his shop, where it had been lying, forgotten, until the Brightstorm name began to enjoy a resurgence after the announcement that Ernest Brightstorm had actually been the first explorer to reach South Polaris. Then the name had become even more renowned after the twins helped rescue the Vane crew on their recent expedition to the east. Seeing an opportunity to maximize his profit, Linwood had offered the box for inclusion in the auction.

Dunstable's Auction House was located at the far northern end of Uptown along Montgolfiere Parade, a high-class shopping area named after an early sky-ship designer and one of the longest and straightest main arteries of Lontown. The area was busy with polished black carts, well-to-do Uptowners strolling in their finest hats, or sipping tea from bone-china cups in the likes of the Copper Kettle Tearooms.

"It doesn't seem right that we're having to buy something back that should be ours by right in the first place," grumbled Arthur.

"I remember the box being on the cabinet in the living room of Brightstorm House, but I can't remember ever looking in it," said Maudie.

"Me neither. Perhaps it includes things Mum collected when she was exploring? Or maybe her favorite sweets or something?"

Harriet laughed. "I can't imagine they'd taste too good after all this time!" she said. "Hold on, I just need to pick up Felicity's new boots from Lakeman's. We've still got a chime before the auction starts, so there's plenty of time to see all the artifacts before it begins."

Lakeman's was the most expensive shoemaker in Lontown, but their footwear was made beautifully to measure and Felicity swore by their shoes' comfort. Arthur and Maudie waited outside while Harriet went into the shop, and they gazed at the neat lines of colorful, fancy laced boots in the window. A brown sign hung above, which stated: Lakeman's—Expert Cordwainers of Lontown.

Arthur hummed softly to himself as they waited,

then realized he was humming the tune from the dream he had been having nearly every night. It gave him an idea: "Maybe Mum's box is a music box?"

Maudie tilted her head to one side. "Perhaps, but there didn't seem to be a wind-up mechanism in the brochure picture. Why do you think that?"

"Do you remember a song Dad used to sing to us when we were little?"

"Dad sang a lot. Which one do you mean?"

"I don't remember a name for it, but I keep dreaming the same song."

"Really?"

"The beat of the earth one." He hummed a few bars more loudly.

"That's strange. I dreamed about that the other day!"

"Did you? . . . Maybe . . ." Arthur shook his head.

"What?"

"I was going to say, maybe it's a sign. That the box is coming home."

"You don't really believe in signs, do you?" Maudie asked, shaking her head. She tended to be more practical than Arthur, looking for answers using logic. "Signs aren't exactly scientific."

"Well, no, but it is strange. Perhaps it's just a twin thing. We've dreamed similar things before."

"Again, not exactly scientific. Maybe you were humming the tune, and I picked up on it and dreamed about it too?"

"But it was so real, almost as though they were in the room singing it."

"They?"

"Mum was there too. I think it means that she wants us to have the box."

Maudie frowned disbelievingly, but he knew she was considering it by the way her eyes gazed up for a moment.

Harriet returned with a chic, black-and-white-striped bag tied with a fuchsia ribbon. "Come on, we're almost there."

Situated between Clarence Valentine Fine Perfumiers and the esteemed Theodosia Brown and Daughters Law Firm was Dunstable's Auction House. It was red-bricked with pointed-arch windows and had complete symmetry in its lines. A black flag with "Dunstable's" written in gold script mirrored the writing on the building's facade. The pillared doorway was framed by two tall, plush ferns in huge gold pots.

Inside, the entrance to Dunstable's had dark wood flooring and picture windows framed with golden curtains. Its scarlet walls were sumptuously decorated with tapestries of Vornatanian landscapes. The group made their way into the main auction hall, which was decorated in the same style but filled with gilded chairs facing a large wooden plinth. The hall was already busy with prospective collectors humming around glass cases that lined the edges of the vast room and looked to be filled with the artifacts to be sold.

"I thought we'd be among the first to arrive," said Arthur, feeling his heart sink at the sight of so many interested people.

"Let's find the box," Maudie said, heading toward the nearest cabinets.

"You go; I'll secure our seats," Harriet said, and she placed her jacket over one of the back-row seats.

"Shouldn't we go near the front?" Arthur wanted to ensure their bid for the box would be seen.

"We're better placed to see who's bidding on all the objects from here. We'll want a full view, in case there are others interested."

"Do you think there will be?"

She put a hand on his shoulder. "Stop fretting. All will be well."

"Arty!" Maudie called out, beckoning him from across the room. "Quick, here it is!"

CHAPTER 3

THE AUCTION

T HE COLORING OF the box's wood was a rich walnut, lighter on the edges where the varnish had been worn from handling. The moth decoration on the lid was stunning, with each saw edge of its feathery antennae intricately detailed, the crackled pattern as if it had been inlaid with liquid ruby. For Arthur, seeing it brought back memories of Brightstorm House years before, with its warm wooden corridors and the scent of books and the smoking hearth.

"Oh, Arthur, it's even more beautiful than I remember," breathed Maudie.

Arthur had to agree, and he was burning with curiosity to see what was inside; the label next to the box merely said the sale included "the box and its contents."

"It's a fine-looking box," said a voice close by.

They were so absorbed that they hadn't noticed a young man standing just across the glass case from them. He wore a soft, kind smile and his eyes were bluer than glacial ice, in striking contrast to his dark eyebrows and hair. He was dressed simply but finely in a white shirt and deep blue suit that looked as though it had been tailored to perfection. Arthur was sure he'd seen the young man before—or perhaps his image in a newspaper?—but at that moment he couldn't place him. There was a gentleness to the way he spoke: "I guess the mystery of what's inside will elevate the price a little."

"You're not going to bid, are you?" Arthur blurted out.

"Oh, please don't worry about me on that front. I look more to the future than the past; I simply thought I'd pop along and take a look at the display. But how rude of me, I haven't properly introduced myself." Without faltering he offered his left hand to shake Arthur's—which certainly impressed Arthur, who had grown accustomed to the awkward, fumbling moments when he met new people and they first realized he had a single arm. "Carinthius Catmole. I'm very pleased to meet you."

A glance was exchanged between Arthur and Maudie. The Catmoles were one of the oldest explorer families in Lontown.

"You're—I mean, we're Arthur and Maudie—" they said together.

"—Brightstorm, I know," he finished for them. "You're quite famous in explorer circles now."

"Really?" Pride swelled in Arthur. It was true that they'd certainly garnered more looks and attention since their well-publicized rescue of the Vane crew on the last expedition, and he was heartened that their adventures were improving the family's reputation and honoring his parents' name.

"Indeed, I've been keen to meet you for some time, but one doesn't just turn up uninvited on the doorstep of the great Harriet Culpepper!" Carinthius smiled and looked back down at the box. "It really is extremely beautiful. You must be very proud of your father's achievements."

"We are," said Maudie.

"And your aunt is Eudora Vane? Am I correct?"

Doing his best not to wince, Arthur nodded.

"I must admit I never paid her much attention until she came back from her recent expedition." Bafflement passed over his face for a moment. "She seems quite different to how I remembered her, I must say."

"You're not kidding," Maudie said under her breath.

On their last expedition, for which an armada of sky-ships set out to find missing explorer Ermitage Wrigglesworth, Eudora Vane's memories had been taken by sapient creatures called darkwhispers. It was just as well, because it meant that the knowledge of the inhabited continent, Erythea, could remain secret, as was the Erytheans' wish. It also meant that Eudora was oblivious to her former crimes and vendetta against the Brightstorm family.

Carinthius smiled. "I only popped in to visit her when she was in the hospital to represent the family and to wish her well. Then one visit led to another, and now . . . Well, you may have heard that we're newly engaged."

The twins both found it hard not to let out a gasp of surprise.

"Er, congratulations?" Arthur said, not meaning for it to come out like a question.

"Thank you. Although, I'm not sure what my future father-in-law, Thaddeus, makes of it. You see, I'm not much of an explorer at all. My heart belongs to Lontown, at the universitas, mainly."

"Oh, yes! You're head of the Biological Institute, aren't you?" asked Maudie.

"Indeed, I'm surprised you know. It's not exactly as glamorous as traveling the length and breadth of the Wide in a sky-ship, but it has its moments. Mostly test tubes and endless reports, though." He winked.

Seeing Arthur's quizzical expression, Maudie said, "I saw his name on one of the doors when I went to look around Lontown Universitas last moon cycle."

Under his breath, Arthur replied, "You didn't tell me you'd been to look around." Why hadn't she told him?

"But of course," said Carinthius, "you're the youngest person to be accepted into the engineering program, aren't you?"

"The pre-program. I'm studying everything from home at the moment."

"Ah, so you get to live the best of both worlds, the double life of an academic and explorer!"

Maudie smiled. "I suppose I do!"

"I'm second-in-command on the Culpepper sky-ship," Arthur blurted out.

"Well, that is some achievement too at your age." Carinthius flashed Arthur a kindly smile. He leaned in a little. "Would it be an awful imposition to ask to see your explorer tattoos?"

Arthur and Maudie eagerly lifted their shirt cuffs above their inner wrists to reveal their Brightstorm moth tattoos.

"Extraordinary. The moth is almost identical to the box," said Carinthius. "That beautiful crackled pattern is perfect."

"Thanks," said Arthur, feeling proud. "This is based on a detailed drawing from my father's journals."

"Our father's," said Maudie.

"That's what I meant." Arthur threw her a scowl.

"Well, I believe I've bothered you long enough. My mother has her eye on an extraordinarily large ammonite that the Acquafreedas found on their maiden voyage, and apparently Wrigglesworth's pen from his scholarly days is here somewhere. I was thinking it might make a nice engagement present for Eudora."

Arthur was tempted to say she'd probably prefer whatever was most expensive, but he resisted the urge. Maybe the new Eudora would like the pen.

"It's been a pleasure to meet you both." With a smile and a nod, Carinthius moved along.

"He's far too nice for Eudora," said Arthur.

Maudie nodded in agreement. "He is nice. It's good to know that not all the original explorer families are like the Vanes."

"Well, the Acquafreedas are kind too." The Acquafreedas had helped them on their recent expedition by lending them a sea-bound ship when the *Aurora* had been stolen by Eudora Vane.

A man with red cheeks who was large in all ways, both wide and tall, pushed through, between them, to look at the box. Arthur stumbled backward.

"Hey!" Maudie complained, but the man acted as though he hadn't even seen her. Arthur recognized him as Rumpole Blarthington, another member of an original explorer family. He wore a long coat jacket with brass buttons and too-big velvet lapels pinned by a silver brooch, and a waistcoat bursting at the seams with highly patterned bronze and black swirls that made Arthur's head swim. His shirt had a lace collar and cuffs, which were the fashion, but Arthur's father had always said they got in the way if you were a *real* explorer. The tall top hat he wore only served to ensure that his presence was conspicuous, and his beard was trimmed sparsely on the jawline but with a sweeping mustache.

"It's not much to get excited about," Rumpole said to a short lady who had wedged herself between Arthur and the man. They matched in their dress: her jacket and her voluminous skirt were patterned with the same fabric as the man's waistcoat, and her blouse was in coordinating lace.

She peered in, lifting a pair of handheld eyeglasses, pursing thin lips. "But think of the resale value, Rumpy. The fuss and interest in this old box are unfounded for sure, but what if it did happen to be something valuable? Then the profit margin could be healthy in the long term!"

Rumpole Blarthington shrugged. "It probably contains some meaningless lump of volcanic rock and they're just not telling us in order to inflate the worth. Perhaps we'll focus on the ammonite. I hear it has healing qualities. I've been trying to get Evelyn Acquafreeda to bring me one for many years, but she keeps ignoring me."

"If you want the ammonite, then you shall have it, pumpkin." They walked away.

"Ugh, I hope Carinthius gets the ammonite, not them," said Maudie. "But at least they seem to have swayed from the box."

"Did you notice the pins on their lapels?"

"Can't say I did. I was more worried about them bidding on our box than what they were wearing!"

"It was odd: a human figure with wings and roots for feet. I've never seen it before."

Maudie shrugged. "Perhaps it has something to do with their explorer symbol."

Making a mental note to look up the Blarthington symbol in their copy of *Exploring in the Third Age* by Ermitage Wrigglesworth, Arthur followed Maudie to view the other treasures up for sale. They found the Wrigglesworth pen; it had an elegant body of mottled brass and a wide gold nib.

"I hope Carinthius gets the pen too. It has more sentimental value than a fossil, and he seems to appreciate that," said Arthur, thinking back to his time with Ermitage Wrigglesworth in Erythea. Ermitage had been an eccentric explorer, and Arthur had enjoyed his company. He still couldn't quite believe Ermitage had enabled Eudora's attempt to try to escape Erythean justice, in the end. But the darkwhispers took Ermitage's memory too, and he remained on the hidden continent; none of the other bidders in the auction room knew that Ermitage was still alive. Nonetheless, Arthur couldn't help but look back on him with fondness when he saw the pen.

Maudie frowned. "Poor Carinthius, marrying Eudora, though."

"Let's hope Eudora's memory never returns, because imagine if she went back to her old ways after they were married. What a shock that poor man would have!" Arthur shivered. "Trust her to marry into a wealthy explorer family, even if she can't remember her life before."

"Yet Carinthius doesn't explore! I bet Thaddeus isn't too pleased about that."

"Thaddeus will only care about the money, their status, and not taking any limelight away from the Vanes. It probably suits him."

"Come on, let's look at everything else. It'll be our only chance before all these things disappear into private hands."

"Apart from the box. That's ours," said Arthur, setting his jaw determinedly.

After doing the rounds, marveling at all the lots on offer, Arthur and Maudie joined Harriet at their seats.

"The sale is going to start soon. How are you both feeling?"

"We have to get the box, Harrie," said Arthur. "There's so much else here, so hopefully it'll pass by unnoticed by most."

"And it's lot eighty-four, so near the end. Most people will have spent their sovereigns by then." With a resolute nod, Harriet added, "Now remember, you're both too young to bid, so I'll be doing it on your behalf."

They agreed, although they both wished they could take part in the bidding because they imagined it would be rather exciting.

Waiting for their lot was like watching sand drip through a timer grain by grain. It was interesting seeing the other lots go through, but all the twins could do was count down to their box.

The Joneses' original cave sketches had fetched a good price, as had the Montgolfiere sky-ship blue-prints. The ammonite and the Wrigglesworth pen had been bought by Carinthius Catmole, so the twins felt a little nervous about the Blarthingtons bidding on the box, but they'd also bought a Wrigglesworth first edition, so Arthur and Maudie hoped they had used up their budget.

The auctioneer banged her gavel for the Fontaine helmet. "An astonishing fifteen thousand sovereigns, I presume bought on behalf of the Geographical Society! Thank you, Madame Gainsford."

Arthur noticed that a few people had turned in their seats to watch them for the upcoming bid. His heart thudded against his ribs.

"Next we have lot eighty-four," said the auctioneer. "The Brightstorm decorative box featuring their family symbol, contents to be discovered by the purchaser."

Feet shuffled and whispers were exchanged.

Maudie squeezed Arthur's hand. "Here we go."

"Bidding starts at one thousand sovereigns," said the auctioneer.

It was a higher starting price than they'd hoped for, but Arthur nudged Harriet to raise her hand.

She shook her head. "I'm going to see how much interest there is. If we act too soon, people could drive the price up quickly."

A hand went up several rows ahead of them.

"Oh, no, it's that horrible Blarthington man," said Arthur, suddenly feeling sick to his core.

"I have one thousand, do I have two?"

Another bidder jumped in at the front.

"Thank you to the lady in row one. Do I hear three thousand?"

While the bidding escalated swiftly to ten thousand, the twins barely dared to breathe. Then there was a long pause.

"Does anyone have eleven?" asked the auctioneer

for a second time. The reserve had been met at five thousand sovereigns, and they'd hoped to acquire the box for that, but Harriet smiled at them and said she had expected it to be a little more and had some funds saved, so it would be fine.

Harriet raised her hand and said, "Ten thousand five hundred."

The auctioneer nodded.

"Eleven!" called Blarthington.

After a suitable pause Harriet rose to the auctioneer's next call of eleven thousand five hundred sovereigns.

"It's so much!" Arthur whispered. The bidding was making him feel as if he'd eaten something that hadn't agreed with him. Harriet gave a swift, reassuring smile but he could tell she was reaching the edge of what they could afford.

The bid bounced between Harriet and Blarthington, increasing in two hundred and fifty sovereign increments, then Arthur could see the Blarthingtons debating with each other in a hushed conversation as to whether to continue.

"The bid is with Madame Culpepper at fifteen thousand sovereigns." The auctioneer raised her gavel. "Going once . . . going twice . . ."

"Sixteen thousand sovereigns!" called Blarthington, standing up. He glanced over his shoulder at them with a sly smile.

Arthur's heart dropped to the bottom of his chest.

"Do I hear seventeen, Madame Culpepper?" asked the auctioneer.

"I'm sorry, I simply don't have any more," Harriet whispered, looking between the twins. After a deep inhale she shook her head to indicate to the auctioneer that she had reached her limit.

"Going once, going twice . . ."

"Twenty thousand sovereigns," said a muted voice at the side of the auction room.

"I'm sorry, did I hear that right? Twenty thousand sovereigns?" asked the auctioneer.

Heads turned in all directions to seek where the bid had come from. A figure concealed in a sweeping, hooded blue cloak nodded in the corner of the room.

"Who's that?" asked Arthur.

"I don't know. It happens sometimes. The bidder obviously wants to remain anonymous," said Harriet.

"Going once, going twice . . ." The auctioneer turned to Blarthington, who shook his head and dropped back in his chair, red-faced. "Sold to the anonymous bidder."

The gavel struck and the deal was done. Violetta's box had gone.

CHAPTER 4

ENMITY IN LONTOWN

ARTHUR, MAUDIE, AND HARRIET remained silent for several moments.

Arthur could see that Maudie was upset—her eyes were glistening, as were his.

Harriet looked crestfallen.

The room buzzed with excitement as the auctioneer attempted to move on to the next lot, but the silence between the three of them was smothering.

Eventually Harriet spoke. "I'm so sorry, I thought we had enough to secure it. Perhaps I shouldn't have given away the water technology. If I'd sold it, I could have bought you the box easily."

"Oh, don't worry. We didn't have it last week, so why should we really miss it now?" Arthur smiled sadly. He didn't want Harriet to know how badly it hurt.

"I feel like I've let you both down."

"It's not your fault," said Maudie. "Besides, I would have felt awful if you'd spent fifteen thousand on an old wooden box."

Harriet looked down at the floor and shook her head. After a moment she said, "Do you want to get out of here?"

Arthur and Maudie nodded.

"Let's go back through the old markets. We can at least spend a few sovereigns on something else to cheer ourselves up."

On the way out they tried to get a glimpse of the blue-cloaked bidder, but the mysterious figure had already left to collect their prize.

The sting of losing the box felt all too fresh, and they walked onward through Montgolfiere Parade in silence. Taking a right into Wyndham Row, they zigzagged through the streets until they were in the bustling old market sector.

"Here, have some sovereigns each and I'll meet you back here in a chime," said Harriet. "I'm going to pop in to see my lawyer, to finalize the agreement with the post office for the sky-aks. Her office is just around the corner from here." She dropped a handful of coins into each of their hands, then paused. "I really am sorry about the box. I never imagined it would have gone for so much, or I wouldn't have got your hopes up."

They both smiled and told her to stop worrying, bid their goodbyes, then distracted themselves in the vibrant market colors and scents of food and spices.

"There's a great scavenger stall here," said Maudie. "A lady who sells mechanical parts that she's picked up from all over Vornatania."

"I hope the secondhand book stall is here today," said Arthur. He loved the old markets because they were a place where people from all parts of Lontown would gather, and you could forget that some areas were clearly more privileged.

"I wonder what that is?" Maudie pointed to a stall where several people had gathered; it was filled with tiny colorful bottles.

"Maybe perfume?" Arthur shrugged.

A man in a leather jacket and tatty feathered hat stood behind the stall. "Turn your average pet into a sapient with Formula Intelligencia!" he called. "This one-hundred-per-cent bona-fide, legitimate, tested, and patented formula is guaranteed to bring that extra spark to your animals, for just one sovereign!"

"That's ridiculous," said Maudie. "As if you could just alter a creature's genetics with a potion from a market!"

Noticing their interest in his stall, the man called over to the twins. "Already own a sapient? Supercharge your sapient with Formula Intelligencia Extra!"

"He must've noticed our explorer tattoos," muttered Arthur. They hurried on past. "And you can't own a sapient. We should tell Harrie so she can report him to the Geographical Society."

"He'll be gone by next week, no doubt," said Maudie. "He won't want to risk angry customers returning when they realize they've been conned."

They found Maudie's scavenger stall, a huge arc of tables with dozens of wooden tubs filled with all manner of metal oddments and spare parts. She bought a bag of pick 'n mix nuts and bolts, then together they looked for the secondhand book stall.

On the way, an excited young woman jumped in front of them with a clipboard. Despite the warm weather, she wore a furry hat with pointed ears on top and a long, colorful patchwork coat. Her dark hair was braided on either side to her waist, her eyes wide and blinking. "Hello!" she said brightly. "Did you know that the human brain is far more powerful than you might realize?"

"Er . . ." Arthur didn't know what to say.

"So powerful that there is a way to communicate through the power of our minds. Far out, right? But it's true. I represent a group called the Wolf-Listeners. Together, we have found a way to channel our inner minds to hear each other's thoughts. You may not have heard of them, but there are creatures in a distant land, wolves with golden fur, who can actually speak through their thoughts!"

Arthur and Maudie exchanged a glance.

"I can tell by your faces that you don't believe me, but the power of the mind has always been there, if you are open to expanding your cosmic energy. In fact, I can tell you right now what you're thinking . . ." She turned to Arthur and put one hand to his forehead and her other fingertips to her own. Squeezing her eyes shut, she said, "Ah, you wish you could have a ride in one of those newfangled sky-ak things. Don't get your hopes up, though." She smiled as though to say *bless him, having such grand ideas*. "And you." She turned to Maudie and planted a hand on her forehead. After a moment she said, "Ice cream."

Arthur stifled a laugh.

"I'm never wrong!" said the young woman proudly. "We meet every Wednesday at the Old Elm Playhouse." She passed them a leaflet printed with the details. "Now, I must warn you that not everyone possesses this uniquely powerful gift, so don't be too disappointed if you're not naturally one of us."

Then she peeled a sticker from her clipboard and slapped it on their shirts. Arthur looked down to see a psychedelic wolf's head. The young woman skipped away.

"That was . . . interesting," said Maudie.

They both laughed.

"Yeah, imagine what Tuyok would have made of that!"

The secondhand book stall was a short distance away, so they pushed on through the crowd. Arthur browsed the collection, looking for anything to do with exploring. He'd once found one of his dad's books here, which even had some of his handwritten notes in it. Luckily, that had been a while ago, before the auction, as no doubt someone else would have tried to sell it there.

It was a warm day, so Arthur took off his jacket and pulled the toggle on the collar of his shirt to roll up his sleeves—an adaption that Maudie had recently invented. "This looks good: *Cave Diving Secrets* by Jonas J. Jones," he said.

Maudie was about to answer when she stopped to observe the woman beside her who had also been browsing the books but had paused to stare at Arthur. Then the woman said, "Such a shame."

Maudie narrowed her eyes. "Why?"

The woman frowned. "Well, he can't do things as well."

"Really?" replied Maudie.

Arthur smiled. "Some things can be a challenge, but I've always found a way."

"Sorry, I didn't mean to offend." The lady blushed.

These days, Arthur rarely wore the iron arm that Maudie had made him because it was a bit heavy and cumbersome; plus, he was older now and more confident at coping with any awkward stares or unkind comments. He knew that there were a lot of things about him that were much more interesting and important. Sometimes when he was out and about, children would come up to him and ask, "What's that?" or "What happened to you?" but they were just being inquisitive, so he would always take the time to stop and explain that he was born with one arm and that it had never stopped him doing anything. It was a piece of him, not the whole him.

Arthur bought the book, then Maudie spotted Harriet in the crowd looking for them. Maudie waved, and Harriet soon joined them.

"How are you both feeling?" she asked.

They said they felt better and had already put the box out of their minds. After buying some sweet popping corn for themselves—and some to take back for Felicity—they reached the last few stalls. At the end of the market a gentleman dressed in a long gray coat was addressing a small crowd. He stood on an old vegetable crate and waved his finger at them.

"Indeed, the crucial focus should be that we maintain our supremacy. After all, wolves can't build cities and technology!" The crowd nodded in agreement and laughed at the idea. "Wolves are savages, and should be treated as such. How could they possibly learn how to civilize? Humans are superior, and must remain so!"

"Come on, let's get away from that," said Harriet. "Time to head back to Archangel Street."

As they walked away, Arthur's gaze lingered on the man's coat, which sported a pin. "I'm sure that's the badge the Blarthingtons were wearing!" he said to Maudie.

Her eyes grew wide. "So it has nothing to do with their explorer symbol . . ."

Arthur turned to Harriet. "Harrie, do you recognize that pin he's wearing? We saw it on the Blarthingtons too."

She peered at the man, squinting. "It looks to be the winged man." She frowned and they continued walking as she talked. "Have you ever heard of the HAC?"

The twins shook their heads.

"Back around the time of the Third Age of Exploration, when sky-ships had been invented and Lontonians managed to explore farther into the Wide, sapients were brought back to Vornatania. Sapients had always been part of the culture, even though early scientists considered it nonsense—folklore. It was around this time that experiments proved their existence and scientists finally came to accept that sapients were real. A small group called the HAC, or the Human Authority Collective, claimed that the sapients were part of some coordinated attack, that the animal kingdom was trying to take over the human world. The explorer community soon quashed their ridiculous concerns and the HAC was disbanded, but it seems someone has resurrected the idea, because that was their symbol: the winged man with roots for feet."

"That sounds a bit worrying," said Arthur, wondering how anyone could feel anything but wonder and respect for creatures like Parthena and the thought-wolves.

"Indeed. There's enmity growing in Lontown, and I don't like it one bit."

Back at number four Archangel Street, they told Felicity about not winning the box. She ushered them all to the kitchen table and served up sweet honeyed tea and generous slices of spiced apple cake.

"Look at all three of you, it's as though the weight of the Wide is on your shoulders. Can't anything be done to cheer you up?"

After a moment of thought, Harriet looked at the twins. "There's only one way to lift the gloom. Seeing as we still have our saved-up sovereigns from the auction, I think it's time. How do you both fancy another trip?"

Like sunshine after a storm, Arthur felt his mood lift. "An expedition?"

Harriet nodded.

"Where?" asked Maudie.

"Well, why don't you two choose?"

"Us?" The twins looked at each other, grinning.

"The Isles of Carrickmurgus!" said Maudie. "We could visit the birthplace of Zollie Ward. She invented one of the earliest working sky-ship prototypes!"

"Or we could go back and see the thought-wolves in the Everlasting Forest," said Arthur. "We didn't exactly explore the area around South Polaris properly last time."

"It would be great to spend more time with the Citadel kings on the way," said Maudie. "But instead of heading south, we could go to the islands off the western coast of Nadvaaryn."

"If we're going to do that, then we might as well head off into the uncharted area to the east of Nadvaaryn, south of Erythea." The thought of flying into the unknown again made Arthur's stomach fill with excited butterflies.

"Arty, have you any idea how risky that would be?"

"It's not like you to be afraid of a little risk, Maud. Have you gone soft in your old age?" he teased.

With a smile, Harriet said, "Why don't you both have a proper think about it, then we can discuss it more."

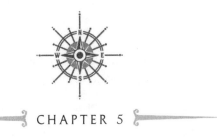

CHAPTER 5

VANE

IN A DARK wood study in the center of Uptown, Eudora Vane looked up from her desk as her father walked briskly into the room. Even though he'd been traveling, he still looked immaculate in his black high-collar waistcoat, crisp white shirt, and diamond cufflinks. His hair, white with age and cropped short, always looked as though he had just stepped out of the barber's chair. He threw his bejeweled cane onto the chair. He'd once told her he'd had it since he was a child, after an exploring accident in East Insulae. It was clear he hadn't needed it for many years, but she suspected he kept using it because he liked to rap it on the floor to call the housekeeper or gain attention—and sometimes just to express his anger.

"I know, don't give me that look, I'm late," Thaddeus said, looking at her with his pin-sharp eyes, then swiftly checking the chime on his gold pocket watch. "But the business in the North took longer than I'd hoped. And I've been securing more funding." He sat down in an armchair and reached for a bottle of brown liquid on the table next to it. "Not only did you come back empty-handed from the last expedition, but you also lost our family sky-ship. New sky-ships aren't cheap, Eudora. Neither are new mines, or payments to officials to turn a blind eye . . . or extended stays in medical facilities."

Eudora straightened the bow on the lapel of her pale-pink jacket. She didn't wear her signature color in public these days, but at home she'd had a whole new wardrobe created by Pompelfrey, her seam-master. She regretted the loss of the *Victorious* in Erythea, but it was a necessary sacrifice to the grand plan. Rather the sky-ship than herself, and her time at the Geographical Society Hospital had been required for keeping up appearances. She had long ago mastered the art of containing her emotions, and although the loss of the *Victorious* had been gut-wrenching, she smiled sweetly and gave Miptera, her silver sapient insect, a quick stroke on her shoulder. "But we now have something far more precious—the promise of Erythea."

Thaddeus gave a nod of acknowledgment, then

poured some of the brown liquid into a crystal goblet. After taking a long drink, he leaned forward. "How have you progressed with your task? What can be done to stop this water engine nonsense?"

Brushing a long curl of blonde hair from her shoulder, Eudora silently gritted her teeth. She hated failure as much as her father did, and she couldn't stomach displeasing him. "It had already gone through before I could stop it. The Culpepper woman used her family lawyer, the unbribable Camille Doherty, who managed to rush it through and find some loophole that meant it didn't need Geographical Society approval. A patent of the people has no ownership as such. I tried every avenue to revert it."

Thaddeus's lips tightened. "That's your mistake. There's *always* another avenue, and if there isn't, you build one, you buy one, you steal one. You rip the ground out with your bare hands and forge one from nothing if you have to." A pulse throbbed in his forehead.

Her father had angry little eyes, but hers were wide, more like her mother's. While people feared him, they trusted Eudora for her innocent, alluring gaze. They made a good team, and they held the Vane name strong at the center of Lontown; between them, they could employ any tactic to get what they wanted.

Eudora smiled. "Or we simply turn the patent to our advantage. Harriet Culpepper would never have sold it to us, and now, while we can't get rid of it or directly profit from it, we can use it freely for our own fleet. It can be our way back to Erythea and into any other parts of the Wide we haven't reached."

Miptera flew from her jacket to take a loop around the room.

"Couldn't you have left that thing in Erythea?" snapped Thaddeus.

Stuttering in flight, Miptera turned and flew back to Eudora's shoulder.

"She's been very useful to me. You've never once considered a sapient, Father?"

"You know I've always distrusted them, and now it seems my instincts were well founded. We should lead by example and rid the family of any sapient connection."

Miptera burrowed beneath Eudora's large bow. "If they are dangerous, then it's all the more reason to keep them close. There are positives to showing authority over the sapient world."

Thaddeus sipped at his drink, considering, while Eudora contemplated what to do if he disagreed. Approval from her father came with a long list of conditions, but she'd accepted that a long time ago.

They didn't often clash over opinions, and while she acknowledged the need to stamp out the sapient threat, Miptera loved her unconditionally, just as Violetta had, and Eudora wasn't giving that up.

The smallest of nods indicated that Thaddeus would allow this one indulgence. Nevertheless, she reasoned, from now on it would probably be wise to keep Miptera hidden whenever he was present.

"The water-technology patent is an annoyance, but perhaps it's a small concern in the overall picture. There are plenty of other uses for pitch within Lontown, and we have your forthcoming alliance with Carinthius Catmole to focus on."

Eudora smiled, and her heart grew lighter in her chest for a moment. It wasn't a feeling she was used to. "It's a marriage, not an alliance." She'd never paid Carinthius much thought before, or any prospective partner, come to that, but he'd visited her in the hospital several times, and it had been so easy to play at being a new Eudora. . . . Things had grown from there.

"Don't tell me you have feelings for him? I've always thought him curious, dabbling in all that science, not a true explorer like the other Catmoles. He should be getting out there and putting his stamp on the world."

"Oh, he'll be easy to bend to the Vane way." Eudora couldn't help but smile again at the thought of Carinthius's innocent-looking blue eyes. He was a good match in beauty and finances, and the fact he preferred to stay in Vornatania with his science would mean she could get on with conquering the Wide without interference.

"Make sure you get it in writing that your children will carry on the Vane name solely. I don't want any of this double-name nonsense. The Catmoles might have more wealth, but I haven't worked a lifetime to play second fiddle to another family."

There was a point when Eudora had considered bringing the Brightstorm girl onto the Vane side. She had the engineering skills of a Vane, so much like Violetta, and Eudora would certainly have a legal claim to adoption as her closest living relative. Not the boy, of course; he was gutsy, and had proved tenacious beyond her expectations, but he was too like his father. No doubt Maudie would have fought an adoption at first, but Eudora was certain she could have molded the girl to her way in time. But Eudora could never ignore the fact that Maudie was related to Ernest Brightstorm, that despicable hypocrite of a man with no family to speak of. The man who had stolen her sister from her.

Now that she had Carinthius, the Vanes could carry on with an untainted bloodline.

Thaddeus took another sip and raised a finger. "And make sure our lawyers double-check the marriage's financial contributions and the pitch mine expansion agreement. We're going to need every sovereign in the coming months. We need to turn our minds to the existence of these so-called super-sapients. They pose a threat to the very essence of our authority in the Wide, and such threats must be squashed like bugs."

Beneath Eudora's bow, Miptera trembled. "Not you, dear," Eudora whispered.

"And how the commoners are becoming confused! There's a growing appetite for sapient pets, sapient sympathizers and wannabes even, calling themselves the cult of wolf listeners." Thaddeus scoffed.

"The thought-wolves could only be heard by the children."

"These creatures pose a threat to human superiority and are what will keep the good families of Lontown from getting the resources we want from a place like Erythea."

Eudora rose from her chair and paced the room. "Everything you say is true, Father, but information is a commodity, as well you know. Timing and maintaining the element of surprise will be key. Erythea will be ours, but we must strike in the right way, at the right time. Plus, something else has come to light." She circled his chair. "There is a way to satisfy our deepest wishes in the meantime."

She pulled a letter from her jacket pocket. She'd been dying to show it to her father since she'd first seen it. It had been a long shot buying the box, and although at first her interest had been merely to prevent the Brightstorms getting what they wanted, she'd also had a hunch on the contents—a feeling that had paid off in dividends. And now a glorious plan was unfolding in her mind, and she had access to one of the best sky-ships in Lontown to see it through. "You won't believe what you're about to read, Father." She passed him the time-worn piece of paper. "It's time to bring down the Brightstorms once and for all."

❖   ❖   ❖

"I recognize that voice," said Arthur.

Maudie coughed. "I recognize that perfume."

They hurried from her room and down the stairs to where they had heard the front door open, followed by footsteps and voices.

They found Eudora in the dining room with Felicity. Harriet had gone out to collect some more detailed maps from the Geographical Society, as they still couldn't decide on a destination for their next expedition.

"Ah, twinnies, I was about to call you." Felicity frowned uncomfortably and mouthed an apology.

Eudora wore her hair down in soft curls, which Arthur didn't think he'd seen before. She was in a simple brown jacket pinned with a white silken scarf. Her sapient Miptera clung, brooch-like, to her upper chest.

Across the room, Queenie watched Miptera with suspicious eyes.

"Harriet's not here," said Arthur bluntly.

"I'm here to see you," Eudora said brightly. "Both of you."

"I'll be in the kitchen if you need me," said Felicity, backing out of the room.

"How can we help you?" Maudie folded her arms.

Despite Eudora's memory being taken by the darkwhispers, the twins kept their guards up. They couldn't forgive the past Eudora for her actions, no matter how pleasant she appeared to be now.

"I have something for you." A package wrapped neatly in brown paper and tied with a red ribbon lay on the table in front of Eudora. She pushed it forward.

"What is it?" Maudie asked with a frown.

With a wide smile, Eudora said, "Open it and see. Hurry, I can hardly wait!"

After a brief glance between themselves, the twins each took an end of the ribbon and pulled. The paper fell open.

It was their mother's decorative box!

Arthur couldn't believe what he was seeing. "So you were the anonymous bidder!"

"I was rooting for you to win the bid at a fair price,

but when it went so high, I couldn't possibly let it fall out of your family's hands again, so I stepped in."

"You bought it for us?" Suspicion laced Maudie's tone, but a smile brightened her lips and Arthur couldn't help but join her delight. Perhaps Eudora *was* changed.

Eudora nodded. "It's back where it should be, in the hands of my sister's children. It's what she would have wanted. Besides, I know I have wronged you both in the past, even if I can't remember the details. But that was another life, another me. I want to make it up to you. My father says that actions count, so here we are."

Maudie touched the decorative pattern of the moth shape on the lid. "Can we open it?"

"Of course! It is yours."

Arthur flipped the lid back to reveal a stack of letters, carefully tied with ribbon.

"Just as Violetta left them. I've not touched them. Tempting as it was to feel in some way close to her again, it didn't seem right. I'll leave you to read them." Eudora stood and turned for the door.

Arthur couldn't help but call after her. He could never forgive her, but didn't everyone deserve a chance to change? "Would you like to stay for some tea? Felicity makes great marsh cakes."

Eudora gave a little smile. "No, but thank you. I

don't want to intrude. I'll leave you in peace. I have business in town anyway."

"Then may we wish you congratulations on your engagement to Carinthius Catmole?" Maudie said. "We met him at the auction and he seems awfully nice."

Eudora's face softened even more and she put a hand to her heart. "Although I can't remember life before the expedition east, I think it must be what my sister felt when she got engaged to your father. I really am very happy, thank you."

And although Arthur and Maudie were both still guarded about Eudora, they felt the sincerity of her words shine through her expression.

"There is one more thing." Eudora took a step back toward them. "I hear that you're planning another expedition, but haven't decided where to go yet?"

They nodded, and Arthur's mind raced: how could she have heard that?

"Word does travel like wildfire at the Geographical Society. . . . Perhaps I may be so bold as to put a suggestion forward. Have you thought about retracing your parents' footsteps into the Volcanic North?"

Frowning, Arthur felt his heart jump a beat. They hadn't even considered that as an option, and yet it seemed so obvious!

"I can only imagine how exciting such a heritage

expedition would be for you both! Perhaps one day Carinthius and I will be lucky enough to have such adventurous children." She put a hand loosely to her mouth. "Forgive me, it's an imposition to suggest a destination. I'm sure wherever you choose will be magnificent. I'll see myself out."

Speechless, the twins stared at each other, then at the bunch of letters.

"The Volcanic North," Arthur breathed. Of course, it was perfect!

Maudie ran her fingers across the moth decoration once more. "Imagine if we could see an actual Brightstorm moth for real! Do you think they're this big in real life?"

"I hope so! I can't believe we didn't think of it before. Perhaps that's what the dreams with Dad and Mum singing were trying to tell us? Perhaps it was their way of calling us to the North!"

"I've told you before, that's totally unscientific, but . . . OK, it is a little mysterious."

"Then finally we've agreed on our next destination?"

Maudie nodded.

"We'd better tell Harriet to start assembling the crew. We've got a lot of planning to do!"

"After we read these." Maudie held the letters in her hands as though they were a precious bar of gold. "To think that our mother tied this ribbon."

The letters were all from Ernest Brightstorm to their mother. They were mostly from his early expeditions, when they had first met each other and formed a friendship. Greedily, Arthur and Maudie read the letters, pausing to read out any parts of particular interest, such as "Dad's written here that he was lost in the marshes for eight days and had to survive on roasted frog, yuck!" And "Look, he talks about visiting the Hawk Isles. That's where Parthena comes from!"

Reading Dad's letters made it feel as though he were somehow in the room with them, and that their mum was too. Just like the dreams.

Even though Maudie was skeptical about the dreams having meaning, Arthur was certain that somehow their parents had been calling them to follow in their footsteps. But Arthur also had a feeling that there was more to discover on the northern horizon. That was what he loved about exploring: there was always something new and incredible waiting to be found.

And they were going to find it.

Weeks passed with Arthur planning the route north and Maudie working with Harriet on new heat-proofing technology, to be ready for the many active volcanoes to be found there. Arthur was taking his job seriously and soon had a room towering with weather charts, historical accounts, maps, and the like. Felicity rushed around shoving food in their mouths, as they were so absorbed in their tasks that they rarely managed to sit down together and eat a meal.

Alongside readying the *Aurora*, Harriet had sent many letters and arranged meeting after meeting in order to assemble the crew. The previous crew members were automatically offered places, of course, but Harriet said she might need a new member or two who would bring different skills and expertise relating to the unique landscape of the north.

After Eudora had gifted them the box, the twins hadn't seen any more of her, apart from the *Lontown Chronicle* articles that liked to predict what the future happy couple's wedding day plans might entail with headlines such as "Will she revert to her signature pink, or won't she?" and "Reception rumored to be held at Carnaby's."

The dreams still came to the twins nearly every night and added to their sense of urgency to get going, but Harriet reminded them that this expedition wasn't a race. They could take their time.

Arthur pored over everything he could find to help plan the route. His father's letters and books were invaluable, and he decided on several key locations as their "must-see" list, including the city of Fellsandur, a chain of small volcanic islands (especially one called the Eye of the Wide, where the lava was said to bubble for all eternity!), a great fjord, and the farthest noninhabited area of the north, Hyrrholm. This was the island where the Brightstorm moths were said to live; the twins' father was still the only one to have mapped it because it was an extremely inhospitable place with acid lakes, boiling vents, steep valley walls, and a treacherous glacier. But that's one reason why the Brightstorm moths were special—they could survive volcanic conditions. In fact, they apparently thrived in them.

One of Dad's letters to their mum was particularly intriguing to Arthur. At first it had seemed to be a letter like any other, written on his way back from Fellsandur, in which he talked about how much he missed Violetta and that they needed to make plans soon. But Arthur noticed a sketch on the back of the page: an island marked as Eldurfoss. It had an intricately drawn jagged coastline, but his father hadn't gotten around to drawing any features on the island. At first, Arthur didn't think much of it; then, when he'd looked to find it on his largest map of the Volcanic North, he couldn't find anything by that name, or an island that even remotely matched the shape.

So, he decided the only thing to do was to recheck some of the smaller maps and look out for it on their travels. If he saw the island, he could at least make sure it was added to the Geographical Society's official map of the Volcanic North. It would be a way of connecting with his father and laying the final piece of a puzzle in place.

CHAPTER 6

NEW CREW

TWO MOON CYCLES after the decision had been made to travel north, a thud sounded on the door of number four Archangel Street. This in itself was curious, as the house was currently raised several feet from the ground in a partial conversion to sky-ship so that Harriet and Maudie could attach the heat panels to the hull. Felicity was out at the market, so, with a frown, Arthur went to the door. It was likely Maudie, messing with him.

"Maud, if you're taking me away from my planning for no good reason, I'll—"

A short, smiling girl stood on the steps. She wore a dark brown jumpsuit with many pockets on the arms and legs. A large metal bow was hooked across her body along with a leather sash looped with a compass and various other small tools. A shiny quiver of arrows lay against her back. Arthur thought she looked a little younger than him.

"How did you get up here?" Arthur said at the same moment that he noticed an arrow stuck into the door, with a rope dangling from it.

"I'm here to join the crew," she said firmly in heavily accented Lontonian, but still grinning an enthusiastic smile. Two thick, dark braids trailed her shoulders from beneath a leather hat with round copper goggles perched on top.

"I'm sorry, but I believe all the positions are taken," he said, trying to recall if Harriet had mentioned any of the crew being unable to make it. However, he didn't want to be rude, so he said, "Perhaps you could leave your name, in case one of our assistants drops out?"

"I think you misheard me. I'm here to join the crew, as in I *am* joining, as opposed to 'can I.'" Arthur struggled to place her accent. It was familiar; perhaps she was from Carrickmurgus? Or the Stella Oceanus?

"Ah, I thought I heard someone!" Harriet called up from below. "I've been waiting for you to arrive! Great. Arthur, it looks like you two are already acquainted."

"Er, not quite."

"Well, then, I'd like you to meet Gan." Harriet gestured to the girl from below. "Toss down the rope."

Gan swiftly threw it, and Harriet deftly climbed up. The pair embraced warmly.

"Let's do this properly: Gan, this is Arthur. Arthur, this is Princess Ganzorig."

"Just Gan will do." Gan shrugged as though the title had been sitting on her shoulders and she needed to dislodge it.

"Princess? Princess of where?" Although Arthur was unsure what a princess should look like, this girl looked more like a young explorer.

Harriet ushered them inside. "Princess of the Citadel! This is Batzorig and Temur's niece, and she's next in line to lead Nadvaaryn."

"The kings' niece?" Arthur wasn't sure if he should bow.

Gan prodded Arthur in the chest with a finger. "You repeat a lot."

"I repeat a lot?"

"Let's get you some food," said Harriet, ushering them further into the house. "You must be ravenous after traveling. How was your journey?"

"Good, thank you. I mainly traveled by horse, and Uncle Batzorig paid passage on a private ship, but where's the fun in that? So I borrowed a fishing boat and sailed to Vornatania, where I found another horse in a fishing village."

"You sailed, by yourself, across the ocean?" asked Arthur, half in awe, half horrified at the wild risk-taking this young girl appeared to be prone to.

Harriet offered Gan some fresh bread, which Felicity had baked that morning. Harriet glanced at Arthur, and, reading his expression, said, "You're rather prone to a bit of spontaneous behavior yourself. Remember the time you charged off on your own in the Everlasting Forest?"

"Yes, well . . ." She did have a point. "You didn't mention that Gan was joining us."

"I thought it would be a nice surprise to have someone around your age on the expedition."

The front door banged shut and Maudie called, "Hey, Harrie, did you shoot an arrow in the door? Neat way to climb up!" She breezed into the room and did a double take at the sight of Gan. "Oh, hello."

Harriet made the introductions.

Maudie's gaze flitted to the tool belt around Gan's waist. Her eyes lit up. "Want to help fix some panels?"

"Hold your horses, Maudie. Let's get Gan settled in first. Besides, I'm assigning her to Arthur."

"You're what?" said Arthur.

"Gan wants to be an explorer, but, as you know, the ways of Nadvaaryn aren't focused on exploration."

"So why is she here?" Arthur said quietly.

"Because the kings think it's the only way to get it out of her system before she settles into her future role."

"Or, I could love it so much they may never see me again," Gan said matter-of-factly.

"Arthur, can I leave you to settle Gan in? Maudie, do you mind if you share your room?"

"Not at all, as long as you don't mind stepping over tools, Gan."

Gan's smile was wide.

"Excellent," said Harriet. "Then let's get these panels finished and put the house back to ground level before Felicity gets back. Then, with any luck, we'll be able to set off next week, after I've interviewed the last candidate."

"But I thought we had everyone?" Surely they didn't need anyone else? Arthur felt comfortable with their usual crew, but now they had Gan, and possibly another stranger.

"This person would fill a specialist role, unique to the expedition. I didn't even realize we might need him until he sent me this letter." Harriet pulled a letter from her pocket and passed it to Arthur. "You'd all better read it too, as I want you to interview him with me. I've invited him to dinner tomorrow."

Arthur took the letter and read the sender's address. Professor Hugo Waynecroft, Volcanologist. Arthur wasn't sure he wanted a stuffy old professor tagging along, but he supposed his knowledge might be useful. At any rate, they could at least get some advice about their destinations, then politely decline.

✳ ✳ ✳

The evening of the dinner arrived. Felicity had all the best crockery out and was flitting about, butterfly-like, between the kitchen and dining room, preparing a range of her best dishes.

"Felicity, it's meant to be your night off," said Arthur, who was helping set the table in the dining room. "You don't have to go to all this trouble."

Parthena flew from the tall cabinet and dropped a napkin on the table, and Arthur said a quick "thank you." Queenie licked her storm-gray paws and observed them nonchalantly with intelligent amber eyes.

"We can't very well have some high-flying

professor of volcanology over and not put on an explosion of taste sensations!" Felicity cried. She glanced at Gan. "Hurry up and change out of your travel things, deary! It's almost time."

Looking up from the table where she was polishing her bow, Gan shrugged. "It took me ages to make this outfit, and explorers need to travel light so I didn't bring anything else."

Felicity shook her head and placed a vase of wildflowers from the garden in the center of the table. "Blessed bunions, at least take off your hat!"

Harriet breezed into the room in her puffy trousers tucked into boots and her shirt hanging over her tool belt.

"Harrie, set an example, will you?" Felicity took her lucky spoon from her apron and began polishing it nervously.

"Felicity, it's only a professor," said Harriet, tucking in her shirt.

"Yeah, you already have royalty at the table anyway," said Maudie as Gan scratched the back of her head with her fork.

"Oh, my silver sovereigns! And shouldn't the sapients be elsewhere? We don't want a stray feather or hair in the professor's dinner!"

Queenie gave a disapproving meow.

"They're fine where they are," said Harriet breezily. "Wait, where's Valiant? He may as well join us too."

"He didn't want to get out of the bath, so I've left him swimming," Maudie replied. A drip of water landed on the table from the ceiling above. "He's rather enjoying himself."

Felicity hurried from the room. "I'm going to turn my croutons," she grumbled.

There was a knock on the front door.

"I'll get it!" Felicity called, spinning on the spot.

Queenie leaped from her chair and padded out to the hallway too. She considered it her job to greet guests and show them the way.

Muffled voices carried through the hallway, including Queenie's loud "Meowt prrwt!"

Then the door swung open.

"Presenting Professor Hugo Waynecroft," said Felicity. A young man, cheeks flushed red, stood in front of her. "He's very young," she mouthed.

Professor Waynecroft wore small, wire-framed oval glasses and had wavy, caramel-brown hair and a goatee. His bow tie looked as though he'd never quite mastered the art of tying it, and his white shirt and tawny waistcoat and jacket had a slight crinkliness to them.

Harriet marched confidently over. "Do take a seat, Professor Waynecroft. I'll introduce you to everyone."

The professor nervously stepped forward and pulled out a chair to take a seat.

"This is Ganzorig of Nadvaaryn."

The professor nodded politely.

"And this is Arthur and Maudie."

"So you're the Brightstorm twins." He observed them curiously with blinking eyes. "I'm sorry, I don't mean to stare, but word travels, even where I'm from."

"It seems your reputation precedes you again," said Harriet, shrugging at the twins.

Professor Waynecroft's cheeks grew redder. "It must put a lot of pressure on you now that your name is so widely known."

"I had never heard of them," said Gan, sitting back in her chair and putting her feet on the table.

Arthur tapped them off and frowned at her. "Don't do that," he whispered. Then he turned back to the conversation but, out of the corner of his eye, noticed Gan do something. "Did you just make a face at me?"

Maudie snickered.

Arthur couldn't believe they'd have to spend a whole expedition with Gan; she was already getting on his nerves, princess or not. He'd loved meeting Batzorig and Temur on their expedition to South

Polaris, but he couldn't quite believe Gan was related to them. She didn't seem to care about anything.

"Apologies, Professor Waynecroft," said Harriet, taking a seat beside him. "The children have pre-expedition excitement."

"Please, call me Hugo."

Felicity brought a pot of soup into the room and ladled it into their bowls.

Harriet clasped her hands together. "You're a little younger than we all expected, Professor. Your letter described a great deal of volcanic experience."

"I grew up in one of the villages in the North, in the Fellsandur region. I started learning young. My parents always taught me to follow my passions, and volcanoes were mine, so it's all I've ever known."

"Your scientific knowledge of volcanoes would be useful, of course, but have you ever been part of a sky-ship crew before? What makes you want to join us?"

Hugo had just taken a sip of his soup and gulped it nervously. Harriet was very direct in her questioning, and Arthur was reminded of the twins' initial inter-view with her when they'd first met. She had a way of shining a spotlight onto your soul, and he could tell from the way Hugo's shoulders hunched a little, and that he seemed reluctant to make eye contact, that he was the nervous sort.

Gan picked up her bowl and slurped, peering over it with her large eyes.

"Well, I . . . I guess it would be a rather marvelous chance to see some of the volcanoes that are especially difficult to reach, and from a new angle."

"Of course, that must be an exciting prospect for you. Now, tell me about yourself outside of your studies." Harriet's voice was bright yet serious.

"Well, I'm, I'm . . . quite quiet, usually. I like the company of books, and I won't get in anyone's way."

"Interesting. Do you sing?"

"Pardon?"

Exchanging a smile with Maudie, Arthur thought back to when she'd asked the same question of them when they'd met. Harriet knew that a good crew was as much about keeping positive and pulling together as its individual skills.

"Do you sing?" Harriet repeated, then nodded, encouraging an answer.

"Well, yes, I suppose I do. That is, in the town I come from, songs form the foundation of our society. It's how we pass on stories to each other."

The door swung open once more and Felicity entered the room with a tray laden with steaming vegetables and meat pies. "Haven't you all finished your soup yet?"

Gan held out her bowl. "I have!"

"A healthy appetite, that's what I like. Come on, Professor, you're eating like a sparrow!"

Cheeks flushing even redder, Hugo spooned the soup into his mouth as hurriedly as he could without being impolite. Then Felicity whipped the bowls away and left them with the second course. "Eat up, now. I'll be back with dessert soon. Chocolate surprise!"

"Are you any good at mending things, Professor?" asked Maudie. "When things break, we need people who can pull together on the mechanical side."

"I'm proficient with my seismic equipment, of course, but I can't pretend to have any experience with mechanics outside of that, I'm afraid."

"Do tell us more of your subject, Hugo," said Harriet.

"Yes, where exactly do volcanoes come from?" asked Arthur quickly, not wanting to feel forgotten in the conversation.

And with that, Hugo was off, telling them in great detail about tectonic plates, something called the core of the Wide, molten rock, lava rivers, ash explosions, and the like. He seemed to relax more as he spoke about his subject, and by the time dessert came, they were all enthralled and couldn't wait to see some of the sights he told them about. Arthur was already thinking about how he might adjust his planned route to make sure they saw everything.

After Hugo had thanked them politely for dinner, Harriet said she would let him know as soon as possible about his place on the crew, as she had much to consider. Then he went on his way.

"He seemed a bit nervy for an adventurer," said Gan, disapprovingly.

"And he didn't have much of an appetite," added Felicity. "You need to keep your strength up on an expedition. Food is everything!"

"And it didn't seem like he'd be able to mend much," said Maudie.

"But he knows so much about volcanoes," said Arthur. "He seems like he already knows the area very well too."

With a smile, Harriet said, "I was pretty certain I'd hire him before he came. Knowledge like that for this expedition could be invaluable. It was really just a formality to make sure he wasn't going to be trouble! But he seems a mild type. So that's it! We have our crew, and if the weather is favorable we'll set off next week."

CHAPTER 7

NORTHBOUND

ARTHUR HAD DECIDED to head northeast of Lontown for the first few days of the expedition. The first place he wanted to see was the birthplace of Parthena, which he knew from his father's letters was a region called the Hawk Isles out beyond the great oak forests, the mountains, and the east peninsula. His father had told them about it, and they had planned to go together one day. While that particular dream had been stolen from them, he would at least be able to carry out a similar one with Maudie.

The rest of the crew arrived the morning they were set to take flight: Gilly, Meriwether, Barnes, Forbes, Cranken, Forsythe, Keene, Wordle, Hurley, Dr. Quirke, and Professor Waynecroft. But an unexpected visitor arrived too, before they set off.

"Octavie!" said Arthur, thrilled to see Harriet's great-aunt. The twins had become regular visitors to her house ever since their trip to find Ermitage Wrigglesworth, who had been an old friend of hers. She was just how Arthur imagined Harriet would be in her later years, still full of energy and enthusiasm, with the same short, choppy hair, but Octavie's being a gray-white color.

"I just wanted to wish you all well and to reassure you that I'll be keeping my ear to the ground here. Harriet told me about the worrying things you heard at the market. And I have another very important task while you're away."

Maudie appeared from behind Arthur, with Valiant on her shoulder. "Hi, Octavie! I've packed Valiant a bag of his favorite treats, and he understands to expect us back in a couple of moon cycles."

"You're not bringing Valiant?" asked Arthur, surprised.

"He's used to the humid rain-forest climate. Lontown is cold enough for him, let alone being too far north, so he has decided to stay with Octavie."

Maudie put Valiant on Octavie's shoulder and gave him a kiss on the head. "I'm going to miss you so much. Will you miss me?"

Valiant took her hand and stroked it in his symbol

for *yes*. He looked sad for a moment, but then Octavie passed him a square of chocolate from her pocket and he was soon chomping happily.

A huge crowd had gathered on Archangel Street. The full transformation from a rather odd-looking house to a sky-ship was rare and had become quite the must-see event.

"Everyone to your stations!" Harriet called, and then she started the extraordinary metamorphosis. The ground rumbled and the crowd gasped as the front of the house folded inward. Great pistons and cogs whirred and crunched until the edges of the house and the door disappeared inside. Shutters opened beside the windows and propellers spiraled from the house, unfolding and turning.

The crew hurried to the attic space, and with the scrape of metal and a sound like a great mechanism clunking and grinding, the roof began lifting backward. The floorboards became the deck as the roof folded in a huge accordion behind them and morning sunlight flooded in. Balustrades took the place of the walls and a panel slid back in the center of the floor. The great fabric balloon started to emerge.

Harriet, dressed in her baggy trousers tucked into long boots, a brown leather jacket, a white scarf, and her signature flying goggles, released a lever and the huge steering wheel rolled into view from beneath the deck. For the third time since they'd known her, Harriet flashed Arthur and Maudie a wide smile and, with a twinkle in her eye, grasped the wheel and pulled levers to complete the transformation and instigate the flight process.

Arthur, as second-in-command, kicked into action, pointing and instructing the crew to their positions on the deck. The crowd on the street *oohed* and gasped as the house lifted from the ground.

Finally, a section of wood creaked and revolved, revealing a shining brass plate that read: *AURORA*.

The great fabric balloon blossomed above.

Making sure everyone was in place, Arthur grasped his own cog wheel.

"Turn! Turn!" he called rhythmically as they turned the cogs to extend the *Aurora*'s wings. Soon there was a loud click and shudder.

The sudden uplift sent a sensation like magic through his veins. It was as though his heart filled his chest with the feeling of wonder for what discoveries and sights would be ahead. It made him feel weightless.

With a happy squawk, Parthena took flight, leading them onward. The *Aurora* rose higher and higher, and the crowd's cheers faded on the wind as they flew over the great dome of the Geographical Society, as was tradition, and then banked around to head north, flying high toward the clouds.

Shortly, the domes and spires of Lontown became a distant memory and they were zooming toward the lush, green oak forests of northern Vornatania. Arthur handed out duty notes, Maudie made her wing checks, and Felicity passed around celebratory tea and marsh cakes.

"How long until we reach Parthena's homeland?" asked Maudie, joining Arthur on deck.

"The wind is with us, so I think by tomorrow. We should get to the mountains by nightfall, so we'll set down on the edge of the forest, then ascend over the mountains during the day to reach the Hawk Isles by sundown."

"The Hawk Isles?"

"It's the region Parthena's from."

"Sorry, I should know these things, but I've been so busy with the thermal panels and studying that I haven't had time to think about where we're stopping!"

Hugo joined them. "I've never been to this region either. Did you say your father traveled there? I'm sorry, I don't recall his name."

"He was called Ernest Brightstorm, and he was a sky-ship explorer too. He wasn't from Lontown;

he came here at fifteen, hitching lifts on carts and walking over a hundred miles because he wanted so desperately to be a sky-ship explorer. But when he got there, he didn't have enough sovereigns to hire a sky-ship, let alone build his own, so he decided his first official expedition to break into explorer society would have to be on foot. He set off for the mountains of northeast Vornatania with a large bag, a small tent, and one pair of boots." It was one of the stories that they had made Dad tell them repeatedly while they sat by the fire in Brightstorm House, on the rug at the foot of their father's armchair. Arthur hadn't spoken of his father like this for so long, he found it a strange relief, as if he had been holding his breath without realizing it.

"He hammered nails into the soles of his boots to act as crampons," Maudie added.

"Really? How extraordinary," said Hugo.

"His aim was to be the first to travel across the mountains on foot and reach the east coast, but instead he found himself lost and dangerously short of supplies."

"The story goes that a moon-bright hawk came during the night and led him out of the mountains."

A squawk of agreement rang out as Parthena flew above them.

"So his first expedition was a failure, and he learned an important lesson about preparation—or so he told us, especially when we didn't want to do our homework.

"The bird wouldn't leave his side until he was safely on the coast, where he caught a lift on a fishing boat all the way back to Lontown. Parthena followed him back, staying a short distance from the boat, then didn't want to leave him even once he was back in Lontown."

Gan appeared with another plate of marsh cakes. She stuffed two in her mouth at once.

"Gan! You'll get indigestion," said Arthur (though he was often inclined to do the same).

She shrugged and said something like, "Felicity's baking is great," but it was a little hard to tell through the chewing.

"May I take a closer look at your route maps, Arthur?" asked Hugo.

"Sure! I wanted to ask you about some of the volcanic spots, to check if I've missed anything."

Maudie stood up and began walking toward the sky-ak on deck.

"Hey, Maud, didn't you want to see the route map too, you've not—"

"Later. I want to do a little work on the sky-ak engine. I've adapted it so they can stay in flight longer. Also, I've got a new invention to start and an engineering paper to finish and send off by pigeon post."

Arthur couldn't help but think that they used to love looking at the maps together, or even sitting in the library of the *Aurora* together, but lately Maudie was so focused on her studies it was as though she didn't care about anything else.

"Everything all right?" asked Hugo.

"Er, yeah, sorry. Just sibling stuff."

"Can't help you there, I'm an only child." He smiled.

"My maps are in the library." Arthur led the way below deck. He pushed open the door and sat at the round table where his maps were laid out, the corners pinned with the books he was currently reading.

"Where did you say you were from, Professor?"

"Do call me Hugo." Hugo sat in the chair opposite. "I live in a small coastal village called Toftvick, not far from the main city of Fellsandur. Right up . . . here." He pointed to the island on the map. "It's pretty cold most of the year, and there's very little to do but fish, think, and grow root vegetables, but of course it's a great region to live in if you're a volcanologist! We don't have any sky-ships up there,

so I have to hire a boat to do my work. We see the odd trade sky-ship these days, but the usual way of travel between islands is by boat. May I ask where our route is taking us?"

"I've put in all the major places my dad talked about in his book and some letters we recently got back."

"Ah, the auction. I heard about that."

Arthur thought it a little strange that he knew

about the box, but perhaps Harriet had told him. "The first volcano of the north is on this island, Rif, so we're going to head there after the Hawk Isles."

"Ah, yes, it's long dormant, but it's impressive, and is of course the first volcano of the Dreki Hyggr!"

"I saw that word on a few maps but couldn't work out which island it meant."

"Ah, that's because it's not just one island. Dreki Hyggr means the Dragon's Backbone in the language of the North Wide. See all these islands stretching across most of your map?"

Arthur nodded.

"That's the Dragon's Backbone. The islands make an arc around two hundred miles long."

"Really?"

"You'll find that the North is a place of story and myth. Every place has some legend behind it that probably doesn't make it into the serious books of the Geographical Society."

Arthur couldn't wait to find out more. "So why the Dragon's Backbone?"

"Because the islands' volcanos look like the spines of a sleeping dragon. Legend has it that there was once a giant one so huge that it could fly around the world in a chime. This dragon was the only creature in the Wide, and it lived for a thousand years before any other creatures. Eventually, tired of being alone, it lay down in the great oceans of the North and became at one with the Wide. The islands are what's left of it."

"That's a great myth," said Arthur, enjoying the thought of an enormous dragon zooming about the Wide.

"Not that there's a real dragon in these parts or anything!" Hugo laughed.

"I've planned to pass over this volcanic island here, called Jordauga, that's part of the Dragon's Backbone. Did I say that right: Jordauga?"

"Almost; the 'j' is pronounced like a 'y,' and the 'au' as 'or.' I've got a small translation book that might help you, if you like."

"Oh, thanks! I've read in one of Dad's letters that you can see the lava inside when you pass over. Will it be safe to fly over the top? I want to see it from the air. We have the heat shields, but I'm not sure they'll be enough, or how close we can get."

"I'm sure we can go above safely, but I can speak with Harriet and advise you on distance when we reach it."

"How about this island marked 'the Lava Plains'?"

"It's pretty barren there, so not the best place for a stop. But good to fly over."

"And what's Fellsandur like?"

Pausing, Hugo had a quick look at the map and calculated on his fingers. "Your night stops are marked in blue, aren't they?"

"Yes."

"Well, it looks like we may just coordinate with their Festival of the Bear when we reach there."

"Excellent! What's that?"

"As you know, the North loves an animal myth. One of the stories is the legend of a great bear as old as time that can set off volcanoes with a single roar."

"Really?" Arthur said, thinking that sounded exciting but terrifying.

"Like I say, the North is full of stories."

"Oh, and one other thing," Arthur said. "I have some more detailed maps of the islands, but one that I came across in my father's letters doesn't fit."

"What do you mean?"

Arthur opened his journal where he kept the letter. "This one, Eldurfoss."

With a frown, Hugo put his small, wire-framed glasses on and studied it. "No, I can't say I recognize it. Perhaps it's one of the Skarr islands, except the cartography is a little inaccurate?"

"But there's nothing by the same name?"

"I don't think so. It roughly translates as 'frozen waterfall,' so it's possibly a cold place."

Harriet peered around the door. "Professor, are you distracting my second-in-command?" she asked sternly. "Arthur, I need you to check some weather projections with Meriwether."

Hugo's cheeks blushed and he jumped up quickly. "Oh, sorry. I need to go and write a letter home anyway."

Before he hurried to find Meriwether, Arthur frowned and quickly traced the drawing in the letter with his finger.

His father was an excellent explorer and an accurate cartographer. It didn't make sense at all.

CHAPTER 8

THE HAWK ISLES

THEY HAD SPENT their first night by a small lake on the northern outskirts of the great oak forests and had taken flight again at dawn.

"There seem to be a few sky-ships in this part of Vornatania today," remarked Arthur, unhitching his uniscope for a closer look. He'd counted four so far.

Behind him on the aft deck, encircled by tools and fabric, Maudie tinkered with her latest invention: gloves for climbing, which she said were inspired by Valiant's grippy paws.

Gan sat beside her, repurposing an old wooden tray Felicity had given her into a target board.

Felicity was handing out brunch buns, her go-to for late breakfast after an early start. Half-bread, half-cake, they were stuffed full of every fruit she had in her pantry at the time, and Arthur thought they were particularly delicious dipped in warm hot chocolate.

"They're probably trade ships," said Felicity, joining Arthur by the balustrades and popping a brunch bun into his large jacket pocket. "There's some good harvests to be found in these parts. It's one of the main sources of food supplies for Lontown."

"Really?"

"Where did you think all the fruits and vegetables come from, eh?"

"I've never really thought about it."

"Did you suppose it just magically appears in those saucepans?" She chuckled and ruffled his hair.

Lush thickets, wheat fields, and apple orchards passed below as the *Aurora* sailed onward through the cloud-dashed sky. Their dad had taken them to the oak forests for a summer trip once. They'd walked until their little legs could go no more, then they'd pitched a tent, lit a campfire, toasted marshmallows, and the twins had fallen asleep on their father's knee while he told them a story.

Ahead, a hazy, blue-gray line came into view in the far distance. Arthur watched as it broadened, grew, and separated into dark, jagged shapes as they neared, until individual mountains were within reach, separated into peaks and passes. The tallest reared above them, snow-topped, but there were areas that were lower in height and passable by sky-ship. On the whole, the mountains weren't as dense and high as the peaks they'd faced at South Polaris, where the only way to get past them had been through caves, but the mountains of northeast Vornatania were more imposing in their sheer volume.

"If my maps and calculations are right, we should be able to follow this line, the Whistle Pass, and make it to the north coast," said Arthur.

"We need to be careful not to get stuck in the rise," said Harriet.

The breeze became biting as they ascended, and clouds would swoop in, obscuring their view one moment, then make way for piercing blades of sunlight the next.

They weren't far into the pass when Meriwether, the *Aurora*'s meteorologist, called out, "What's that down there?"

Leaving Queenie to keep the wheel steady, something the sapient cat had been perfecting of late, Harriet and Arthur hurried to the side. Maudie jogged over, a small fire wand in hand, from where she'd been heating material for the gloves. They all peered over.

Hidden in the nape of the mountain was an enor-

mous, angular, gray building in the shape of a squared off "U" with a large chimney, or vent, at the back.

Arthur squinted to see below. "What is it, Harrie? It's not on any maps I've seen."

"Nor I. It seems far too large for a home, and it's far too clean to be a pitch mine."

"It looks like some sort of factory," said Maudie.

Ω"Me?" He hadn't expected Harriet to let him make such a big decision yet. Straightening his shoulders, he considered the options, wanting to make the right choice. He was curious to know what the complex was, but it could simply be some boring factory, and he didn't want to lose time. "We'll push on. Perhaps we can investigate on the way back, or after we return to Lontown."

With a nod, Harriet returned to the wheel and took over from Queenie.

Chimes passed as they crossed mountaintop after mountaintop, until eventually the triangular peaks flattened and the air became fresh and raw with the scent of the ocean. The ground fell away in a sudden cliff and sparkling waves danced below. With the chill of the mountains behind them, the afternoon sun warmed the wooden deck, and Felicity kicked off her shoes and began dishing out afternoon crumpets loaded with butter and jam, washed down with lemon tea.

The crew sat on the deck, munching. Hugo was a short distance from the rest, which Arthur noticed he often was, so he thought he'd join him.

"What are you writing?"

Hugo obscured the note with his hand. "Not much, just a letter home."

Arthur nodded and looked out at the huge

expanse of water before them. He had only been polite, inquiring about the note, but now he found himself burning with curiosity. What was Hugo writing, that it needed to be so private? "We should be at the Hawk Isles soon."

"I'm looking forward to seeing it," Hugo said, folding the letter and putting it in his jacket pocket.

Parthena landed on the deck beside them, then Felicity joined them, and they all talked courteously about how nice the food and weather were, but Arthur couldn't help wondering whether Hugo was hiding things from the crew, and what those secrets could be.

A short while later, Parthena let out a loud cry, and Harriet called, "Land ho!"

Arthur and Maudie dashed to look, and they saw a lush, green island coming into view. Hurrying to get his map, Arthur showed Harriet where he thought the location of a suitable landing plateau should be.

It was late afternoon when they slowed the engines and made a gradual descent onto a hill with a large, flattened area at the top. They overlooked a misty valley with hundreds of tiny specks circling the air above. Arthur mistook them for insects at first, then realized it was a distant spiral of birds meandering in the updraft.

Parthena landed on the deck beside Arthur. He narrowed his eyes. "Are you waiting for permission? Go, join the others for a bit!" He laughed, and Parthena stalked a few steps along the deck, spread her wings, and with a cry of delight headed into the valley.

Sunset warmed the treetops and picked out the silhouette of the *Aurora* as the crew lit a fire on the plateau and cooked vegetable sausages on sticks. Gan was with Maudie, laughing and teaching her how to shoot an arrow straight into the target she'd made from the tray.

"Arty, come and have a go, this is so fun!"

"Yeah, that might be a bit of a challenge," he mumbled, feeling a bit annoyed that they were already having a great time without him. He was also trying to work out how he might tackle a bow and arrow with one arm.

"Get the iron arm!" Gan called.

Not one to give up on a challenge, Arthur decided to forget his current annoyances and join in. He soon worked out that the best way to shoot an arrow was to use his iron arm as the bow hand, and his left arm to pull. After a bit of practice, he was at least *almost* hitting the target.

Maudie's shots were as bad as his, but Gan's hit

the bull's-eye almost every single time, and Arthur had to admit that for all her clumsy, messy appearance she was a brilliant shot.

"I could make a bow for you to use without needing your iron arm," Maudie said, squinting her eyes in thought. She took her notebook from her pocket and began sketching while Gan and Arthur carried on shooting.

Soon, the sun had disappeared completely and the gray-blue light of dusk settled on everything. The birds flew into the mountains and trees, and Parthena rejoined the crew on the sky-ship, settling into a satisfied sleep beside Arthur in his bunk. It had been a better start to the expedition than he could have imagined, and he fell into a sleep that felt like home.

The song came almost immediately as he closed his eyes, but it didn't jar him into opening them; he let it in, savoring every word as his parents sang to him.

The beat of the earth is strong, strong,
Forged from the roars of time.
Hum! Hum! Thrumming high.
It calls, we call, the voices.

✵   ✵   ✵

As night deepened, the last embers of the campfire on the plateau went out, bats returned to roost, the moon crested in the sky, and all that could be heard for miles were the repeating chirp of crickets in the valley and the sway of wind through the hillside trees.

Two sky-ships flew a short distance away from the *Aurora*.

Eudora knew that using Carinthius Catmole's sky-ship would be perfect for the expedition. His parents had had it built for him, and as Carinthius was rarely inclined to go exploring, it was in pristine condition. His family was wealthy and the build quality was exceptional, a Pelastria teak deck and mahogany hull, almost as good as the *Victorious* had been. It had taken Eudora a while to convince Carinthius, but as always her smile and gentle persuasion won through, and eventually he'd let her make a few modifications herself. Its engine, rebuilt to employ the new water technology, was muted compared to how it used to sound when it was fueled by pitch. And there was a hatch now integrated into the hull for ease of loading supplies and . . . other things, she thought with a smile.

The other sky-ship following the *Aurora* had quite surprised her. She'd found out about it back in Lontown, a rumor of another sky-ship preparing for the journey north. Wondering if they'd merely started a trend or if there was more to it, she'd sent Smethwyck on a mission to discover more. A mysterious man had arrived at the docks and hired a sky-ship to go "as far as it takes" northward. Initially furious, she'd deployed a few bribes to get the manifests of all the sky-ships due to leave. Upon receiving them, she soon realized the situation might be used to her advantage.

From the bow, Eudora observed the silhouette of the *Aurora* parked down below. She wouldn't have risked being so close by day, but that other sky-ship was keeping its distance and she couldn't resist a quick assessment with her own eyes. The *Aurora* was a curious vehicle, some said quirky, some said elegant, but to her it looked confused, as though it didn't know what it was meant to be—a kind of confusion that she had never experienced herself.

No, Eudora had always been certain of her path. She was a Vane, and that meant upholding the values that generations had worked so hard to build: strength, accomplishment, recognition, power, dominance, and legacy. Sometimes when she thought of it, her heart felt heavy. Why hadn't her sister, Violetta, seen the truth of how things were? There was a natural social hierarchy to Lontown, and that was how it was meant to be. It wasn't their fault that they were born on the right side of it.

Violetta had fallen out with their father first, as a young teenager, when she'd started questioning the way the family did things. Their mother, Scarlet Vane, formerly Nithercott, wasn't around enough to address Violetta's growing disobedience. As long as Scarlet Vane could go to her bridge club and continue dining on Montgolfiere Parade with her exclusive group of Uptown friends, her default reaction at home was that she agreed with Thaddeus on everything. She didn't have time for the business side and she left the exploration to her husband; she used to say her job was to be the flawless face of the Vanes, which was incompatible with what she called "frolicking to dirty locations through storms." Eudora, however, prided herself in proving her mother wrong and showing that style and exploration could not only be achieved at the same time but could even become iconic when displayed together.

While Scarlet ignored the family dissonance, Thaddeus had little tolerance for insubordination and brooked no criticism of the Vane way. And when Violetta ran away with Ernest, Thaddeus savagely cut her connection to the family; he never spoke of her again.

"Excuse me, Madame Vane." It was Smethwyck.

Smethwyck had always been a loyal servant to the Vane family, acting as lawyer and second-in-command on her expeditions. In some ways it was unfortunate that Smethwyck had actually lost his memory to the darkwhispers in Erythea, along with her crew. She'd had the good sense to leap into a trunk to protect herself from those creatures' mysterious mind-altering abilities, but the others weren't as quick-thinking, so she'd had to fill in a lot of gaps for him. It was an arduous task, but she was pleased to see that even without knowing their history he was still ever obedient and groveling to her every whim.

"What is it?"

"Would you prefer a tri-lock system on the enclosure, or a standard one-bolt? The welding is almost complete, and the crew are applying the final touches. I've told them they won't sleep until it's completed."

"Tri-lock," she said, observing the silhouette of the dormant *Aurora* against the low moon in the far sky.

"And when they've finished, they are to work on the chains."

"Chains, Madame?"

"I'm not taking any risks. Double the lines."

Smethwyck bowed his head and retreated below deck like a worm slithering back into a hole.

Although she had kept her distance from the *Aurora*, Eudora wasn't overly concerned about the Catmole sky-ship being seen; there had been several trade sky-ships in the area and, anyway, she was certain her memory-loss performance had convinced them that she no longer posed a threat.

Eudora set the sky-ship to auto cruise, sat on the armchair by the wheel, and took a letter from her pocket. She'd read it many times, hoping to solve its puzzle. But the last piece of the jigsaw still alluded her.

It was just like Ernest Brightstorm to plague her thoughts, even though he wasn't alive anymore.

But her beloved Violetta was in this letter too. Perhaps that's why she found herself reading it over and over.

"If only you'd listened to me and stayed away from that nobody," she whispered. "It could've been us together, taking on the Wide."

She flipped on her pocket light and read the letter once again.

My only Violetta,

As always, I send this with my deepest wishes. I've decided to call my sky-ship the Violetta, *to feel as though* you are with me, not a thousand miles away.

Things in the north have taken some interesting turns. As I head into the region unwalked by human feet, as far as we know, I believe I have stumbled upon a most extraordinary discovery: a creature of sorts, something so precious and important that I fear that I cannot write any more here.

I am still confident that by sending the letters care of my Lontown address they won't fall into the wrong hands, but with the overt resistance from your family, I think extra caution is needed. Although I have only observed it from a distance, I believe this creature to be a real yet mythical being, sung about in lullabies and passed down through legends. I will stop there and hope I have not said too much. As you know only too well, exploitation of the Wide has made many a wealthy family within Lontown, and it's not something that would be given up easily.

I have kept my small crew on the black beach of the new island, as I feel the secret may be too important to share, even with them, and have drawn a map to mark the area as unsuitable for sky-ships to safeguard for the future. I've decided to turn back for Lontown. I think the time has come for you to make your move. This finding may be so significant, so incredible, that I feel we should be together in this, a way to start our lives together with conviction and wonder. I'll be back in two moon cycles, if *the wind is favorable, and I propose we leave immediately to return to the deep North, where we can make the full discovery as one. Then we will decide what we want to do, together.*

> *Yours always,*
> *Ernest*

Unclenching her grip on the letter, Eudora stroked Miptera on her shoulder. The silver insect slept on her shoulder, clacking her mandibles as she dreamed. The audacity of Ernest Brightstorm to think he could break the Explorer's Code like that! All new discoveries had to be logged by law—anyone with true explorer blood would know that.

But her plan was coming together.

"Soon," she said. And then, more absently, "Soon."

CHAPTER 9

MANY MOONS AGO

OVER THE NEXT few days, the *Aurora* pushed on across the ocean into the North. The crew spent two nights taking shifts and sleeping while in flight, as there were no islands in these parts for stopovers.

Arthur and Maudie continued to hear the song every night.

They sat on Maudie's bed reading the letters once more, in case they had missed some reference to the song. Each chose a letter to double-check before moving on to the next.

"How are the gloves going?" Arthur asked absently.

"Good, thanks." Maudie looked up. "They involve a lot of micro-engineering with the material, but Harrie has some great microscopic tools in her kit.

They're based on analysis of Valiant's paws and what makes them so adept at clinging to trees. They seem to defy gravity."

"That's pretty genius, Maud," he said, glancing at her.

"Yeah, well, I was thinking they might come in handy in the North and . . . you might be able to use one on your next expedition."

"Yeah, we might be able to," he said, turning back to his letter.

Maudie paused as though about to say something, then returned to hers. After a moment, she said, "I still can't find any clues, but there is definitely something strange going on, for both of us to be having the same dream so often. For argument's sake, if Mum and Dad are somehow behind this . . . what do they want from us? Perhaps there's something in the letters that means we need to take them to the North."

"Maybe . . ." started Arthur as an idea came to him. Then he shook his head. "No, it's daft."

"Go on."

"Well, I had a thought that although Mum and Dad lived in Lontown, maybe the North is Mum and Dad's true home. What if the spirits of our parents are out there, and they're calling to us through the song? They likely learned the song while exploring the North. Perhaps they want us to bury the letters where they explored together, like laying them to rest, as one."

Maudie smiled. "That's not daft. I think that's a lovely idea."

It was nice to spend some time chatting like they used to. They seemed to be ever more consumed by their own tasks, and despite being on the same sky-ship, some days their paths barely crossed, with Maudie perfecting her climbing gloves or in the engine room and Arthur with his head in a book or going about his duties.

"Do you think we should mention the song to Harriet?" Maudie asked.

Arthur had wondered about it for a while, but he didn't know what Harriet would think. Possibly that they were losing their minds? "I kind of like that it's something secret that's between us. For now." Deep down, he wanted to hang on to this thing that was keeping them connected. There had been an invisible barrier between them on this expedition and he couldn't work out what it was.

Maudie nodded. "I wish I could remember the full song."

"Me too, but it always seems to end after two verses."

"I did remember one more detail last night, though, from when Dad used to sing us the song," said Maudie. "After he would finish singing, he would tuck us in, turn out the pitch lamp, and pretend to walk to the door . . . but then he'd turn and pounce on us with a roar and tickle us until we were laughing so much it hurt!"

"I do remember that, now that you say it! He'd say it wasn't him, it was the Great Bear." They smiled at the memory.

Then a call came from the deck, so they hastily put the letters back in the moth box and hurried up top.

Hugo beckoned them over. "See that island? The Volcanic North starts there."

"Is that Aor?" asked Arthur.

"It is indeed. The start of Dreki Hryggr—the Dragon's Backbone. Aor is an ancient volcano. It's been over ten thousand years since it last erupted, so it is classed as extinct. They say it was the first-ever volcano of the Wide; but again, it's one of those things sung about up here that no one really knows."

Arthur and Maudie exchanged a glance.

"So you probably know the words to many of the songs from these parts?" Arthur said. "You did say you grew up here."

"A few. Why do you ask?"

"Just curious," said Arthur. "Would they be in any books?" The more he thought about it, the more he thought the song their dad had sung to them as small children, the song they were hearing every night now, simply must have been something that he had picked up from his travels in the region.

Shaking his head, Hugo said he didn't think so. "These are old rural traditions, not the stuff scholars have much interest in."

"How about fables like the one you mentioned to me after we left Lontown, the legend of a great bear who can set off volcanoes with a single roar?"

"You liked that one, eh?" Hugo smiled.

"Arthur loves collecting details of the Wide," said Maudie. "But you never told me about that," she added, turning to him.

"I didn't think anything of it at the time," Arthur said quietly, knowing they were both wondering if it could somehow relate to the song and their dad pretending to be a bear when they were children.

"So how does the fable go?" asked Maudie. "Tell me the story."

Hugo took his wire-rimmed glasses off and cleaned them with a cloth from his pocket. He glanced at Harriet and looked down, awkwardly blushing.

"Well, the story goes that once, many moons ago, when everything was being created in the Wide, as continents were forming, lakes were filling, and forests were growing, a great bear was born from the belly of the earth. Being at one with the Wide, it possessed special gifts: it could talk, becoming the voice for all the creatures, plants, and flowers. It knew the past, felt the present, and could sense what was to come. And most importantly, so the story is told, it could sense the truth of a human soul."

Arthur and Maudie were wide-eyed.

"The earth-bear lived in peace and harmony for centuries, protecting the earth and the creatures of its land. But one day, a human discovered the earth-bear. They wished it harm, wanting its special gifts and powers for themselves, so they disguised themselves as a great wolf of the land so that they might get close. But the earth-bear roared and saw the truth of who was inside the disguise. It saw their ill intention."

"What happened?"

"It swallowed them whole. And that's what's known as the tale of the earth-bear. Of course, everyone knows it's just a fable, a metaphor for the Wide and some such, or a story used to make sure children behave. It's a good story nonetheless."

But Arthur couldn't help but wonder if this earth-bear could be real. The thought-wolves were real, and the darkwhispers were too. What if they could find it?

And another thought occurred to him: what if the mysterious map of Eldurfoss that didn't seem to match up with any of the official maps had something to do with it? He decided to study it again at the next opportunity.

Through his uniscope, Arthur took a closer look at the volcano island of Aor. It rose majestically from the water with a concave section at the top that looked as though a giant had come along with a great spoon and taken out a scoop. The vegetation was a lush green and small puffs of low clouds hung around the center. Turning his uniscope to check the horizons, he noticed a couple of sky-ships in the distance again. The shapes weren't familiar, but they were too far away to see any details. He was becoming suspicious that they weren't trade ships at all, or perhaps one of them wasn't. He'd voiced his concerns with Harriet, and she had said that she agreed and was going to keep a close eye on it. One of the sky-ships always kept the same distance away from them: just close enough to spot, but too far away to identify.

They set down by the coast to refresh the water for the engine and to see if they could gather any food. Hugo wanted to take some readings and gather rock samples, and some of the crew were keen to see the view from the highest point of Aor, so they hiked to the top. Felicity was excited to discover her favorite variety of black grapes growing on the sunny, south-facing slopes.

The panorama from the volcano's rim was beautiful. They were still blessed with fair weather. The sun shimmered on the endless turquoise ocean all around and feather clouds smudged the lucid blue sky like chalk. Arthur was thrilled to discover a lake in the depression at the top, and Gilly went straight off to take fauna samples. To the north, some of the other islands that made up the Dragon's Backbone could be seen arcing into the northwest.

After stuffing their faces and filling their pockets with as many grapes as they could, they made it back to the *Aurora* in the late afternoon. The ship immediately set off for the next islands in the chain, hoping to make a landing by nightfall.

Arthur was on a break, so he decided to head to the *Aurora* library to check the strange map of Eldurfoss again. He laid out his large map of the Volcanic North on the table, then took the smaller map of Eldurfoss on the letter and held it beside the map, looking for any similarities between the shapes. "Where are you?" he muttered.

The final destination on the map was an island called Hyrrholm. The island had been well documented by his father because it was where he had encountered the Brightstorm moths. Beyond the island was more sea, then ice, until North Polaris, which was seldom explored because there was no land in the region, only ice. The Acquafreedas had been first to reach North Polaris, several years after the Brightstorm expedition had documented the farthest reaches of land in the Volcanic North; the Acquafreedas' steadfast determination to resist sky-ship travel through the ages and stick with seagoing vessels had paid off.

Arthur had an idea. He went to Harriet's study to borrow some grid paper, then returned to copy the outline of the island on a smaller scale so he could trace it and then overlay the shape on the large map to see if it matched. Despite turning it in all directions, there was still nothing like it.

Where was this island? If only he had a clue, they could make a diversion on the way to seeking the Brightstorm moths on Hyrrholm. But as they landed for the evening and tiredness consumed him, Arthur admitted defeat and went to sleep.

CHAPTER 10

THE PITCH MINE

IN THE DAYS that followed, they passed over many more islands of the Dragon's Backbone, but Arthur was dismayed that none of them matched the unusual shape of the hand-drawn map of Eldurfoss on his father's letter.

The cheerful weather left them, and the sky darkened through the morning, becoming a dull steel-gray, and there it stayed for the next day as they headed farther north.

The dreary days were perfect for catching up on reading, and Arthur was currently enjoying the book he'd picked up at the market, *Cave Diving Secrets* by Jonas J. Jones. It was full of interesting details about the subterranean creatures of the Carrickmurgus caves, which had been discovered living without sunlight. There were some incredible underground cave sketches, and a surprisingly enjoyable section on Lontown law detailing how the independent status of the islands meant that explorers had to be mindful to leave everything as they found it and not damage or alter the caves in any way. He thought that Jonas Jones sounded like a good person in the way he wrote so respectfully about the caves and the creatures.

They eventually reached a large island called Lida, to the west of the Dragon's Backbone. Wretched and made of endless rock, it matched the sky's somber manner. They'd passed over a village on the coast, but otherwise the island was uninhabited. Barren, flat-lying basalt extended, unrelenting, as far as the eye could see. The crew had planned to stop on the island, but Harriet kept flying. Arthur began to understand why the Volcanic North was one of the least explored, albeit accessible, areas of the Wide.

Even the *Aurora*'s engine seemed muted and silent as it trudged on. Gan had taken to lying on the deck, arms spread wide, rolling her eyes and declaring she was bored, then asking why there weren't any horses on the islands to ride.

Hugo, still wearing his crinkled beige suit and bow tie, sat beside Gan, sketching a diagram. "It's actually rather fascinating. Flood basalts are thick sequences of flows that can cover hundreds of thousands of square miles. It's all to do with the molten basalt lava's low viscosity."

Gan let out a loud yawn, and Arthur exchanged a smile with Maudie, who was finishing her second pair of climbing gloves. Arthur actually found Hugo's explanations interesting, but he could also relate to Gan's need to be on the move, experiencing new places and seeing the unexpected. So much of exploration required putting the chimes in traveling in order to reach the rewards. He'd offered Gan some books on the Wide to read, but she'd snubbed them and gone back to shooting arrows.

Arthur noticed Harriet instruct Queenie to hold the wheel steady, and she moved to the side with her uniscope.

Joining her, Arthur strained to see what she was looking at.

"That sky-ship is still following us," she said flatly.

"I knew it!" said Arthur.

"At first I passed it off as a trade ship, as there have been a few in the area, probably on their way to Fellsandur, like us, but I veered off the direct route a little on a hunch. And this particular sky-ship has done the same."

The sky-ship was close enough to make out the

basic shape when Arthur looked through his bino-scope: single balloon, large oval hull. But he still didn't recognize it.

"And there appears to be something ahead," said Harriet.

When he turned, Arthur saw that the land dipped as though a great hulk of it had been gouged away.

"Now that looks like a pitch mine to me," said Harriet, shaking her head. "I'd heard they were edging farther north. Let's slow the engine and take her down a little."

As they descended and focused in on the pitch mine, Arthur heard faint music drifting on the wind. It was the song, the one from his dreams!

Pausing, he glanced at Harriet but there was no reaction on Harriet's face. Was it all in his imagi-nation? However, clanging sounded on the deck as Maudie dropped her spanner and looked to Arthur.

Before they could do anything, growling filled the air. It was like thunder, but it wasn't coming from the clouds, it was rising from below, the grumble of rocks roiling and bouncing, trembling at the mercy of a greater force.

Rushing to take a look, the crew witnessed the ground below shaking.

"It's an earthquake!" Hugo called.

The roar grew like a great, angry, spitting fire. Then a loud cracking sound ripped through the air as the ground began tearing in a jagged split, the fissure leading to the pitch mine.

The rumble relented as the *Aurora* flew directly above the mine. The small collection of huts and sheds below had collapsed into a chaotic jumble of debris.

"What if there are people down there?" said Arthur.

The crew on deck rushed to the side, all their faces anxious and full of concern, scanning the scene below.

"The only way of knowing if it's occupied is to go down," called Harriet.

Arthur pulled out his binoscope and frantically searched. Not spying any more movement, he ran to Harriet at the wheel. "I can't see anyone, but they may have been trapped inside."

Harriet pulled a lever to slow the engine. "One thing's for certain: we can't pass over and pretend we didn't see anything. We'll make sure the earthquake has stopped, then we'll find somewhere to set down."

Arthur nodded. Terrified as he was of finding dead or badly injured bodies, he knew that they had to help. He went back to the ship's edge to see if he could find a suitable landing spot.

"There seems to be a path down to the mine," he called. "And that area close to it looks like the flattest place to land; everywhere else looks too jagged and could damage the hull."

Carefully, the *Aurora* descended beside the crater of the mine. When the engine was stilled, a stream of instructions cascaded from Harriet's mouth, ending with, "Dr. Quirke, bring your medical bag, and Gan, you stay on the *Aurora* to be ready to help if needed. Everyone else, follow me."

The crew cautiously but swiftly disembarked and hurried down the path toward the fallen buildings of the mine. The largest of the buildings had completely collapsed and was a pile of rubble, wood, and glass. The crater was eerily quiet after the quake, and they paused at the edge of the ruins, listening for any cries for help. But there didn't appear to be anyone there.

"It looks as though the mine was exhausted and abandoned several months ago," said Harriet. "But we'll search, just in case."

After several minutes of calling and pulling back debris, they agreed that it was unlikely that anyone had been there.

"Look at this sign," Meriwether called, flipping a large metal sheet. It stated, "N23 Mine, property of Vane Incorporated. Closed."

"Typical. The Vanes get everywhere," said Maudie.

"At least we checked, for our own peace of mind," said Harriet. "Plus, it would also have been a serious infringement of the Explorer's Code not to. Come on. Let's get back to the *Aurora*."

But as the words left Harriet's mouth, the ground shook. A small shudder at first, then the rumble grew to a thunderous roar all around them.

With lightning reactions, Harriet pulled Arthur and Maudie to the ground and wrapped her body over them as best she could, protecting them from the rain of dust and mud falling from the edges of the steep walls all around them.

Through a gap in Arthur's fingers, the canyon blurred as it shook. He caught a flash of silver—perhaps light catching debris? He couldn't be sure.

Eventually, the growl of the earth subsided.

Harriet stood up and shook the mud and dust from her body and hair. "Is everyone all right?" she called.

A thick cloud of dust hung in the crater, and the crew spluttered and wheezed their answers. Everyone appeared to be fine, aside from the odd cut or bruise.

"Hopefully that was just a small aftershock. Let's get everyone back to the *Aurora*," said Harriet.

After they had unpeeled themselves from the

ground, and the dust had settled, they turned to head back on the path—and were left speechless.

Sheer walls hundreds of feet high surrounded them, and the route back had crumbled away. The *Aurora* was now teetering close to the edge above.

"At least we've got Gan up there," said Harriet, once the shock had worn off. "She can throw us some rope. It's a steep climb, but if a couple of us make it up we can fly the ship down to get the rest."

"Er, Harrie?" called Gilly. He pointed a finger to Gan, who stood sheepishly beside him. In their original rush to search for survivors, nobody had noticed her follow along at the end.

"I didn't want to miss out on the rescue," Gan said, scuffing her feet.

With no one up on the *Aurora*, there was no way to get back.

"Perhaps we can call Parthena to help," suggested Arthur.

"She's clever, but flying the *Aurora* might be a bit beyond her," said Felicity with an awkward laugh. Arthur appreciated how she would try to make them feel better even in the direst of situations.

"I meant, perhaps she could toss down the rope."

"We'd still need someone to tie it to the *Aurora* so we could climb up." Harriet frowned. "We could send her for aid, but that would take too long." She clapped her hands loudly. "Everyone, I want you to have a good look around and see if anything has been left at the mine that might help us. Gilly, Meriwether, Wordle, Hurley, and Forsythe, search the huts over there. Barnes, Forbes, Cranken, Keene, and Dr. Quirke, rummage among what's left of the sheds. Felicity, Arthur, Maudie, and Gan will search the main building along with me."

"Er . . . excuse me, Captain Culpepper. What would you like me to do?" asked Hugo.

"Readings. You are our ship's volcanologist and I expect you to let us know how long we've got down here before the earth shakes again."

"Oh, yes, of course. I'm on it."

Every bit of the main building had collapsed, so soon Harriet's small team were mostly pulling up pieces of wood and shifting debris in their search for useful items.

"Gan, I didn't ask you to stay up there because I thought you weren't good enough to help; I did it in case something like this happened." There wasn't scorn in Harriet's tone, or disappointment, it wasn't her way; she was direct, but with compassion.

"I'm sorry, I wanted to help."

Arthur, however, couldn't help but scowl. He

sidled up to Maudie and whispered, "I guess the princess isn't used to being told what to do."

"What do we do now?" asked Maudie.

"Hope there's not another quake. Because if there is, then that's joining us, and this expedition is over." He pointed to the *Aurora* teetering on the edge above.

✳ ✧ ✦

Miptera clattered through the porthole into Eudora's cabin and landed with a metallic ting on the edge of the enormous teak table.

"You've been gone a while," Eudora said curiously, while pin-marking a point on the large map of the North she had laid out on the table. Miptera scuttled across, wavering from side to side, before settling in front of Eudora and gnashing her mandibles erratically.

"I don't care if you're hungry right at this moment, I'm busy." Eudora tapped her out of the way and continued.

Miptera's tiny claws pattered away, then a crash sounded and black ink spilled not far from Eudora's hand.

"What's gotten into you?" she snapped.

Miptera tilted her head, then looked to the ink splotch.

Eudora leaned in curiously. "Lida?" It wasn't far ahead, and it was the current known position of the *Aurora*. Miptera had been out on a spying mission.

"Are they in trouble?" she asked.

The excited drum of Miptera's feet told her she was right.

Eudora frowned, then frowned more deeply, before remembering that frowns were aging. She looked to the map and the island of Lida. "Well, now . . . What to do . . . What to do . . ." she said quietly.

CHAPTER 11

A LOOMING SHADOW

HUGO HAD BEEN diligently prodding the ground with an extendable metal probe attached to a handheld box of dials and springs with a small rotating drum. Every now and then he would pause to scribble in his journal. Noticing Arthur's curiosity about the device, Hugo said, "It's my portable seismometer. Not as accurate as my bigger machine, but it should help us assess whether the shocks are over."

After a short while he called out, "I think the danger has passed, Captain Culpepper!"

"Thank you, Hugo, and please stop calling me Captain. Harriet is sufficient."

Hugo blushed and accidentally dropped the meter end of his seismometer, just catching it before it hit the ground.

"I think he'd rather it be Harrie, personally," Maudie whispered to Arthur.

"Huh?"

"Surely you've seen the way he looks at her when he thinks she's not looking?"

Frowning, Arthur tried to work out what Maudie meant.

She rolled her eyes and pulled him behind a boulder, out of sight of Hugo and Harriet. "Boys are so blind. Arty, I think he likes her."

"Of course he does. Everybody likes Harriet."

"No, I think he *likes* her."

"Really?"

They peeked around the boulder and observed as Hugo fumbled awkwardly to put his seismometer away.

"See? Sweaty, nervous palms."

"Maud, we're stuck in a canyon. We've all got sweaty, nervous palms!"

But there was something overly jittery in Hugo's behavior that Arthur had noticed in general. He wasn't sure whether he should mention it yet or not, but he suspected it could be for a different reason. "Maud, I'm not sure that I trust him."

"What do you mean?" She frowned.

"What if he's nervous because of something else?"

"Go on?"

"He's sent several carrier pigeon notes since we left Lontown. He says that they're for family, but nobody else sends that many notes. You've seen him watching Harriet, but I think he's watching all of us. Harriet is concerned about the sky-ships keeping just out of distance. She's been passing them off as trade ships so the crew doesn't get alarmed, but what if . . ."

"I see what you're getting at, but what reason could Hugo possibly have to be in league with another sky-ship? We're not part of a race, we're not competing to find anything that's not already been discovered."

"But what if—"

"Arty, I know what you're going to suggest, and I don't want to hear it out loud because that might make it true. I don't know if I can face another clash with that woman."

Arthur huffed; he had to say it. "What if Eudora hasn't changed, and she can remember?"

"Then why give us the box?"

"To keep us believing her."

Maudie shook her head. "If she had remembered, wouldn't she expose the discovery of Erythea?"

"Not if she is biding her time for . . . some reason."

Suddenly Felicity's voice boomed nearby. "Oh, my

days, I knew I shouldn't have left my lucky spoon on the sky-ship!" She joined them, then narrowed her eyes as they stopped talking. "What am I interrupting, twinnies? I've known you long enough to see that you two have business on your minds."

Arthur glanced across to see Hugo looking to the southern sky. Arthur followed his gaze, and he suddenly felt as though a bucket of ice had been poured over him.

The sky-ship that had been in the distance was now hurtling their way. As a cold sweat prickled his skin, Arthur couldn't help but think back to the moment on their first-ever expedition when the *Aurora* crashed in the Everlasting Forest and Eudora Vane and Smethwyck had arrived, goaded them—and left them to perish in the frozen, perilous conditions.

Steadying his nerves, he reminded himself that they'd survived that and they'd find a way out of this too.

Of course, that would depend on what the crew coming toward them were planning. This canyon was far more exposed than the Everlasting Forest had been, and the approaching ship could have guns.

He glanced across at Harriet and saw her expression of disbelief. She looked to the twins and hurried over. "Surely not her again," she said. "Maybe a trade ship saw us and is coming to assist?"

Nevertheless, she sprang into action and ordered everyone to find some cover using anything they could find. The crew grabbed fallen doors, scrambled under broken chairs, and hurried behind piles of rubble.

Like thick, viscous oil, the ship's great shadow spread its gloom over the bottom of the crater.

"Everyone stay under cover!" shouted Harriet. "I'm going to face them!"

Peeking out from his hiding place—a propped-up door where he crouched with Felicity and Maudie— Arthur tried to make out the figure leaning over the edge of the sky-ship, but they were too far away. The muscles in his stomach clenched. They were like fish caught in a net, awaiting their fate.

The next words out of Harriet's mouth were not what he'd expected: "Batzorig? What in all flying fortune are you doing here?"

Blinking and looking between each other, Arthur, Maudie, and Felicity pushed their door shield to the ground and stumbled over to join Harriet gazing above in astonishment.

"Uncle Bat?" Gan crawled from beneath a piece of corrugated iron.

"Ganzorig! You're all right! Are you all in good health down there, Harrie?"

"Yes, everyone is fine, thank you, just minor grazes. But we could do with a ride out of this canyon."

"I'll send down a ladder; hurry on up!" He signaled to the ship's crew, who began letting down a long rope ladder.

"What are you doing here?" Harriet called up. Although by her knowing tone, Arthur could tell she had an idea.

"I received a pigeon with your hurried SOS call for help."

Harriet glanced over at Hugo. "One of Hugo's messenger pigeons must have flown down from the *Aurora* for him to send a message," Harriet murmured to Arthur. "That was quick thinking."

Although Hugo looked slightly confused.

"Let's get you back to the *Aurora*," called Batzorig. "Then we'll find somewhere safe to fly to so we can talk."

"Why is he here? He doesn't even own a sky-ship," said Gan, baffled.

After everyone had clambered onboard, Batzorig's sky-ship ascended out of the canyon. The deck was adorned with colorful, patterned rugs with plush purple and crimson cushions dotted all around.

Fringed scarves draped the balustrades with ornate gold lamps swinging in between. It felt like stepping into a little piece of the Citadel in Nadvaaryn.

"Welcome aboard the flying *Altan*!" Batzorig declared. He wore his elegant red robes with gold embroidery, but his trousers were rolled up to his knees and he wore a pair of sturdy walking boots.

Harriet clasped his hands and kissed him on both cheeks. "It's really good to see you, old friend."

"And you too, Harrie."

Arthur and Maudie also greeted Batzorig in the traditional way. They had never felt more relieved to see that warm smile beaming at them, framed by his pointed gray beard.

"You named the sky-ship after your horse," Arthur remarked, remembering the king's beautiful chestnut horse from Nadvaaryn, which he'd suspected was sapient.

"You have a keen mind, young Arthur. The power of four legs now embodied in flight!" He put his hands on Arthur's shoulders. "My, how you have grown! You were a mere boy when I met you, now . . . well, I see a young man before me." He turned to Maudie. "And you are quite the young lady! Perhaps you can teach my Ganzorig a thing or two?" He glanced over at Gan, who had taken herself off to a corner of the deck.

"She's been teaching us a lot, actually. Like how to shoot arrows," said Maudie.

"Ah, yes. I'll wager she is the finest archer in the Citadel."

They were soon back at the *Aurora*, which the Culpepper crew swiftly boarded, then both sky-ships took flight again to regroup in a safe place. Meanwhile, Dr. Quirke hurriedly checked the crew over for any cuts that needed bandaging.

The *Aurora* led the way, over the north coast of Lida, across the muted gray waves and into the darkening sky, until Harriet spotted a rocky, uninhabited island, just big enough to land two sky-ships.

Dusk was almost upon them when they landed, so Arthur, Maudie, and Harriet made a campfire while Felicity fussed about what she could serve that would be worthy of King Batzorig, and the two crews carried out their maintenance checks and duties. Batzorig insisted that Felicity have a break from cooking after their ordeal in the canyon and instructed some members of his crew to prepare a meal.

Uncharacteristically, Gan hadn't spoken to anyone since Batzorig had rescued them. She had refused to wash and had folded her arms and sat, pouting grumpily, staring out at the sea while the others helped with the fire. Soon, Batzorig's crew brought out silver platters toppling with dried fruit, golden grains, plump dumplings, and ornamental jugs filled with rich plum sauces. Together, the crews sat around the fire and feasted, faces glowing with orange light.

Although relieved that they'd been wrong about Eudora following them, Arthur and Maudie were still burning with curiosity about why Batzorig was here, so far from the Citadel. He had always been amused by Lontonians' need to explore, as he felt Nadvaaryn had everything anyone could wish— why leave?

"Harriet has been writing letters, keeping us updated with your latest travels, although she was very mysterious about the details of your expedition to the Stella Oceanus."

"It was quite an expedition, and we thought it would be hard to top South Polaris," said Maudie, glancing at Harriet because she was unsure about how much she could say about Erythea.

"We often talk about the Citadel," said Arthur. "We'd love to visit again someday."

"You know you are always welcome." Batzorig

glanced in the direction of Gan, who had turned her back to the fire and faced the opposite direction to everyone else. "I think someone is not pleased to see me."

Harriet narrowed her eyes and with a wry smile said, "Might that have something to do with your motive for being here? Because here we are, unexpectedly dining with a king who snubs the way of exploration, over a thousand miles from the Citadel." Leaning in, she lowered her voice. "I'm taking it that it was your idea to keep an eye on Gan?"

Batzorig stroked his beard and nodded. "Temur told me it was a bad idea."

"So he's still back in the Citadel?" asked Arthur.

"He said that one of us had to remain sensible."

"That's Temur, always the voice of reason," said Harriet. "Well, whatever your motive, we are extremely grateful for your intervention."

"I'm sure you would have found a way out without me."

"It would certainly have taken us much longer!" said Harriet, laughing.

"Temur told me it wouldn't go down well if Ganzorig found out I was following her. But she's our princess! I just wanted to keep a distant eye on her and make sure she was safe. At first, I was going to turn back once she got safely to Lontown, but then I persuaded myself to follow you a little further, and so on, and here we are. I was hoping she would miss home and turn back before she even reached Lontown, and I'd be right behind her, waiting."

"When I was a young explorer, nothing would have stopped me," said Harriet.

Arthur knew that feeling. If Harriet hadn't hired them for the crew to South Polaris, they would have swum there if they'd had to.

"She's an independent girl, but she needs to get it out of her system now, so that she can prepare to run the Citadel one day. A leader can't simply abandon their people every time they want to spread their wings. It is fine for you, of course; you don't have the same responsibilities to your people, but Ganzorig has a set destiny, whether she likes it or not." He frowned and shook his head.

Arthur guessed that Gan wasn't keen on her prescribed destiny.

"So I agreed to one expedition before she has to take up her duties, and of course you, Harrie, were my only choice of captain if I was to allow her to go. One expedition, and definitely no explorer tattoo! Although yours are very nice," he added, quickly glancing down at Arthur and Maudie's wrists.

"Where did you get your sky-ship?" asked Maudie. "I thought you didn't have any in the Citadel."

"I bought it from a Lontown spice trader and made a few adaptations so it felt more homely."

"Well, I must say, I'm pleased to see you," said Harriet. "But if my parents had decided to follow me on my first expedition, I may have acted the same as Gan. She'll be feeling that you don't trust her. She needs space to grow up and decide what she wants—and make her own mistakes."

"As ever, you are the wisest of humans, Harrie." Batzorig sighed. "I will speak to her and explain, but there is one problem that I think young Arthur will understand the most."

"What's that?" asked Arthur.

"I have, how would you Lontonians put it . . . caught the insect."

Arthur frowned. "Insect?"

Harriet chuckled. "He means, caught the bug."

"Don't tell Temur, but this has all been the most fun I've had since I rode the Great Plains of Nadvaaryn in the coast-to-coast race as a boy. Of course, I had to disguise myself so that my parents never found out."

"Batzorig of the Citadel enjoys exploring new shores? That's something I didn't think I'd hear!" said Harriet.

"The cold air of the North is a little shocking, but if it is all right with you . . ." He leaned in and with a twinkle in his eye said, "Perhaps I can venture a little farther north with you? I'll tell Gan it is still to keep her safe. If I tell her I'm having fun, she will never be willing to take on her responsibilities!"

"Of course I don't mind, but I think you need to explain why you're here to Gan first. Perhaps tell her what she's done well."

Batzorig nodded and made his way over to Gan.

Arthur thought it would be brilliant to have King Batzorig around for a bit longer. His smile and laugh were infectious and could light up a moonless sky, and it made Arthur feel closer to the memories of the trip to South Polaris and the thought-wolves. They certainly needed *something* to lift the gray gloom of the past few days; in fact, Arthur's whole body felt suddenly lighter now that his worries of Eudora playing games again had disappeared. He could focus on the song and the call to the North.

Batzorig and Gan walked along the beach a little, and after some heated waving of hands, they eventually hugged and rejoined the group.

"Now, isn't it a tradition to sing on an expedition at times like this?" asked Batzorig.

Through smiles, a sad look was exchanged between the crew as they all remembered Welby, who would usually lead the songs with his banjo.

"Hugo, how about you?" said Harriet.

Hugo jumped and dropped his plate.

"Captain, I mean, Harriet?"

"You told me you know a song or two. Perhaps you could take the lead this evening?"

Although impossible to tell due to the fierce glow of the fire, Arthur was certain that Hugo's cheeks would be glowing even more brightly.

"Unless you weren't being truthful," Harriet teased.

Hugo cleared his throat. All eyes fell on him.

Silence hung like an unwelcome visitor for several moments before Hugo's shoulders lifted in a deep breath and he began singing.

Arthur and Maudie gasped and locked eyes. It was the song they'd been hearing!

Hugo had no reason to be shy about singing: his voice had great depth, with a rich yet soft, soothing quality.

He stopped after the first two verses and made an excuse about not remembering the rest.

The crew clapped for him vigorously.

"So I think we can conclude that it's definitely a Northern song," said Maudie, leaning in to Arthur.

"It's strange hearing someone else singing it, though."

Then Batzorig stood and declared it was his turn to show everyone how it was done. He began singing a raucous traditional song about charging horses as he clapped on his knees and danced around the circle simulating a galloping stallion, while Gan hung her head in her hands in embarrassed disbelief.

Not long after, as merriment turned to the soft silence of contented bellies, joyful souls, and drowsy yawns, the crew began turning in for the night.

Arthur and Maudie followed Hugo, as they wanted to find out more about the song.

"Well done on the singing," said Maudie. "But where is that song from?"

"Oh, it's just one of the lullabies of the North. Most parents in the North, from Fellsandur to the last villages, have sung it to their children at some point."

"And you can't remember the rest of the verses?" Arthur asked curiously.

"My memory is a little fuzzy; it's been a while since I last heard it, but it was the only song that I could think of when Harriet put me on the spot! It was either steady myself and sing, or run to the sea and vomit with nerves. I couldn't decide which was worse, for a moment, but singing won. Why do you ask?"

"Oh, nothing, we're just curious," said Arthur, wondering if now that they were farther north, the song's reach and power might be growing.

CHAPTER 12

THE FESTIVAL OF THE BEAR

THE FOLLOWING MORNING, the sky remained a uniform gray, the sea beneath matching it with dreary swash. By the time a beam of sunlight broke through the clouds the following afternoon, the *Aurora* and *Altan* crews' eyes, greedy for color, lapped up the sight.

They were almost at the largest island on Arthur's map of the North and heading for the city of Fellsandur. By the time it came into view, the clouds had almost completely lifted, giving way to a warming sun and an aquamarine sea, sparkling with flecks of white light.

As they descended, the picturesque city of Fellsandur came into view. Set in a huge bay, flanked by gentle green cliffs and fields of yellow flowers, its colorful array of buildings rested by the shoreside. Some were white with rich russet and cobalt roofs, others with cheerful orange, yellow, or green walls. The houses were spread out, so it didn't feel squashed, like most areas of Lontown tended to be, where buildings were packed side by side and often fought for space. Here, mossy hillocks punctuated the town, making it feel spacious and welcoming.

They set down in the bay as the sun dipped low and smudges of pink and orange warmed the sky in the west. Their arrival caused a stir in the population, as many came out of shops and houses to walk up the jetty to greet the sky-ships and see what they might bring. A couple of trade sky-ships were in the docks already, alongside colorful fishing boats. Flags and lights looped the bay, a jaunty violin played somewhere not far away, the streets were busy with people, and there was a general jovial atmosphere to the town.

"Looks like we made it in perfect time for the Festival of the Bear!" said Hugo.

Like a moth to a pitch lamp, Gan jumped off the *Aurora* before Harriet had even lowered the plank, her face beaming with a broad smile. She looked over her shoulder and beckoned Arthur and Maudie to hurry up.

"Have you got any sovereigns for food?" Maudie asked. "Harriet said she wants Felicity to enjoy the festival, so the crew are to buy food in the town."

"Ah, this is your lucky day," said Hugo. "The festival is always free. People contribute whatever they've grown and made, and everyone can enjoy and choose what they'd like."

"But what can we contribute?" Arthur turned to Harriet. He didn't want the people of Fellsandur to think they were impolite.

"I have a fresh batch of marsh cakes," said Felicity.

"And I could offer rides in the sky-ak," suggested Harriet. "Off you go, enjoy yourselves."

Maudie hurried down the plank onto the jetty, but Harriet held Arthur back a moment.

"Arthur, will you keep an eye on Gan, please? I think she looks up to you, and you can see she has a tendency toward impulsiveness. She's young and needs to be free, but I shall feel better if you have her under your wing this evening, and I know Batzorig will appreciate it too. I've already told her I'm going to ask you and that she should stay close."

Arthur said that of course he would. It felt a little strange to be asked, as he didn't exactly feel his track record of decision making made him the best role model, but perhaps he had come further than he thought.

He jogged after Gan and Maudie, who were already near the end of the jetty.

A wide path wove along the shoreline and into the town, the center of which was paved with rainbow stripes of color snaking between the shops and leading to a tall, sky-blue building with a conical roof.

"If I ruled the Citadel, I would paint it like this!" said Gan.

"I wonder what that building is?" asked Maudie.

Arthur had read a little about the town in one of Dad's books. "I think it's called the Circe of Jord. It's where they gather to say thank you to the seasons."

A young lady in a bright yellow skirt, blue shirt, and knitted orange hat smiled and said something in a language they didn't understand. She held out a tray of small white meringues glazed with shiny red icing to look like a paw print.

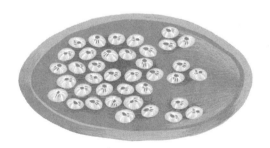

"Thank you," they said, bowing their heads and taking one each. They were melt-in-the-mouth delicious, light and chewy and filled with a sweet berry jam.

They moved through the crowds, being offered all kinds of treats: savory twists made to look like trees, glazed apples, boat-shaped donuts, warm spiced nuts, cheeses on wooden sticks, and bread rolls stuck with juicy currants made to look like a bear's face. They passed a stall with paper bears with small mechanisms that made them dance on the table.

"These are incredible!" said Maudie. "Look at that tiny motor, and how cleverly it operates the hidden strings!"

"Please, you take," said the woman at the stall, who was dressed in a brown furry jacket and had bear ears attached to her head with a band.

"Really? Thank you," said Maudie, dipping her head and smiling from ear to ear. "You want to ride?" She pointed to the bay where Harriet was giving sky-ak rides. The woman smiled and nodded, hurrying off.

"I can't eat another thing," Arthur groaned after they'd only got halfway along the path.

"Really?" said Gan, stuffing another meringue in her mouth.

Suddenly, drums, flutes, and violins started playing and everyone moved to the sides of the path. A procession started at the Circe of Jord and began moving along the path. Something huge and dark was being carried at the front. As it neared, they realized it was a great model bear held high by five people with long sticks: two on the front paws, two on the back, and one controlling the head. The limbs were partially automated, giving it a lifelike appearance, and as it passed it let out a mechanical *"Roar!"*

"That's brilliant!" said Maudie as the bear danced onward.

People in colorful waistcoats and billowing skirts followed the bear, holding poles aloft with what appeared to be all manner of natural objects suspended: seashells bound together to resemble fish, flower garlands arranged to look like foxes, wheat wreaths entwined to form birds.

Arthur turned to Maudie. "What do you think they are?"

"They're meant to be visual interpretations of the soul," said Hugo, who had joined them in the crowd along with Felicity, Meriwether, Gilly, and Dr. Quirke. "It's to show the bear that they are respectful protectors of the Wide and that their souls are good."

"Now, that's a lovely idea," said Felicity, who had been adorned with a garland of shells.

They enjoyed the procession for half a chime as the town paraded by, singing and dancing in their colorful costumes. After a while, Arthur glanced over his shoulder and realized he couldn't see Gan. "Maud, can you see Gan anywhere?"

"She's probably gone off to find more food."

"I'd better go and have a look. The parade looks like it's coming to an end, so I'll meet you back at the *Aurora*."

Arthur moved through the crowd searching for Gan. Maybe she'd gone to join Batzorig, who had been helping Harriet with the sky-aks . . . but he could see them on the jetty, chatting and watching the parade.

Then he caught a glimpse of dark hair and a metal bow. He pushed on through the crowds toward her. "Gan! There you are!"

"Arthur! Look what I've got!"

She thrust her wrist at him. "It's my very own explorer's tattoo!"

Arthur felt his stomach lurch. Batzorig had specifically mentioned at the campfire that a tattoo was something he definitely wouldn't allow! An outline of a horse's head was on her wrist, with stars for eyes.

"You went and got a tattoo?!"

She shrugged. "So? You've got one. All the explorers do."

"You're younger than me, and you're not a full explorer, you're crew, and . . . I can't believe you did this while I was meant to be looking out for you!" Harriet and Batzorig were going to be so angry with him.

"Relax, Arthur. You're so uptight! I'll cover it up, if you're so worried about what Harriet and Uncle Batzorig will say."

"Great, so not only did I take my eye off you and you went and did that, but now you want me to keep what you did a secret?"

Gan grinned. "Exactly. What's the big deal?

"Shall we go and join in the dancing?" Gan pointed to a group dancing with the bear on the beach.

"Er, most definitely not. Let's get you back to the *Aurora*." Arthur followed her up the jetty, wondering how he was going to explain this one to Harriet. When they got back to the sky-ship, Harriet was chatting on deck with Meriwether and Felicity, and Batzorig had already retired to his sky-ship. Arthur decided to deal with Gan's tattoo in the morning.

He couldn't sleep, so he laid his maps on his bed, then popped into Maudie's room to get the moth box and read through the letters again to see if there was anything that might remotely refer to the mythical bear or the map of Eldurfoss. But he couldn't find anything.

He wrote down the two verses of the lullaby that he knew. Perhaps there were only two? Yet he couldn't help feeling that there were more. . . . He'd learned over the past few years to trust his instinct, and, just as he knew there was more to the song, he could also feel that all three mysteries on his mind—the missing island, the bear, and the song—were all pointing in the same direction; he just didn't know what that was. Whatever the answers were, with absolute certainty he knew that the song was calling them farther north, either to bury the letters and lay his parents' memory to rest or to find the missing island and the mythical bear.

Frustrated and unable to still his thoughts, Arthur put on his boots and went back on deck. Sometimes he liked to lie there in the night with Parthena and look up at the stars, but when he stepped out of the hatch, someone was already on the deck, facing out to sea. His first thought was that it was Harriet, who was also prone to restless nights, but the silhouette didn't look right for her. A carrier pigeon flew away from the person's hands. Arthur ducked behind one of the sky-aks and watched. The person was dressed in light trousers and jacket, highlighted by the moon. It was Hugo.

As he turned, Arthur noticed a soft smile on his lips.

A strange cold feeling washed over him. Although tempted to reveal himself and question what Hugo was doing, Arthur remained behind the sky-ak. Was Hugo's innocent-looking, shy persona all a front that was covering something more sinister? Could it all be a show? His mind prickled with questions.

Whatever was going on, he would sleep on it and speak to Maudie tomorrow.

CHAPTER 13

THE EYE OF THE WIDE

THE NEXT MORNING, they waved goodbye to colorful Fellsandur and ascended across the hills beyond the town. There was a spot on the large island that Arthur had planned into their route called Saell Fjord. His father had mentioned it in his book about the North. The translation of it was "Fortunate Fjord" or "Happy Fjord," and the legend was that if you passed through the fjord from south to north, you left all your worries of the past behind so that you could focus on the future. It was apparently a local tradition to walk or row the length of the fjord to pass from childhood to adulthood. Arthur figured that flying the length in the sky-ship would count too.

He stood next to Harriet at the wheel. Dr. Quirke

was close by, bandaging Gilly's ankle after he'd sprained it dancing at the festival.

"We will find the moths, you know," said Harriet. "Even if Hyrrholm is a bit of a challenge to navigate. Hugo told me he's never been to Hyrrholm because it's the most inhospitable place in the North. He says no one ever goes there. I think he was trying to put me off."

"Really?" Arthur said, wondering why Hugo would do that.

"I've looked at your father's map of Hyrrholm, and there are deathly sheer walls, a great valley filled with acid lakes and boiling vents, not to mention a volcano that we know very little about because no one has ever been there! But when were we ever deterred by a bit of hardship?" The sunlight sparkled on the flying goggles resting on her head, and her eyes shone with their own inner light. Arthur loved that Harriet was so unafraid of facing even the harshest challenge.

"I'll check with Meriwether," she continued, "but if the weather stays fine and the wind keeps in our favor we should make it in half our predicted time. Two days, I reckon."

"Great!" Arthur couldn't wait. It might mean they would have a bit of time to seek out the missing island.

He hadn't had an opportunity to tell Harriet

about Gan's tattoo yet. There was always someone around, and he was too embarrassed that it had happened on his watch. Gan kept the tattoo covered but kept winking at Arthur knowingly, to the point that Maudie became suspicious that something was going on. She called Arthur to the stern to ask about it as they flew into the fjord.

"She slipped away during the parade and had a tattoo done!" Arthur hissed, shaking his head.

"You're kidding me!"

"Batzorig is going to hate me."

"It wasn't exactly your fault. She's the sort who will do whatever she wants regardless. A bit like someone else I know," she said with a knowing nudge.

"Yes, but I'm second-in-command now, and I should be, I don't know . . . responsible, or something."

"What's done is done. Whether you tell Harriet and Batzorig now or later won't change what's happened."

"Well, thank goodness this will be our only expedition with her; she's too much trouble," he groaned, then laughed. "See what she's done? I'm already thinking about our next trip, and we're not even halfway through this one!"

Maudie gave a hollow laugh in return that made him frown. Then she said, "Don't worry. You may as well enjoy the view for now; it might be the only opportunity we have to see it."

They entered the fjord. Mile-deep, lush green mountainsides gave way to a crystal-blue river meandering through the landscape in soft sweeping curves. Lemon-gold sunlight lit snow-dusted peaks, and waterfalls from melting glaciers spilled down the steep edges. Gilly, the ship's botanist, had told Arthur that he hoped to catch sight of some sea lions and seals, so Arthur and Maudie had their binoscopes ready as they flew through the middle of the valley.

Arthur's mind drifted back to the evening before. Checking over his shoulder to make sure Hugo wasn't close, he whispered to Maudie, "Do you think there's something going on with Hugo?"

"Aside from the way he goes pink whenever Harriet walks past?"

"I saw him on the deck after everyone was asleep sending a messenger pigeon."

She shrugged. "He said he likes to write to his family. You're not still worrying about Eudora now we know the sky-ship that was following us was Batzorig?"

"There are still other sky-ships in the area."

"Yes, and we've just been to the largest town in the Volcanic North, so it was always likely we'd see a few. I think you need to relax and stop fretting or you'll miss out on what we're meant to be doing—enjoying an expedition in our parents' footsteps. After all, it might be the last time we get to do this for a while."

"What do you mean?" he asked, startled.

"Well, it's expensive to get a crew together, and we've got Welby House to think of and everything."

"Yes, but your sky-aks are doing well in Lontown, and we can sell photographs from the trip, and Harriet can do a few lectures at the Geographical Society . . ."

"Yes, I suppose." She gazed down into the valley, her thoughts unreadable to Arthur.

Parthena, who flew in the wake of the *Aurora*, seemed to be watching them closely. Sometimes, Arthur wished she could talk. She could feel things that he couldn't work out yet.

The twins spent several minutes scanning below for signs of wildlife, but Arthur chafed at the silence between them. "Hey, Maud, we'll be at the Eye of the Wide soon, and then it's only a few days' flight to Hyrrholm, where we should find the Brightstorm moths."

"I can't wait to see them in real life." She smiled. "Do you think they'll be curious enough to land on us and big enough to cover my hand like Dad told us?"

"I hope so."

The fjord had an air of silence and calm, the light vivid and crisp making the green of the mountainside radiant and the blue of the river brilliant. It was as though it existed in its own chime.

Looking over his shoulder to check that no one was near, Arthur said, "Have you heard any more of the song?"

"Every night, but still only two verses."

"Me too. But I have a theory."

"Of course you do." She glanced at him and grinned.

"The island that Dad drew on the back of one of the letters? I've got a hunch that that's where we might find the bear."

"You're convinced the bear is real, then?"

"Just a feeling. But imagine if we saw the Brightstorm moths, and then we looked for the island and found the bear too! And imagine if it was a supersapient like the thought-wolves!"

"OK, so what clues do you have?"

"I have the map."

"Which just has the outline of an island on it, with no directions or notes?"

"Well . . . yes."

"Anything else? Any mentions in Dad's books or journals?"

"Er . . . no."

"So we have nothing to go on apart from flying blindly around the North trying to find a small island of the same shape as a half scrawled map. And you think that's enough to convince Harriet to extend the trip?"

"Well, when you put it like that . . ."

She gave him a hard pat on the shoulder. "Good luck with that."

Meriwether said hello as she checked the barometer at the stern, then moved on. Gilly exclaimed excitedly that he'd seen a rare black-and-white whale.

"You *could* help me look for more clues," Arthur said as they scanned the water below.

"Arthur, you've read the letters a hundred times and you never stop poring over the books and maps. Some things in this world really are just stories. The moths are real; let's focus on them."

Sometimes it was frustrating trying to convince Maudie of things he just *knew*, his gut feelings. She was always so practical—*too* practical. How many times did he have to be right before she took his instincts seriously?

On the other hand, he thought, sighing, perhaps

she *was* right and he was getting carried away, putting two and two together and making five.

"It'll be amazing to see the moths in real life. Like you said, it's what Mum and Dad wanted; it's why we're hearing the song," Maudie said, and glanced back at her tools laid out on deck, as though she wanted to get back to them. "We need to go to the place they discovered together, bury the letters, and move on with our lives."

With that, Maudie walked away. "Call me if you see the whale."

Something in Arthur snapped. All the little comments she'd been making lately suddenly fused in his mind. "Hey!" he said, jogging after her and pulling her back. Harriet and Gilly looked over, so he lowered his voice. "What are you on about, *it might be the last time we do this,* we have to *move on with our lives,* and what was that half-laugh you did when I mentioned our next trip?" He planted his fist on his hip.

Maudie moved back toward the edge of the sky-ship, and Arthur followed so they were away from curious eyes.

"I'm not going on the next expedition."

It felt as though she'd just punched him full force in the gut. "Don't be daft," he said dismissively.

"I'm going to be at the universitas soon, next year.

They're bringing my application forward because of the breadth of my experience with the sky-aks and everything."

"Yeah, well, that's all right, because you can just carry on studying on the sky-ship."

"Arty, I won't be coming. I want to go and study in person."

"Stop saying that," he said more forcefully than he meant to, but the panic he was feeling was like one of Felicity's pots overboiling.

"You do realize exploring is *your* dream, not mine."

"But we're . . ." He could hardly speak. He noticed Maudie's hands trembling.

"I've been trying to tell you." Her voice wobbled. "I want to be with other young engineers. Learning together where we can bounce ideas around and share knowledge."

"We do that," he said desperately.

"I know, and you're everything to me, but . . ." She let out a loud sigh. "I can't talk about this right now," she said and hurried away, disappearing below deck.

It was as though someone had pulled the planks

from beneath him and he was suspended in the sky, about to fall.

Harriet called him over to the wheel. "Is . . . everything all right?"

He felt numb. Perhaps Maudie hadn't really meant it. She'd probably change her mind by the time they were back in Lontown. Yes, that was what would happen. He shook his head and looked to Harriet. "Yes, I'm fine."

"Are you sure?" she asked slowly.

He nodded. He so desperately wanted to tell her about how he felt, and about the songs, and the drawing of the island, but he thought that would really make him seem as though he was losing the focus of the expedition.

"OK. If you're really sure, then would you take the wheel for a while? I'm going to check in with Meriwether on the readings. Just hold her steady in the central line of the fjord, you'll be fine."

He grasped the wheel tightly with his hand. It always made him feel steady and in control, as if the *Aurora* were a real person who had his back. As the sun grew higher in the morning sky, the shadow from the ship's great balloon reached him.

Parthena landed on the deck and gave him a curious "*squark.*" *Was he all right?*

"I'm fine," he said quietly to himself. "Yep, totally fine."

※　※　※

By early evening they had reached another volcano that formed part of the Dragon's Backbone. Jordauga, the Eye of the Wide. Harriet was back at the wheel again.

"Is that another pitch mine down there? I wouldn't want to work that near to a volcano," said Arthur. He was still feeling a bit wounded from the morning, but he was mostly managing to block it from his mind. He and Maudie had kept their distance since, with Maudie working on her invention in the library.

Harriet looked through her uniscope. "Yes, I believe it is! It seems to be in operation too. Thaddeus Vane has never cared much about the safety of his workers. You won't hear about it in Lontown, but a few cases were brought against him on that issue. They were quickly swept away; it just took a few sovereigns."

"Why doesn't that surprise me?"

"Mind you, it's not only the Vanes. There are several prominent explorer families who invest in the mines. It seems that they really are expanding northward. I hope the water engine will change things and stop the demand, but I guess that might take a while." Harriet shook her head. "Come on, we're almost at the volcano and I want to ascend a little. Hugo is confident that we'll be safe with the heat shields, but I want to be cautious. Maudie, can you activate the shields, please?"

"I'm on it!" she called, coming up from the library.

With Harriet holding the *Aurora* steady, they slowed to a near crawl as they crossed over Jordauga. The crew were gathered on the bow to see the spectacle, although Maudie kept a slight distance from Arthur and was chatting with Gilly. They let out a gasp as they reached the peak and bubbling red lava came into view in the vent of the volcano. Gan joined Arthur. "Wow, it looks really angry!"

The molten lava churned with burning fury as they approached.

"My dad wrote about this volcano in his journal. He said that the people who live in the area believe there are spirits in the fire and that the very soul of the earth is here. If you look down into it, you are looking into the actual eye of the Wide."

"Maybe it is an eye!" said Gan. "The big evil Eye of the Wide! Mwahaha!"

Arthur laughed and found he was warming to

Gan, however much of a liability she was. Then Gan appeared to remember she was still cross about Batzorig continuing the journey with them. She glanced back at the *Altan* flying to the south and resumed her scowl.

It was a magnificent sight below, the colors so vivid, like the raw power of the Wide's soul was before them. He wondered how Dad must have felt seeing this for the first time. He turned to tell Harriet to let Queenie take the wheel so that she didn't miss it, then noticed Hugo quickly sending off another pigeon with a letter at the stern.

Where was that pigeon headed? Arthur wondered. He squinted at the horizon behind them, and he spotted a dark dot in the distance. It had to be another sky-ship!

Molten hot fury seemed to explode in his core. Perhaps it was the fact he had boxed up his emotions from the morning, or that he was just so outraged by what he had realized.

"Hugo's a spy!" he shouted to the whole crew, before he'd even had time to question his decision. "He's sending letters to Eudora Vane, I know he is!" Arthur blurted. "All this meek, shy professor front is just an act!"

Maudie rushed over. "Arty!" she said with hushed urgency. "You might want to stop and think."

But a tightened coil had unleashed within him and he couldn't stop, especially not with Maudie standing in front of him, thinking she had any right to tell him what he should or should not do. "Hugo is a spy!" he repeated, louder.

"Arthur?" Harriet frowned. "That's quite an accusation. What's going on?" The crew were silent and stared between Arthur and Hugo. Gan took a couple of meringue sweets from her pocket and stuffed them in her mouth as though they were snacks for a show.

Hugo blushed and looked like he'd been caught with his hand in Felicity's secret stash of chocolate-coated honey biscuits.

"Everybody return to your duties," said Harriet. "Maudie, can you take the wheel with Queenie? Arthur and Hugo, I think we'd better have a talk in my room."

"Er, perhaps Maudie should come too," said Hugo meekly.

Did Hugo think Maudie could calm him down? Arthur wondered, indignant. Well, he'd picked the wrong day for that.

"Very well. Felicity, Queenie is capable of keeping the sky-ship steady, but if you could just stay with her, please?"

Felicity nodded, her grasp tight on her lucky

spoon, looking as taken aback by the unfolding events as the rest of the crew.

They followed Harriet to her cabin. "All take a seat." She leaned against her desk and folded her arms as they slumped into chairs. "Arthur, could you please explain your unexpected outburst?"

"Hugo keeps sending letters when he thinks no one is looking, and I don't trust Eudora. I think she's following us for some reason, and I think he is helping her and feeding her secret information." The words came out like an avalanche.

"They're just letters to my parents." Hugo turned his hands upward in innocence.

"Then why send them when you think no one is looking? Why did you cover it with your hand when you were writing it?"

"I'm a private person, and I've never met this Eudora, I promise you."

But Hugo's eyes were darting and Arthur wasn't convinced. "I don't believe you."

Hugo loosened a breath, his shoulders dropping as he closed his eyes in resignation. "All right. Perhaps it's time."

CHAPTER 14

HUGO

HUGO TOOK A deep breath and looked at the floor. Then he turned to face Arthur and Maudie. "I knew your parents."

"You knew our parents?" repeated Arthur, not quite able to register the words. It was the last thing he expected Hugo to say.

Hugo smiled, and his features softened as though a great burden had been taken from his shoulders, and for once his cheeks didn't flush red. "I did. In fact, I've known your father since I was born. I'm his younger brother."

Maudie scrunched up her nose and frowned. "Dad had a brother?"

"I'm sorry I didn't tell you who I was sooner, but yes, I'm your uncle."

Arthur glanced at Maudie. Why had no one ever told them they had an uncle? They both looked to Hugo for further explanation.

"So Hugo Waynecroft isn't your real name?" asked Maudie.

"No. It's Hugo Brightstorm. Although our family name before Brightstorm was Brierson. I'm sure you know that your father chose Brightstorm as his explorer surname, and we all decided to follow suit back home."

"So you're not Hugo Waynecroft," said Arthur, his brain spinning. "And you're not Eudora's spy?"

He shook his head. "No, I'm definitely not Eudora's spy. I chose the name Waynecroft because it sounded Lontonian. I thought I'd better not use Brierson in case Ernest had mentioned that name to you, but by your expressions I'm guessing he didn't."

"Wait, how can we be sure you're telling the truth and this isn't all part of some elaborate plan of Eudora's?" Arthur leaned back and crossed his arms. He looked at Hugo differently now, and noted the red tinge of his hair—not quite the rusty brown of his father's, but similar. And Hugo's freckles were more prominent now that he'd had some sun on the trip—that used to happen to their father too. And now that he thought about it, he could see it in the line of Hugo's jaw and the eyes hidden behind the wire-rimmed glasses. And his smile seemed to warm a room, just like Dad's. It was doing it now. Arthur and Maudie locked eyes, the tension from their argument at the fjord dissolving for the time. Could they really have an uncle?

"Because it's the truth," said Hugo, shrugging his shoulders. "My parents are at their summer house close by, on the island of Snae Strond. If you need confirmation, we could go visit them, and they'll tell you everything. They are who I've been sending notes to."

In his heart, Arthur could feel the truth of Hugo's words, and a mix of emotions swirled like rapids within his head. He was certain it was the same for Maudie.

"Our grandparents . . . are alive?" she asked.

Hugo nodded.

Arthur had so many questions that he didn't know where to start.

"Well, this is not how I thought this was going to go," said Harriet, unfolding her arms. "Would you like me to leave you to talk?"

"No," the three of them said at once.

Then Hugo did blush red.

"So, you're not a professor?" asked Maudie.

"Oh, I am a professor. In our own small universitas in the north of Vornatania, close to Fellsandur."

"Why didn't you contact us before; and why didn't you tell us who you were when you first arrived?" asked Arthur.

"It was important that I got to know you first. To find out what you were like. Ernest always kept in touch, with photographs and letters, and he visited when you were tiny, but you wouldn't remember. But after what happened in South Polaris you were hard to track down. News from Lontown can take a while to reach these parts; we tend to keep ourselves to ourselves as much as possible. We assumed you would be taken under the wing of your mother's family, the Vanes, and we knew how that would be. They have quite the reputation even outside of Lontown. Then I saw you were with Harriet and off on another expedition, so there's not been much opportunity to seek you out."

Arthur wondered how things might have turned out if Hugo had appeared the day they found out about their father and were taken from Brightstorm House by the Begginses. They had a Brightstorm family they'd never known about—a family that was part of their dad.

"I was in Lontown on other business when I heard you were back in the city and planning to travel north like your parents, so I sent the letter to Harriet, and well, here I am. I was going to tell you soon, I was just waiting for the right moment; perhaps a starry night on the deck or something, rather than being shouted at for being a spy."

They all smiled.

"There's something else important I need to tell you now," said Hugo.

Somehow Arthur knew, because it had been rolling through his mind ever since Hugo had told him about the legend. "The earth-bear isn't only a story, is it?"

Hugo looked at him with surprise, then glanced at Harriet.

"It's all right, Harriet can be trusted with anything," said Maudie.

"Yes, I can see that." Hugo nodded. "Your suspicion is right. The earth-bear is real. It's the main reason I had to make certain I could trust you. The earth-bear has been protected here since your parents discovered it. It's been fairly easy to keep it that way, since nobody believes there is anything of worth in this area. Not unless you are young explorers on a mission to follow in your parents' footsteps, that is."

"Then the legend is true!" said Maudie. "Can it talk? In our language, not just in thoughts?"

Hugo nodded. "From what we know, the earth-bear is an ancient creature, old as the land itself. It has a deep connection with the Wide; that's why it sings of how it came to be."

"Then it's been the earth-bear singing the song, not the ghosts of our parents!" Maudie was amazed.

"What song?" asked Harriet. She looked as though she was finding it impossible to keep up.

"We wanted to tell you, but we thought you might think us unhinged! We've been hearing a song. First it was in our dreams, but then it was . . . also when we were awake. We thought it might have been the ghosts of our parents calling us to explore where they did . . ." Arthur felt a bit foolish, but he supposed the reality of the earth-bear was just as strange a concept. "It started before we'd even decided to come north."

Frowning, Hugo became lost in his thoughts for a moment. "Curious! I know its song can travel—I believe that's why the legend started in the villages—but over such a distance? It's as though it wanted you to come here for some reason."

"The thought-wolves can communicate over great distances too!" said Arthur excitedly.

"Yes, I read about these wolves in the *Lontown Chronicle*. I believed the earth-bear was a unique type of sapient, but perhaps it makes sense there are more. And you met these thought-wolves?"

Both twins nodded, and Arthur opened his mouth to mention the darkwhispers too—but then he remembered that Erythea was still a secret, so they should check with Harriet first.

"Then you can imagine such a creature might be seen as a prize by some in Lontown," Hugo mused.

"It certainly would," agreed Harriet.

"So that's why our parents chose to protect it?" asked Arthur.

"Ernest was an explorer for all the right reasons. He loved the feeling of adventure and discovery. He was never interested in harming or exploiting anything he came across. But as much as he wanted to tell the world about the creature for all the right reasons, Violetta warned him what people like her father and sister might do. They would see such a creature as a prize and slaughter it for its fur, or try to make a stuffed trophy from it, or keep it locked up and charge admission to view it. So your parents made a promise to the earth-bear, and they decided to let me in on the secret. Lontown being so far from here, they wanted someone a little nearer whom they could trust to keep an eye out too. We didn't even tell our parents for a time, but then we needed more eyes in the area and we knew they wouldn't tell a soul."

Although it was incredible to find out they had a Brightstorm family alive, they couldn't help but wonder why their father hadn't told them, why Hugo or their grandparents hadn't approached them before. The awkward pause and the twins' slightly aggrieved expressions told Hugo their thoughts.

"Your dad wanted to tell you, but he had to hide his family connections to keep you and the earth-bear safe. He didn't trust the Vanes enough to even let them know who his family was—he knew the Vanes would investigate them to try and discredit him, and he didn't want to garner attention and risk discovery of the earth-bear. Ernest always said he would tell you when you were old enough to truly understand the gravity of the secret and the ways of the Wide. He was going to wait until you were thirteen."

It did make sense, and the twins couldn't be cross with their father for making that decision if he was just trying to protect them, but it still left them feeling hollow. They had missed out on ever having the conversation with their father.

"Can we go and meet the earth-bear? Do you visit it often?" asked Arthur.

Hugo shook his head. "I've never seen it. I'm not as brave as your father was. I've heard it's wild and rather fierce. I wanted to come with Ernest one day, but then South Polaris happened and I couldn't face it on my own, so I've been keeping it safe from afar, doing what I can to make sure no stray sky-ships head this way."

The thought-wolves had been terrifying when Arthur had first met them, but they had become their closest allies and had ended up saving them at South Polaris. The darkwhispers had been fearsome too, feeding off memories, but even they had helped him by showing Welby's memories. He wondered what the earth-bear would be like?

It was all so much to take in.

"Snae Strond isn't far from here," said Hugo. "We can visit on the way to Hyrrholm, if you'd like to? That last letter to my parents was to let them know that I was going to tell you, and that I'd hoped you'd agree to visit."

Harriet clasped her hands together. "Arthur,

you're in charge of navigation. I have no objections as captain; so, would you like to readjust the route?"

He looked to Maudie. He was desperate to finally get to Hyrrholm and see the moths and now to search for the earth-bear, but Snae Strond was near—and to think, they now had three new relatives!

"Let's go meet our grandparents!" he said.

CHAPTER 15

SNAE STROND

SUNRISE PEEPED OVER the eastern sea as they reached the shores of Snae Strond, a vast, snowy island, flatter than much of the landscape they'd seen, but with pretty fields of purple flowers and houses made with grass roofs.

Hugo had sent a pigeon ahead to tell his parents they were arriving, so as the sky-ships descended into the bay, two excited figures were waiting to greet them.

The twins and Hugo were first to disembark from the gangplank of the *Aurora*. The twins exchanged nervous glances as they walked toward their grandparents. They were both tall, their fore-heads and eyes creased with years and their skin sun-weathered and freckled. Their grandfather had a neat, full beard and wore a fawn-colored, thickly knitted turtleneck sweater, and their grandmother wore a long wool cardigan to her ankles. She was round-faced and her hair was bunched up loosely. She grabbed her husband's hand and squeezed as they approached.

Hugo embraced each of them warmly, then turned to the twins. "This is my mother, Anna, your grandmother, of course, and this is my father, Jon, your grandfather." Before Hugo could say any more, Anna hurried over to Arthur and enveloped him in a squeeze, and Jon did the same to Maudie. Then they hurriedly swapped, filling the space with excited chatter and a cacophony of questions and remarks about how much like their father they were, and how they were so delighted to finally meet them. Arthur smiled as his grandfather's hands enveloped him like great mittens, his warmth surrounding him, and memories of his dad flooded back.

The crews of the *Aurora* and the *Altan* joined them to a flurry of introductions.

"All are very welcome!" said Anna. "Our stores are full and our home is yours too."

"Care to explain why they almost hugged you in half?" Gan asked Arthur.

"Oh, you were still pouting over Batzorig, so I

didn't get a chance to tell you, but it turns out that Hugo's our uncle," said Arthur.

"But I thought you said he was a spy?" Gan's face dropped with disappointment. "That would've been far more exciting."

Batzorig laughed. "I fear for the future of the Citadel!"

Arthur thought that if you were to write down everything you would wish for in an ideal grandparent, their Brightstorm grandparents were it. They were full of smiles and stories, their faces warm, weathered with age and experience, their words kind and their hearts full. They still had lots of energy and spent the morning showing the crew around, feeding them, showing them family heirlooms such as Ernest's first hiking boots from when he was three, and pressed flowers they'd collected in books together. At lunchtime, they took them a little farther along the bay to where a hot spring pool looked out over the sea.

"Now, let's get you washed and into some clean clothes, you all have that several-moon-cycles-in-the-sky look!" said Anna. "There are plenty of bathing suits in the sheds over there and room to change. Leave your dirty clothes in the wash bins and Jon and I will see to them."

They hurriedly got changed and Arthur was the first one back outside, where he joined Anna.

"This will relax every muscle in your body!" she said, walking with him to the pool. "It's the reason we like to spend the summers here. Of course, the northern summer is much cooler than a Vornatanian summer."

Batzorig joined them, followed by Felicity, Maudie, and soon the other crew members.

Gan came out of the shed wrapped in a towel.

"Pop your towel on the ledge and dive on in," Anna said to Gan, smiling warmly.

As Gan took off her towel, her horse tattoo came straight into view.

Batzorig saw it in an instant. "Ganzorig! What in all the great kings and queens of the Citadel have you done?!"

"Ah, well, maybe I should explain," said Arthur.

"No need." Gan ran toward the pool and leaped in the water with a "Woo hoo!" When she surfaced, she called back, "Don't worry, Uncle, it's not permanent! It's painted on with a paste of crushed leaves that stains the skin. It'll be gone in a week or so."

Arthur and Maudie exchanged a shocked glance, then chased after her and jumped in the pool.

The water was glorious, and the heat was perfect, hot enough to bring a warm glow to their cheeks. It felt like the most luxurious bath Arthur had ever had. He swam over to Gan. "You mean it's temporary? And you had me thinking it was permanent!"

Gan nodded with a cheeky grin. "I couldn't help myself. If you could have seen your shocked little face when I showed you. And technically you never asked if it was permanent."

Maudie looked at Arthur and splashed him. "The apprentice likes to mess with the teacher, it seems!"

"I'm no apprentice," Gan grumbled, at the same time that Arthur protested, "Hey, I'm no teacher!"

"Really?" Maudie asked with a glint in her eye.

"Well, go on, jump on in, the rest of you!" said Jon.

The rest of the crew joined them, then Anna and Jon.

"This is amazing!" said Arthur.

"My feet have never felt so good," said Felicity.

"We call it Aegirsyn Laug, which in Lontonian would be the 'see sea spring,'" said Jon. "Because you can see the sea from the spring."

"Where do you live in the winter?" asked Maudie.

"Not far from Fellsandur, in a little village out of the city."

"Is that where Dad was born?"

Anna shook her head. "We're both from Chesterford in Vornatania originally, but we were each drawn to the ways of the North, so we moved here when Ernest was young. All the islands are independent; no one belongs to anywhere here, and you get a wonderful mix of people. Fellsandur was, and still is, a place for everyone. Residents are from Carrickmurgus, East Insulae, even as far as Nadvaaryn."

"Of course, no one ever ventures much farther north than Fellsandur because sky-ships aren't exactly your average transport and pitch is expensive. We use our sailboat, but we're used to the weather and waters of the North. This island you're on now was found by Ernest," said Jon proudly. "He built these huts."

Arthur thought this was the sort of place it would be difficult to leave. Indeed, the thermal spring felt so good that the crew stayed in there for over a chime, until their muscles were languid and their fingertips wrinkly as raisins.

Anna left them towels and clean, dry clothes in the sheds. They kept a large collection of extra clothes there, having hosted a lot of families over the years and also because they both loved to knit. Anna said she even had a solar-powered dehydrator machine for those who had long hair to dry.

They spent the rest of the day walking on the beach and spotting blue dolphins in the bay, then Jon insisted that Felicity take a rest and that he cook for everyone. After a supper of grilled halibut with spruce tips and freshly baked sourdough rolls, they put on chunky, knitted cardigans and made a fire on the beach.

The waves tickled the shore and Arthur and Maudie stood chatting to Harriet.

"Your grandparents seem so happy to meet you." Harriet smiled. "It can't have been easy, but they must have understood that severing ties was something your father needed to do in order to keep the earth-bear safe from the Vanes and other Lontonians. Nonetheless, it probably hurts a little. Trust me, I know how you are feeling, but once you understand why the decisions were made, it becomes easier."

It had escaped Arthur's mind that Harriet had been unaware of her Erythean heritage until their last expedition, but the reasons for her being kept in the dark made sense when you took the time to understand. "It's funny," said Arthur. "We grew up thinking explorers were the people connecting the world and building bridges through travel, but after Erythea, and now knowing this . . ."

"Yes," said Maudie, "Dad agreed with the Erytheans in principle, that Lontonians might not be safe to introduce everywhere."

Harriet nodded. "He must have been mindful of the risks they posed to local communities in their exploration."

Arthur wondered how many others thought like them and what that meant for their own responsibilities as explorers.

"Perhaps there is much to be said for making sure Lontown is good and safe for others before venturing elsewhere on its behalf."

There was so much sense in Harriet's words and she always spoke with such truth, strength, and kindness. Arthur didn't know what they would have done without her the past two years. What Arthur didn't find easy was why the Wide had to be this way. Full of secrets and judgment.

"You might never understand why some humans are the way they are, why some societies develop with a deep sense of superiority over others," Harriet went on, as if reading Arthur's mind. "But I do know that it's people like your father and mother, the Erytheans, and the kings of the Citadel who change things."

Pride for what his father stood for and what his parents had achieved, considering what they were up against, made his heart feel as though it took up half of his chest. And here he was, on this strange island on the edge of nowhere, a home he never even realized he had or needed until now.

But there was a reason they had come here: the earth-bear had called them, and he knew that the only way to find out why was to finish their journey to Hyrrholm. They had to find the earth-bear and speak to it.

Somewhere, from the distant shore, carried across the waves, the song came to him. He looked at Harriet, but there was no change in her expression. Maudie's eyes, however, widened in the moonlight when he looked across at her sitting by the fire.

Perhaps the earth-bear wanted a new guardian to take on the role their parents had left behind? Perhaps coming here and living with their Brightstorm grandparents and Hugo was simply destiny, everything coming together the way it was meant to?

Maudie walked across to join them.

"Can we leave to seek the earth-bear tomorrow, please?" asked Arthur.

Usually decisive in her thinking, Arthur could tell that Harriet was wavering. "Harrie?"

She sighed. "I'm not sure if I'm the right person to ask anymore."

"What do you mean?"

"You have an uncle in Hugo and your Brightstorm grandparents are here. I can't help but think . . ."

"But the *Aurora* is . . ." He wanted to say *home*, but was it? Harriet had been looking after them and had offered them a home because she was kind and amazing like that, and they'd had nowhere else to go. But now that they did, she could be free of them. Was that what she was trying to say? His throat became tight.

"I agree with Arthur that we should seek it

tomorrow," said Maudie, and Arthur was grateful to her, because he felt as though saying anything more would burst a dam that he hadn't even realized was there.

Harriet turned to the sea. "Of course we can. If it's . . ." Her voice faltered, which the twins had never heard, even in the most perilous of situations they'd been in. "If it's all right with your Brightstorm family, we'll head there tomorrow."

❋   ❋   ❋

The next morning, Arthur awoke early, keen to get going, but Harriet was up earlier and already on the *Aurora* deck, making checks.

"Morning, Arthur. I've decided we will proceed with a skeleton crew. Meriwether is detecting small levels of ash on the wind, nothing to be overly concerned about, I'm sure, but if it became severe it could be dangerous for the water engines. If we have to abandon ship, there isn't room enough for the full crew on the sky-aks with all the materials we needed for the journey, so it will be myself, you and Maudie, of course, Felicity, Hugo, and Gan."

"Gan? Are you sure?"

"Batzorig will drive her batty if she stays here.

Did you hear him last night telling Anna and Jon how of course the Citadel would do things differently, like this, and the Citadel would do things even better, like that!" She laughed. "Thank goodness he is so charming and your grandparents are so gracious and patient, as there could have been a very different mood to the evening!"

"She'd probably stow away anyway," Arthur said, smiling and shaking his head.

"The rest of the crew seem happy at the prospect of staying here longer, and of course I've not mentioned the earth-bear. I'm afraid I will need to tell Batzorig, because I want his permission for Gan, but Hugo has agreed it's the right thing to do and that Batzorig can be trusted."

Arthur nodded, then Anna called from the shore to tell them breakfast was ready around the fire.

Arthur and Maudie sat with Anna and Jon on the pebbles beside the lapping water, eating cooked tomatoes and scrambled eggs.

"I know it's early days and we've only just reconnected, but both Jon and I feel like we've known you forever."

Arthur felt the same. They were such happy company to be in.

"You know, you could consider making this your

home too," said Jon. "You could travel back to Lontown whenever you like, of course. There's always a warm bed waiting for you here with us, and don't forget that your Uncle Hugo also spends a lot of time here in the North."

"Thank you," said Arthur. "That's very kind of you. It's certainly something for us to consider." The idea of his home now seemed unmoored. The only home he'd truly been able to rely on was Maudie, and if she was set on her own path . . .

By midmorning the Brightstorm grandparents had packed the *Aurora* with fresh supplies: bread, butter, cheese, shiny red apples, and tomatoes grown in their greenhouse. The smaller crew waved goodbye to their friends and then took off from the sunny shores of Snae Strond, sailing onward, toward Hyrrholm.

CHAPTER 16

HYRRHOLM

As THE *AURORA* pressed on in a northwesterly direction, the song became louder and more frequent, so Arthur studied his maps of Hyrrholm again to distract himself. They would need to be careful, as the north half of the island was marked with dangerous sulfur lakes and searing hot-gas geysers. But his father's journals indicated that the moths were on the south side, so he hoped the earth-bear would be there too. Then they wouldn't have to venture into the more perilous northern half.

The temperature dropped during the night and snow fell as morning arrived. A white, wet haze hung in all directions, making it difficult to see the vast ocean below. Before they'd left, Meriwether had insisted they take their cold-weather gear, as a northern summer could turn within a chime, so they all dressed in their fur-lined jackets and pants. Arthur put a pair of large woolen mittens Jon had given him on his hand and over the end of his right arm to stay warm while he cleared snow from the wings. The wind picked up and bore them on faster toward the island.

By midafternoon of the next day, the sky remained uniformly white, and the cloud level had dropped, so they descended a little to fly a short distance above the ocean. Eventually, a dark shape arose from the cold mist.

"Look!" called Arthur from the bow. "Hyrrholm!"

His pulse was racing. They had reached the home of the Brightstorm moths at last.

"We're really here!" said Maudie, as she hurried below deck to retrieve the Brightstorm moth box containing the letters.

Parthena skimmed the waves close by and let out a joyful cry.

They descended to the southern beach, where the sand was peculiarly black. Hugo told Arthur that when the island's volcano had erupted, the lava had reached the water, cooled rapidly, and shattered, eroding to sand over time. There were tall gloomy shapes visible in the mist—the outline of mountains, perhaps the volcano.

After landing, Harriet insisted that Arthur and Maudie be the first to step onto Hyrrholm as a symbolic gesture. They stood grinning on the gangplank and together took a step onto the black sand.

Harriet, Felicity, Hugo, and Gan all clapped from the balustrades, then followed them down.

"To think, our parents were here together once too," said Arthur, his heart swelling in his chest.

"I know! It makes them feel close, doesn't it?" Maudie squeezed his hand. She clutched the box close to her. "Do you think we're doing the right thing, burying the letters?" asked Maudie.

"We'll soon know, if the song stops." Arthur smiled. "Although I'm going to keep the letter with the mysterious island on it, so maybe you should keep one too?"

Maudie nodded.

"Do you think the earth-bear could be watching us?" Arthur scanned the landscape, looking desperately for any sign of movement.

Maudie sighed. "The rocks look hazardous, and the earth-bear might feel threatened by us. This is going to be tricky."

Harriet joined them and surveyed the upcoming landscape with her binoscope. "Felicity and Gan are going to stay and keep watch on the *Aurora*. We'll have a preliminary scouting mission first, and we should aim to be back before two chimes. I've promised Gan that if it's all OK she can come out with you tomorrow."

"Here," said Hugo, passing them all climbing boots. "I borrowed these from Snae Strond. These will be better for climbing over the rocks."

"And I have my new climbing gloves in case we get to any really tricky parts," said Maudie.

They changed their boots, then headed off into the tumble of rocks and crags while Felicity made a beachside fire and prepared food for their return.

"From your map it shouldn't be too far to the area your father marked as being the site of the moths. I'm judging less than a chime on foot."

Arthur agreed. "Have you got the box, Maud?"

She nodded and tapped her backpack. "I've put it in here."

It was heavy going and slippery. All the while they listened for the earth-bear and any sign of the moths, but the island was eerily quiet and the sky was empty aside from Parthena. Eventually they reached an area where they descended again and the ground widened and flattened out before rising steeply in the distance.

"That must be the edge of the valley up there," said Arthur pointing, then comparing it to the map. "The edges look too steep to see what's inside."

"This is it, then. They should be somewhere here!" Maudie said excitedly.

They put their backpacks down and scanned the area and the sky. But all was quiet and there wasn't any sign of creatures anywhere. It all seemed lifeless.

"Perhaps we're in the wrong place?" asked Arthur, turning the map in his hands. They searched for a while around the sharp rocks and the moss, then sat on a boulder.

Maudie sighed. "Or maybe they've moved on, or become extinct, or something horrible."

"Or perhaps we need to let the sun go down?" suggested Harriet. "Moths don't tend to like the day. I'm not so sure about getting back over the rocks to the beach when it's too dark, though."

Disappointment was a lead weight in Arthur's stomach. He had imagined burying his parents' letters somewhere magical and lush, a flight of moths fluttering reverently above, and now he felt a little foolish for taking his wild dreams seriously.

"We could build a fire while we wait and make a torch to help us get back? It shouldn't be too much longer," said Hugo.

"Yes! Can we, Harrie?" asked Maudie, excitedly. "We've come so far."

Harriet smiled and agreed, so they made a fire and waited until the sun began setting. But there was still no sign of the moths.

"Maybe we should bury the letters now," said Maudie. "It'll be better to do it while we still have light."

"Anyone bring a shovel?" asked Arthur, and the others shook their heads. Why hadn't they thought of that?

"Here, we can use my wrench to dig," said Maudie, unhitching it from her belt.

Arthur nodded and they dug a small hole in the softest piece of ground they could find.

They took the moth box from Maudie's backpack and placed it on the ground before them.

"Would you like to say anything?" asked Harriet.

Maudie drew a breath and nodded.

Arthur said he'd go first. "We never got to know our mother, because she died when we were born, but our father told us about their adventures together, and he always said that Maud was a natural-born engineer, just like her."

Maudie took over. "Our dad was the best dad we could imagine, and although we didn't get him for long, he taught us that family is important, and that as long as you have at least one person in your life to call family, then you can get through anything. Luckily we have quite a few more now, so that's . . . er . . . good! Thank you all for bringing us to this place."

"Even if it is a little bleak, and desolate, and I can't feel my fingers because of digging that frozen earth!" said Arthur.

"Yes, so can we please see the moths now?" added Maudie, and they all laughed—which felt right because their father had the warmest laugh, and perhaps he was here, watching them and laughing with them.

Arthur and Maudie knelt and put the box on the ground. Together they each put a hand on the lid, ready to open it.

Then something extraordinary happened: the moth design on the box's lid shifted!

The twins peered at it, blinking disbelievingly.

"Did you see that?" Maudie breathed.

Arthur nodded as the edges of the pattern lifted. "The whole thing is moving."

Slowly, the wings peeled from the box.

"Perhaps there are hidden mechanics?" Maudie said, bending to look.

The moth lifted its wings together, then extended them wide again, as if it were waking from a deep sleep. It pushed itself up to its feet. They couldn't believe what they were seeing.

"What's happening?" Arthur asked, mesmerized.

"That doesn't seem mechanical to me," said Maudie. "It's coming to life!"

"But how?"

The moth observed them with intelligent eyes, unfolding its wings, then closing them.

"I think you're right!" said Harriet. "I know your mother was a fine engineer, but that doesn't appear to be mechanical. Did your mother have a sapient?"

Like a key turning in his brain, Arthur recalled a conversation they'd had with their father when they were young. "Yes, I think so; Maud, didn't Dad say she had a great moth sapient companion?"

Maudie nodded. "We assumed it had left or died when she died, long ago. How long can moths live?"

"Surely this couldn't be the same moth? After all this time?"

"It has to be! Mum's sapient—she's been with us all along!"

"Incredible." Harriet shook her head. "It must have been in a kind of stasis for the past . . . what, fourteen years?"

"Absolutely astounding," said Hugo, putting on his wire-rimmed glasses to get a closer look.

The moth's black wings, etched with the red jagged pattern, seemed to fire into life, becoming more vibrant and animated with every moment.

"Her name—what is her name?" Frantically, Arthur tried to remember if their father had ever mentioned any . . .

"Could it be . . . Urania?" asked Maudie tentatively.

At the sound of her name, the moth's feathery antennae flickered. Then with a flutter of her wings she flew to land on Maudie's shoulder.

Maudie giggled. "The word is etched into Mum's toolbelt," she explained. "I've looked at it nearly every day since I was small and never paid it much thought."

Urania's antennae brushed Maudie's cheek, then she flew to Arthur's shoulder and did the same.

The emotion Arthur felt at that moment was something he'd never felt before—no, he surely *had* felt it before, just out of reach of his memory. It was something akin to being held as a baby, feeling utterly secure, safe, and loved in the arms of his mother. He knew that Maudie had felt it too because of the way she gazed over at Arthur, her eyes gleaming. It was as though Urania had kept the last touch of their mother safe and had given it to them now as a gift.

Suddenly, with a flutter of her wings, Urania took flight. She looped around the clearing, landing briefly on the plants and rocks in an excited dance. Then she began spiraling into the air, higher and higher.

Somewhere, humming started.

"Can you hear that?" Harriet asked, looking around.

"Yes," said Hugo, curiously.

"What's happening?" asked Arthur. A strange electricity seemed to fill the air and the mountain rippled.

Harriet grabbed their hands. "Look!"

The steep wall of rock before them began quivering. There was no rumble beneath their feet, so Arthur was certain it wasn't an earthquake. Urania flew before the wall.

Then something took flight a short distance away

and joined her. "It's another moth!" called Arthur pointing excitedly.

"Over there, Arty—two more!"

They were all similar in size to Urania, large enough to cover an adult hand.

Urania flew back and forth, as moths rose from the rocks around her, joining her in flight, their wings illuminated with the ruby pattern when they moved.

"There are thousands of them!" said Maudie. "They were just cleverly camouflaged before."

Then the words of the song began, carried from not far away.

> *The beat of the earth is strong, strong,*
> *Forged from the roars of time.*
> *Hum! Hum! Thrumming high.*
> *It calls, we call, the voices.*

"Maud, it's the song!" Arthur whispered to her.

"Is it coming from the moths?"

He turned his head as though to locate the sound. "I don't think so. It's as though it's traveling on the wind from that direction."

Harriet scratched her head. "Is this the song you've been talking about? It's beautiful."

"You can hear it now?" asked Maudie. Everyone

spoke softly, suddenly under the spell of what they were hearing.

"Yes!" said Hugo, his arms stretched wide in amazement. "I know it. It is the Firesong!"

"Harriet and Hugo can hear it too!" Arthur said, pulling Maudie onto a boulder so that they could hear where the song was coming from. The moths fluttered and danced rhythmically above, as though also under the spell of the song. There was no way they could single out Urania anymore.

"It's coming from far off over there somewhere," said Maudie, pointing north to the crater.

> *When the stars were to begin*
> *Flame on shoulder, water of hand*
> *They called to the great sky,*
> *"Bring, begin! Buds, grow! Sea, land!"*

"Perhaps we could find the source. It must be the earth-bear. It can't be far away," said Arthur.

Harriet cleared her throat. "In case anyone hasn't noticed, the sun is very low. Don't you think rather a lot has happened today already without extending it to search for a possibly dangerous sapient in the dark?"

"Please, Harrie, just half a chime," Arthur pleaded.

The moths suddenly dispersed, disappearing over the cliff wall.

She sighed. "You two are very persuasive sometimes. Come on, then, but when I say we turn back I don't want to hear another word."

"The earth-bear must live past those cliff walls, inside the valley, but how do we get in?" Arthur spread his dad's map of the island out on a boulder. "There must be a way in. Perhaps a place where the walls aren't so steep and we can climb . . ."

"I have my climbing gloves," said Maudie. "But I only have two pairs."

Harriet gave a definite *no*. "We need to stay together."

They walked for a chime, but still couldn't find a viable place to get inside without needing some specialist climbing gear. "Maybe Dad had better equipment than us." Arthur sighed. "Didn't he tell you how he actually got in to see the bear, Hugo?"

Hugo shook his head. "He said the less I knew, the safer it would be. My role was only to keep watch in the Fellsandur area for any expeditions that might be heading this way."

For another chime they walked back and forth without seeing any possible way to climb into the valley.

"We could fly the *Aurora* inside," Arthur suggested.

"It wouldn't be safe to do so," said Harriet. "That map makes the valley area look very treacherous, and I wouldn't want to risk the *Aurora* being exposed to toxic fumes from the acid lakes."

All of a sudden, Arthur and Maudie heard the song again. This time the ground rumbled softly, as though the very earth growled at them. They all crouched low and clasped the ground. The rumbling soon subsided.

"We need to get back," said Harriet.

"It's fine; that was just a small tremble!" said Arthur. He didn't want to give up again. He could feel in his bones that the rumbles weren't from any normal earthquake. It was something to do with the earth-bear.

"Arthur, I know it's disappointing, but it's late and I told you not to argue on this point."

"Harriet's right," said Hugo. "We can try again tomorrow, if the tremors stop. The last thing we want is an eruption."

"But you said there have been no eruptions for thousands of years in these parts," said Maudie.

"Exactly," Arthur added. "What if the rumble is part of the earth-bear calling us? If we keep stopping every time that happens, we'll never find it!"

The ground shook again.

"I'm sorry, but we're heading back," said Harriet. "Now."

* * *

Felicity jumped up when they arrived back. "Ah, there you are! Gan and I were going to get a search party together if you were much longer! Did you feel the ground rumble?" She buzzed around them, passing them warm milk, hot potatoes from the fire, and cooked apples with melted caramel inside.

They told Felicity and Gan about seeing the moths and hearing the song as they filled their bellies, their legs tired from clambering over rocks.

They were about to go to bed when soft rumbling shook the ground, more urgent than before.

"I don't like the sound of that," said Harriet, her eyes wide in the firelight. "Hugo, can you take some readings straight away, please?"

Hugo nodded and hurriedly retrieved his machinery from the *Aurora*.

They all watched while he busied himself. "Curious. The volcano seems to still be dormant. But some of my readings don't make sense. I'm afraid to say that things are looking a little . . . *confusing*."

"What does that mean?" It was the last thing Arthur wanted to hear. They had to go back and search for the earth-bear in the morning.

"It's hard to know. Without getting closer and taking more readings, I couldn't say."

Harriet frowned. "We'll keep a careful eye on the situation. You'd better all get to bed."

CHAPTER 17

SEEKING THE EARTH-BEAR

ARTHUR COULDN'T SLEEP. As twelve chimes approached, the song was calling to him almost constantly. Even Parthena was agitated, skittering atop his maps on the table.

"Hey, girl, careful." Arthur suspected that Parthena, being sapient, had perhaps been hearing the singing all this time too.

He stroked her head, but she kept scuttling across the maps. He frowned. She paused and pecked the back of the letter where Arthur's father had drawn the map of the island called Eldurfoss.

"I know you're trying to be helpful, but that island doesn't seem to exist here. It's probably in another area in the Wide that Dad explored some other time."

But Parthena persisted and stabbed her beak at Eldurfoss once more, then tapped the large map of Hyrrholm with her claw, tilting her head.

"Are you trying to tell me those maps are connected?" Arthur studied them once more, looking between them, hoping that something would jump out. It was like the spot-the-difference puzzles in the *Lontown Chronicle* he used to do with Dad, except *everything* on the maps was different: there was nothing remotely similar about them—not the shapes nor the landmarks. The only thing that they both had in common was a compass in the top right corner.

Then Arthur noticed something peculiar: his father had omitted to write "north" and "south" on the compass of the Eldurfoss map, there was only "east" and "west."

A wild idea came to him and his pulse quickened. Could it be? "Parthena, I think I've got it!"

Hurriedly, Arthur stole out of his room toward Maudie's. As he passed Harriet's office he heard voices, and he paused to listen.

"You're telling me there are subtle changes in your readings," said Harriet.

"Yes, but such precursors can occur for months, even years, before any eruptions, and this isn't an area like any other," said Hugo. "I believe the earth-bear regulates it, and what we're seeing might be caused by our presence."

Harriet sighed. "I just don't think I can take the risk. Not on my watch of the twins. I'll tell them in the morning. It's too dangerous here. We have to leave."

Disappointment sank through Arthur's bones. He slipped down the corridor to Maudie's room and, as silently as he could, opened the door.

"Maud, are you awake?" he whispered.

"Yeah, that song won't leave me alone," she said softly. "Come inside."

Arthur inched over so as not to wake Gan, who was asleep in the bunk opposite Maudie, hugging her arrows and quiver. He sat beside Maudie on her bed.

Maudie propped herself up on her elbows. "Why doesn't the song ever finish? There's a final part that Dad used to sing us, I'm certain of it . . . but I can't remember the words."

"Me neither, but listen, I think I've worked something out with the missing island map, something that will help us find the earth-bear. But we've got a problem. I just heard Harrie and Hugo talking. She thinks the volcanic readings are too dangerous here, and she doesn't want us to go back and search again."

"But if we turn back now, we'll never know!"

"I'm not leaving without seeing it."

"Arty, we've been here before and look where that got us. Remember when Tuyok was shot because we decided to sneak onto the *Victorious* in the frozen South?"

"Yes, well—"

"And when you accidentally stowed away on a stolen sky-ship bound for Erythea?"

"But that—"

"And then we followed you, which ended with me being shipwrecked and lost in the jungle."

"Maudie—"

She shook her head. "Things don't always turn out well when we go against Harriet."

"I know, but if Harriet had heard the song as long as we have, she'd know how much the bear wants us to find it. If it controls the volcano, like Hugo says, then it'll keep us safe, I'm certain." He drew up and straightened his shoulders. "You know I'm going to try, with or without you."

Maudie's frown deepened into a scowl. "Why do you think you're always meant to be the spontaneous one? Perhaps I've already made the decision myself to go, whatever Harriet says."

"You have?" He had expected more resistance from her and didn't know whether to be impressed or affronted. "So you're in on this, whatever the consequences?"

She nodded. "Yes. We should leave before sunrise."

"Excellent!" said Gan, who had still appeared to be slumbering in her bunk.

"I thought you were asleep," said Arthur flatly.

She opened her eyes. "My horse would have sneaked in more quietly."

Hurriedly, Maudie brushed past Arthur to sit beside Gan. "Please, Gan, it might be dangerous. You can't come."

"I could always ask Harriet," Gan said with a smirk. "Look, you both think you're so good at being secretive, but I have keen ears and I've heard you talking about the song for ages. I'm not missing out now that it's getting interesting."

After a long huff, Arthur resigned himself to the fact that they had to let Gan tag along. He looked to Maudie and shrugged.

"She's a princess, Arty! What if something happens to her?"

"Then we'd better make sure nothing happens."

Maudie fumbled on the bedside table for her ribbon and tied her hair. "If we're lucky, we can find the earth-bear and hurry back by midmorning. We'll leave a note to say we went fishing along the bay."

"Harriet will see through that straight away." The idea of deceiving Harriet didn't sit well in Arthur's stomach. But what choice did they have? He knew that if they left this island, they wouldn't come back. It was their only chance. "I can't think of anything better, so fishing it is."

"But we still don't know how to get beyond the ridge," said Maudie.

"Ah, that's what I was on my way to tell you. I've got an idea." He smiled.

They decided it was best to leave as soon as possible. They crept out of the sky-ship onto the black beach and, by the light of a small lamp, began clambering across the rocks. Parthena flew soundlessly above them, pausing occasionally to hover in pockets of wind.

By the time they reached the site of the moths it was the pale blue light just before sunrise.

Arthur took his father's book from his bag and unfolded the map of Eldurfoss. "I noticed last night that the compass doesn't have a north or south drawn on it. Dad purposefully left them off, as though those directions are irrelevant. So I got to thinking: what if we've been looking at it from the wrong perspective? If north and south don't relate to this map, and it only runs east to west, what if we're not looking down on the island, but from the side?"

He held the map vertically in front of them. The line that Arthur had assumed was the northern edge of the island—with its distinctive bumps and curves—was exactly the same skyline as the ridge!

"That's brilliant!" Maudie hugged him.

"So the map you're holding is the ridge; but how do we get through the rock?" asked Gan.

"Well, I'm not sure, but the only mark on this map is the small x where Dad wrote 'Eldurfoss.' We assumed that was just the name of the island, but what if x marks the way in?"

They studied the rocks before them and then looked back to the map.

"That area there is this peak, then it flattens off a little, then the triangular piece of rock, so . . . I would say it's just beyond that snowy rise there?" Maudie pointed to a bank of snow.

Parthena took flight with a loud cry and headed over the bank, and the others eagerly followed.

"Be careful over here, the ice patches are slippery!" said Arthur, leading the way.

As they reached the top of the snowbank, another area of the ridge came into view.

"There! That's it!" he said.

A great frozen waterfall shimmered in the morning light, coming from over the ledge of the great rocky wall above them.

Everything fell into place. "Eldurfoss!" Arthur said. "Hugo told me on the journey up here that it meant frozen waterfall! Eldurfoss wasn't really an island name. Dad just disguised it to look like one."

"Ah, only a true explorer would get that," said Gan. "That's a clever trick!"

They hurried down the rocks until they stood before it.

"What now? Are we supposed to axe our way

through it?" Maudie was already unclipping equipment from her tool belt.

"Arrows will be swifter," said Gan, unhitching her bow from across her body and keenly pulling an arrow from her back. "I will create a split in the ice, then we can smash through."

"Not so fast, dynamo," said Arthur, putting a hand on her arm to push the arrow down. "Look!" He pointed to the base of the fountain where the ice formed a skirt before the rocks. When he reached the side, he saw there was a gap big enough to fit through. He edged into the space behind the waterfall, and it opened up into a cave tunnel, so he beckoned them through.

Maudie lit her pocket fire wand and they clutched one another's hands as they stepped into the cave, silently moving onward into the darkness. Eventually, a dim glow appeared at the other end. The song echoed from the walls.

"The song—I can hear it too!" said Gan.

The light from the cave's exit blossomed brighter.

"Be careful when we get out the other side," said Arthur. "There are acid lakes, and sheer drops, and—"

They pushed through mossy vines and stepped out into an enormous enclosed valley. Lush birch trees and ferns grew amid numerous rocky hillocks and boulders. The pinkish glow of sunrise filled the sky above, and in the near distance at the north end, a dormant volcano rose from the ground to the height of the valley walls. There were no exploding vents to dodge or acid lakes to avoid. It was an oasis.

"Whoa, this is awesome!" said Gan.

"It's nothing like the map!" said Arthur.

Parthena swooped over the valley ridge to land atop a nearby birch tree.

Maudie hooked Arthur's arm. "If you think about it, it's pretty obvious. Dad wanted to put people off ever wanting to explore here, so of course he would make it look as inhospitable as—"

Her arm tensed suddenly, and they all came to a jarring halt. Because there, around a mile away, past hillocks and above the tree line on the volcano bank, was an enormous bear.

CHAPTER 18

ROAR

GOOSEBUMPS PRICKLED THEIR skin. Even though it was some distance away, the bear looked immense: the combined height of Arthur, Maudie, and Gan at least, its shoulders wide as a cart and limbs like oak trunks. It was facing away from them, having reared up on its hind legs. Its thick, dark-brown fur was unlike anything Arthur had ever seen on a mammal; it appeared to be etched with strange, jagged markings, similar to the Brightstorm moths' wings.

"I'm not sure this was a good idea," whispered Maudie. "It's much bigger than I thought. Let's back away slowly. I don't think it's seen us yet."

"No way," said Gan, grinning at the sight.

"You might want to consider that a little bit of fear can keep you alive," Arthur muttered to Gan. "But

what's it doing?" Arthur thought it looked as though the earth-bear was preparing to pounce.

It lunged forward and landed with a crash that sent vibrations through the ground beneath their feet. As it did, a flurry of Brightstorm moths filled the air.

The earth-bear jumped up and scooped a handful of moths between its paws, then appeared to eat them.

"It's attacking the moths!" Arthur squeaked. "Why would it do that? It's meant to be a protector of the Wide!"

"It also has to eat." Gan shrugged.

"But it's eating the Brightstorm moths!" said Maudie incredulously.

"I get the circle of life and all that," said Arthur, "but still . . . Wait, do you think it eats *humans*?"

"Probably only boys," replied Gan.

The earth-bear suddenly lifted its head and sniffed the air. They all tensed as they waited for it to turn their way. But it bounded to the left and out of sight behind a patch of birch trees. They followed, but when they turned the bend, the earth-bear had disappeared.

Arthur wasn't sure whether to feel relieved or frustrated. "Where's it gone?"

The silhouette of a great bear suddenly appeared on the brow of one of the rocky hillocks up to the left.

"There it is!" Maudie pointed. "It's as though it's waiting for us to come to it."

The earth-bear stood proudly, its nose high, not looking at them . . . although by now Arthur was fairly certain it knew they were there.

"Let's go, then!" said Gan.

They scrambled up the hillside, but when they reached the top, the earth-bear had disappeared again. Parthena squawked from high above.

"I think it might be leading us toward that rocky area by the volcano," said Arthur, pointing to movement down below. "Do we keep following it?"

But Gan was already charging down the other side.

"Anyone would think it's been calling to *her*!" Arthur snorted.

"She's certainly fearless," said Maudie.

They hurried after the bear until they reached the rocky edges of the volcano.

"It's disappeared again!" said Arthur. "I think it's . . . playing with us?"

"As long as it's not like a predator playing with its next meal . . ." said Maudie, looking a little pale.

Then, like an explosion of thunder in a cloudless

sky, the earth-bear leaped from behind a cluster of boulders to land before them. With a yelp, Arthur, Maudie, and Gan stumbled backward, but they were now pressed against the rocks, with nowhere to run, drowned by its shadow. The earth-bear was even more enormous up close. It towered above them, looking down with fierce black eyes. Its markings were magnificent, the jagged patterns cutting through its thick umber fur all around its body, with a curious spiral around its neck area.

It paced before them, its enormous paws thumping into the earth, shaking the rocks around them.

"Try not to show fear," Arthur whispered, thinking back to when he'd met Tuyok in the Everlasting Forest.

Then the earth-bear opened its mouth and spoke. "You are the children I've been calling?" Its voice was female, but it had countless layers and tones to it like a crowd of voices speaking as one. "But there are three of you?"

"Yes, you called us," said Arthur, thinking *please don't eat us* repeatedly. "But you can trust Gan too."

The bear lunged forward and narrowed her eyes. "Humans! Who can trust humans? I make up my own mind on whom I can trust." The bear resumed her pacing.

"The legends say she can read you with her roar," whispered Arthur to Maudie and Gan. "Remember at the festival? The people who carried their souls to show their intentions?"

"Just as I know how the earth came to be and I can feel where it is going, I see you," the earth-bear said. "As the inner forces of the Wide remain hidden by the great crust, I can unveil them. As the deepest parts of your souls remain hidden by your bodies, I will unveil them." As she spoke, the markings on her fur flared with orange and red.

Swallowing hard, Arthur found there was no moisture in his mouth. This was far more terrifying than the thought-wolves had first been. Self-doubt crawled over his skin and burrowed into the pit of his stomach. What would she see in his soul? What if he wasn't as good as he hoped? Did he have the courage to face his truths?

"Who are you, deep inside?" The earth-bear narrowed her onyx eyes. She fixed on Maudie. "You will be first."

If Maudie was scared she didn't show it. But Arthur knew she had no reason to be afraid. She was a good person, a natural-born engineer who had already invented something that helped people in Lontown.

The earth-bear stood before Maudie, her fur puffed out. She reared back slightly.

"Oh, my," Maudie said in a half squeak.

Then the earth-bear sprang forward and unleashed her roar.

Arthur threw his hand to his ear as air rushed past and noise pounded the three of them like a hurricane. Resisting the urge to clamp his eyes shut, Arthur saw that the markings of the bear burned as though a furnace heated them from within, fiery gold and scarlet glowing brightly.

Maudie stood firm; the only sign of her fear was the way her hands were clenched at her sides.

When the earth-bear finished, she said, "Your

heart is true." She bowed her head to Maudie, who responded with the same, appearing calm but with sweat beading her brow.

Next the earth-bear turned to Gan, who had her hands on her hips and was somehow managing to look both terrified and excited by the prospect.

The earth-bear unleashed her roar once more. "Your heart is true," she said once again. She bowed her head to Gan, who looked over at Arthur and Maudie and flexed a bicep.

"That was intense!" Gan cried.

Every footstep the earth-bear took toward Arthur felt like a lifetime. There was no escape. It was his turn. Somewhere, as though from a distant land, he could hear Maudie telling him to relax, that he had nothing to worry about. But he suddenly felt hopeless in his abilities. Did he have courage? He wasn't outwardly gutsy like Gan, or solidly sure of himself in the way Maudie was.

The earth-bear stood before him, her breath hot. Arthur's heartbeat reverberated in his chest and made every cell pulse to its rhythm. Everything fell away from his vision apart from the obsidian eyes of the earth-bear staring at him.

Her jaw widened.

And she roared.

The earth-bear became part of him, as though they were entwined in a strange cosmic glue together, one and the same; he was both looking at the earth-bear and looking at himself, small and cowering below. "Who are you?" the earth-bear asked.

Flashes of his life pulsed through his brain, and images that he didn't recognize, places in the Wide he hadn't seen, children he didn't know, creatures he had never dreamed of. Time lost its meaning and Arthur felt he was a boy, a young man, and beyond all at once; it was a feeling beyond articulation.

The roar ceased. Arthur heaved long breaths, suddenly feeling like there wasn't enough air in the Wide to fill his lungs.

Rather than dipping her head, as she had to Maudie and Gan, the bear took a step toward him.

"Did I fail?" he breathed. Would she see him as meat now that she'd realized he wasn't good enough? What would death by earth-bear be like?

The bear's eyes narrowed, then her hackles relaxed and her expression became soft. "Not all courage is loud," she said gently. "Your heart is as true as the dawn."

"I think I'm going to faint," said Arthur, his back sliding down the rock as though it were butter.

CHAPTER 19

THE MEASURE OF WORTH

WHEN ARTHUR CAME TO, he felt foolish for fainting.

Maudie stared down at him, her expression shifting from panicked concern to relief. "It's all right, you more than passed the test. The earth-bear told us she had never seen a heart so aligned with the earth, whatever that means."

"How long have I been out?"

"Only a few minutes." She smiled and passed him a flask of water from her belt. "It was the earth-bear calling us with her song all along. We've been waiting for you to wake, because she wants to tell us more."

The earth-bear was sitting a short distance away while Gan chatted incessantly to her about Nadvaaryn and what it was like. Arthur heard her suggest that perhaps the bear might like to visit.

The earth-bear simply smiled and nodded to Gan's words. She glanced over, seeing that Arthur was awake. "Ah, our young friend is back. Now I can continue. Gather close. It is time for you to hear the full Firesong."

She began singing.

The beat of the earth is strong, strong,
Forged from the roars of time.
Hum! Hum! Thrumming high.
It calls, we call, the voices.

When the stars were to begin,
Flame on shoulder, water of hand.
They called to the great sky,
"Bring, begin! Buds, grow! Sea, land!"

They came with the wind, wind,
Like dark woe slaying wisdom.
While the stars all danced as one
It calls, we call, the voices.

Then the chains of men laid down,
Cold of heart, imprisoned shores.

They laid claim to the great sky.
"Bring, submit! Hold, fear! One, all!"

The beat of the eight is strong, strong,
Forged from the roars of time.
Hum! Hum! Thrumming high,
It calls, we call, the Firesong.

That was it! The words now so familiar, but finally complete.

"It *is* the song Dad used to sing us!" Arthur exclaimed. Questions tumbled in Arthur's thoughts as he tried to make meaning of the words. What did the chains of men mean, and what was the beat of the eight?

"It's called the Firesong?" asked Maudie.

The earth-bear nodded.

"Why did you call us here with it . . . ?" Arthur wanted to use the earth-bear's name, but was unsure if she had one.

Reading his thoughts, the earth-bear said, "You may call me Gaia."

"Thank you. Why did you call us here with your Firesong, Gaia?"

"The Firesong is not mine, it simply is. It is the past, it is the present, it is what could come to be. I will not tell you why I called you with it." The bear rose and stretched. "I will show you why."

Then Gaia brought her body low to the ground.

"She wants us to ride her!" said Gan excitedly.

"Yes, I do," said Gaia.

Arthur had no idea how they would get onto the great bear. She was much bigger than the thought-wolves they'd ridden on the Ice Continent.

But Gan had already taken a running leap and pulled herself up.

Maudie made a cradle with her hands, helping Arthur up. Then Arthur and Gan pulled Maudie up by the arms, and they were all on the back of the earth-bear.

"Hold my fur tight," she commanded.

With a mighty lurch, she was off. The three of them yelped in surprise at the speed as she charged

forward. They pressed their bodies into hers and took in her scent, which was something like warm earth and fresh meadows all at once. The rhythm of her great strides rocked beneath them like a heartbeat. They clung tighter as she climbed upward, before she eventually came to a halt over the other side of the crest.

From their position, they could see a great indent below by the coast where an area of the ground had been dug away as though by human hands. They climbed down from the bear and passed Maudie's binoscope from one to the other for a closer look.

"But we thought no one lives on this island," said Arthur.

"They have only just arrived to test the soils on this island in the past moon cycle. I've managed to hide from them so far but it's only a matter of time. Mines have been encroaching on the North for several years now," said Gaia. "It has been a concern of mine for a while. The pitch deposits are rich here, but deep. The encroachment of mines on the whole region is causing instabilities in the earth's structure, causing violent earthquakes and putting species at risk of extinction. If they carry on here as they have farther south, they will clear unique habitats that have existed for thousands, if not millions, of turns.

The destruction is spreading like a virus through the Wide."

It was awful to hear how bad it had become.

"The thought-wolves told me to call on you for help."

Arthur realized that the thought-wolves and the earth-bear must be able to communicate telepathically, even from opposite ends of the world.

"I'm sorry if I scared you with my roar," she continued. "I had to check I'd found the right children, that you are true and worthy and can help. Your parents were great protectors of this island, and the thought-wolves said they would trust you with their lives, as I did your parents."

They retreated a little way back down the ridge into the valley.

"Well, we learned before that the Vane Corporation is behind this," said Arthur bitterly, as they came to a stop. The trio slid from Gaia's back onto the lush soil.

"What can we do?" asked Maudie. "It's not like asking nicely will work."

"You could set some traps and scare them away!" suggested Gan.

Arthur searched his brain for an answer. "The problem isn't just about this mine. It's all the mines north of Vornatania that need closing down. In fact, all the mines in the Wide where the Lontonians are harming the land need to be closed down."

"Maybe Harriet would know what to do?" suggested Maudie.

Arthur needed to think, so he paused to rest on a nearby boulder. The earth-bear stretched her front legs, and Parthena was perched in a tree a few feet away, preening.

The earth-bear had come to them, and Arthur was determined to prove their worth. "Hey, Maud," he said, a sudden memory coming to him. "Remember that book I picked up at the market?"

"The Joneses and the caves one?"

"Right, it was called *Cave Diving Secrets* by Jonas J. Jones."

"Yes, but how exactly is that relevant?"

"There's a whole chapter on Lontown law. It says that islands with independent status are protected by law. That explorers must leave everything exactly as they find it on such islands, with no damage or alterations!"

"It's written in Lontown law?"

He nodded. "Which means it's part of the Explorer's Code! And what is the one thing the Vanes uphold?"

"Their status in society?"

"Exactly! So, imagine if it were exposed that they'd broken the Explorer's Code on numerous occasions? I'm sure that brilliant lawyer that Harrie knows will help bring them to court!"

"That's genius, Arty!"

Gan cleared her throat. "I have no idea what you mean, but it sounds clever."

Arthur stroked the earth-bear's fur. "Gaia, we can help you! We'd need to get back to Lontown, but I promise you, it is possible."

Gaia dipped her head, which Arthur interpreted to be in both relief and gratitude.

"Thank you. I am glad the Firesong was heard."

Absorbed in their conversation, no one noticed the figure stepping forward from the boulders behind them.

But then she cleared her throat lightly, and all turned to stare at her.

At first, Arthur thought it must be Harriet, having tracked them down after their lie about going fishing in the sky-ak.

Then, like plunging into icy water, he realized he was looking at Eudora Vane. She smiled at them. Parthena cried out and took flight, quickly disappearing from view.

The earth-bear snarled, "Is she friend or foe?"

"Friend, of course!" Eudora said brightly.

"What are you doing here?" Maudie asked suspiciously.

Many possibilities ran through Arthur's head all at once. The Vane Corporation was responsible for many of the pitch mines, so perhaps she was here on business? Or maybe she was looking out for them, making sure they were safe, like Batzorig had been for Gan? Or perhaps . . . The thought that rang the truest made his body feel brittle as ancient bones: Eudora had planted the idea to come here, to the Volcanic North. Had she lured them here for revenge?

"I wanted to keep an eye on you and make sure you were safe. So, I've been following you—at a distance, of course."

"You've been following us all this time?" Maudie asked, before saying to Arthur in a hushed voice, "Then it wan't just Batzorig and trade ships we were seeing."

"When I heard there was a big bear in these parts, I simply had to make sure you were safe. I must say I'm surprised at Harriet, letting you go off alone like this into such a wild, unstable area."

Their faces told her that Harriet didn't know.

"It's all right. We'll keep it as our little secret."

Eudora's gaze fell on the earth-bear. "What an extraordinary beast, and it seems so tame. I must have imagined it just now, but I could have sworn I heard it . . . *talk*."

"That was me," said Arthur forcefully. He prayed that Gaia wouldn't speak again.

With a smile and a loud sigh, Eudora reached a hand to her long, brown cape. Her fingers pinched the end of the ribbon tie. "I think I'm tired of the games now."

As she gently pulled the ribbon, her cape fell from her shoulders to reveal immaculate pink trousers and a matching fitted woolen jacket in exactly the same shade: Eudora Vane's signature pink from before Erythea.

And with that, Arthur and Maudie knew for certain that Eudora's memory had returned.

She looked down at them with eyes that seemed to glimmer and flash with savage laughter.

"She's back," said Maudie, her voice barely audible.

CHAPTER 20

BOOM

"**D**OES SOMEONE WANT to tell me who this is and what's going on?" said Gan. "And most important, how has that woman managed to stay so clean?"

Eudora smiled with sweet menace. "When I saw the manifests for your ship and the *Altan*, I presumed Batzorig's intentions must have been to follow you, Princess. I knew I could follow the *Altan* instead of the *Aurora* and keep an even farther distance so you wouldn't suspect a thing. How did you think they knew to rescue you when you got into danger on Lida?"

Arthur remembered seeing the flash of silver after the earthquake on Lida. Miptera had acted as spy before; it had to have been her. "But . . . why help us?"

She leaned in. "Perhaps I needed you to make it a little farther."

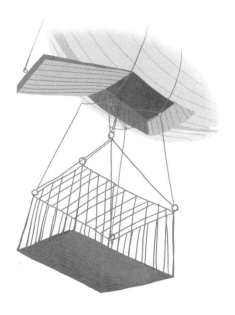

Sensing that things were about to escalate rapidly with Eudora, Arthur turned to Gaia and yelled, "Foe, she's definitely a foe! Run!"

But before anyone could move, a great shadow melted over them and a sky-ship rose from behind the rock ledge. Smethwyck was leaning over the deck's railing with a gun trained on them, smirking broadly. A huge cage was suspended beneath. They wouldn't be able to land, but that didn't mean they still couldn't capture Gaia.

"I wouldn't try to escape if I were you," said

Eudora smoothly. "And I don't *want* to kill the beast. A talking bear would be worth much more alive, but if I have to I will kill it and take its rather fascinating pelt as a consolation."

The earth-bear growled deeply, making the smaller rocks around them jitter.

"We can do this the easy way, or, shall we say, the slightly messier way," said Eudora, her eyes sparkling with a mixture of menace and relish, her lips and cheeks rosy.

"Nobody move!" said Arthur. He glanced at Gaia. "That thing is a gun: if it fires, it will kill."

Eudora perched on a boulder. "I must say, when I read the letters in the box I was thoroughly bored . . . until I came across the mention of something in the North that needed protection. That was far too deliciously intriguing to pass up. I didn't imagine in my wildest dreams that it would be a secret this magnificent!"

"You read our mother's letters!" said Maudie. "You didn't buy the box for us. You just found what you wanted and then used it to manipulate us." She clenched her fists.

Gaia bristled beside them.

"But I still don't understand: why suggest we come all this way?" asked Arthur. "Why not set off on your own to discover what our father was protecting?"

"And pass on an opportunity?"

Arthur noticed a member of Eudora's crew had a camera ready above. "What do you mean?"

"Indeed, this is the perfect opportunity to destroy the Brightstorm name for good, to discredit you and make sure you are ejected from the Geographical Society forever."

"She can't do that, can she, Arty?" Maudie whispered.

"Are you clear on the Explorer's Code, the rules for exploration set down by the Geographical Society?" asked Eudora, tilting her head with a smile. "There is a sharing of information clause, put there to protect the safety of future travelers. If you discover something of note, importance, or danger, it is your duty as a member of the Geographical Society to report it upon your return."

Arthur took a step forward. "We're not back yet, so who's to say we weren't planning to report this?"

"Your father's letter made it clear that he was withholding a secret about the Volcanic North. Now that I have evidence of what it is, I can expose the secretive misdirection Ernest Brightstorm was capable of. As my memory returned so miraculously while away in the North—" She gave them a faint wink. "—I'll also be able to reveal that you have been withholding information about an unknown continent, Erythea!"

"So you've been pretending about your memory all along!" said Arthur, wishing he'd trusted his gut feeling. How did she always manage to reel them in? She was a master of manipulation.

With a small shrug of her shoulders and a wry smile, she said, "Fun, wasn't it? But think back to Erythea. Did any of you actually see the darkwhispers take my memory?"

Looking at each other, Arthur and Maudie knew she was right. Cold sweat ran the length of Arthur's spine. She had emerged from behind the *Aurora* when it crashed at the darkwhispers' site. They'd been focused on, and devastated by, what had happened to Welby at the time.

"Information is one of the most powerful weapons one can have. The ability to use it and to trade on it is one of the reasons why humans are superior to all other creatures. Now you are here, and I have your father's letter, so it won't take much to convince the Geographical Society that you knew about this bear all along. It will be quite plain to everyone that you were continuing to keep your father's secrets from the rest of the Lontown community."

"Perhaps the explorers will understand *why* we

had to keep Erythea secret, and why our dad was protecting the earth-bear!" said Maudie, scowling.

"Protecting dangerous creatures that pose a threat to Lontonians?" Eudora wagged her finger and shook her head.

Gan tugged Arthur's sleeve and whispered. "Er, much as I like a challenge, perhaps a retreat is in order?"

Arthur knew in his heart that Eudora was right and that the Geographical Society and Lontonians would be affronted at being kept in the dark.

"But wait . . . what's that sound? Do you hear a crashing?" asked Eudora softly, standing once more and pretending to listen to the wind. "I do believe it's the sound of the Brightstorm legacy falling around you."

No one had noticed the earth-bear's fur pattern igniting from within. The cracked-lava pattern on its body burned scarlet, and the spiral on its neck became vibrant orange with fiery light. She roared, the impressive sound radiating toward Eudora and taking in the full measure of her worth, her inner secrets and desires.

When she had finished, a strange silence hung until Eudora laughed lightly. "You're all noise and no substance, dear thing. But when we have you on show in Lontown the people will pay a fortune to see you do such delightful tricks."

The earth-bear looked to the children. "She has courage. But her truth and intentions are as dark as a bottomless night. This human poses a threat not only to creatures but to other humans as well."

Arthur nodded. "I'd say you have the complete measure of her."

"Shoot to injure, but keep it alive!" Eudora shouted.

Chaos arrived in the blink of an eye.

Gaia's fur shone with brilliant red-yellow fire-light as it was pierced by gunshots. The earth-bear roared with ear-splitting ferocity, so intense and powerful that a shock wave pulsed through the air, propelling everyone off their feet. Arthur, Maudie, Gan, and Eudora smacked into the rocks and boulders. The sky-ship was thrust back across the sky. Then shocked silence fell, but only for a split moment before rocks rumbled and the volcano on the northern part of the island growled as though a monster had been unleashed in its belly.

A deafening *boom* exploded from the volcano, followed by eerie stillness as everyone turned to see an enormous, thick mushroom cloud of ash and gas erupt from the vent.

Even the earth-bear seemed shocked at what was happening.

There was no time to acknowledge the cuts and bruises they'd all received from the fall.

Thick lava poured out of the crater, bleeding in red wounds down the side of the volcano. Red fire sparks and burning rock shot into the sky. It was one of the most dangerous kinds of eruptions: a gray eruption. Hugo had told them about such occurrences when they'd first met, and they knew that everything from fine ash to fragments of solidified lava as big as cannonballs would be thrown everywhere.

"We need to get out of here, now!" shouted Maudie.

The sky-ship had made its way back above them and was rocked again in the sudden wind.

"Madame Vane!" Smethwyck called. "The rope ladder!"

"Not without the bear! We have time!" Eudora called. "Shoot it!"

More shots fired. The bear darted from place to place as shots missed her by inches.

"Useless idiot! Throw me the gun. I'll do it myself!" Eudora screamed.

Molten rock now burst from the top of the volcano in a great lava fountain. Ominous thuds sounded somewhere nearby as rocks fell, and Arthur looked up frantically to make sure none were heading their way.

"Go! Fly to safety!" he called to Parthena. She hesitated but he heaved his shoulders forcefully and she took flight.

The sky-ship shuddered in the air and spun as though it had been knocked by debris. More shouts came, ash started to rain, and Eudora Vane focused on her prize.

Meanwhile, Arthur, Maudie, and Gan grabbed each other and sprinted east, heading back for the ice waterfall entry as huge rivers of lava began flowing down the volcano sides toward them.

By some luck, the debris that fell around them was mostly ash, but the ever-thickening haze was making it almost impossible to see.

"What if we're heading the wrong way?" Arthur called.

They called for Gaia to help, but there was no reply—only the sound of more shots firing.

Dust rained down on them, and their clothes flapped in the wind. Terror and ash combined to make it hard to breathe. The murky fog enveloped them.

"Don't let go of each other!" Maudie shouted, her voice strained.

"It's no good. We can't see!" said Arthur. "We might be going in the wrong direction."

They jerked to a stop.

Suddenly, red flashed among the gray above them and fear seized them all as something hurtled toward them.

"Debris!" Arthur yelled. Their hands clenched, knowing there was no time to jump out of the way.

But the object didn't strike them; it suddenly paused midair. Wings fluttered.

"Urania!" cried Maudie, as more moths appeared through the gloom.

The cloud of Brightstorm moths' wings seemed to shine brighter than ever through the ash cloud. Urania turned and flew onward, the other moths following her.

"Come on!" said Maudie. "She's leading them, showing us the way back to the waterfall!"

Every inch of their bodies covered in ash, the trio kept their gazes firmly fixed on the ever-shifting flock of moths as they hurried on over rocks and through shrubbery until their muscles burned and they could barely stay upright. But they had to keep going.

Just then, the direction of the wind suddenly

changed, and the ash cloud lifted. In the near distance, behind the next hillock, the cave of the frozen waterfall came into view.

"There it is!" cried Gan.

They hurried up the set of boulders between them and the cave, but at the top they froze in disbelief. A river of slow-moving lava was blocking their escape.

CHAPTER 21

LAVA

"IF WE DON'T make it back to the waterfall, we're done for!" said Arthur. But the flow of lava was too wide for them to jump across.

"What do we do?" cried Gan, looking around with desperate, wide eyes. This was the first time Arthur had seen her looking fearful and uncertain.

"We'll have to create something to get across!" shouted Maudie. "Look around!"

There were only rocks too small to help and boulders that seemed too big to move.

"Maybe we could roll this one?" suggested Arthur, seeing a tall stone by the edge that might bridge the gap just enough for them to leap over.

They braced against the stone.

"Heave!" Maudie shouted. But despite giving

every drop of energy they had left, it didn't move even a fraction of an inch.

The panic was now all-consuming as they struggled for answers.

"Parthena!" Arthur screamed, hoping she had kept safe from the blast and was still nearby and could get help. But there was no call in reply. "She must have left the valley."

"Gaia!" cried Maudie. "She could easily jump across!"

"Of course!" said Arthur.

They called and called her name.

"What if Eudora shot her?" said Maudie.

Lava was swelling where it had reached the wall, forming a deadly lake that was bulging back toward them.

"She's not coming," said Arthur, feeling their last hope slipping from them. He tried to focus, to not think about the fact that they had led Eudora straight to Gaia—after all their father had done to keep the earth-bear safe.

They whipped off their fur coats, lightheaded from the heat of the surrounding lava and their exertion.

"We'll have to find another way out," said Maudie. "Let's head back west."

But as they turned, they saw that another lava river had appeared behind them. They were trapped.

Desperately, they called Gaia's name again.

Then movement caught their attention on the rocky brow. For a second their hopes rose, before they quickly realized the figure was too small to be the earth-bear. An ash-covered Eudora Vane stumbled up the rock screaming for Smethwyck and the sky-ship to return. Her pink outfit was caked in gray, as was her disheveled hair. Seeing them, she drew herself up tall and, despite her own predicament being almost as bad as theirs, she threw them a sly smile.

With restrained fury, Arthur said, "Even now she hates us and is happy to see us in danger." But he couldn't waste energy on her, not when they needed all their focus to get themselves out of there.

The next moment, with a rush and swirl of ash, Gaia seemed to materialize behind Eudora. Eudora was swift to react, pivoting to point her gun at the earth-bear looming over her. The two stared at each other.

"Get me out of here, bear, and I will spare your life," Eudora said.

Gaia turned her head and called over to Arthur, Maudie, and Gan. "I will save you," she turned her gaze back to Eudora, "after I have dealt with this . . . *creature.*"

"Be careful!" Arthur called. He knew only too well how ruthless Eudora could be.

The great earth-bear and Eudora stalked each other in a circle like predators, eyeing the other warily. Arthur glanced at the lava lake as it edged nearer.

Gaia reared back on her legs. Eudora raised her gun higher, pointing it at Gaia's chest.

Suddenly a sky-ship emerged over the southern edge of the valley. Everyone looked toward it.

"Please let that be Harriet and not Smethwyck!" said Maudie. But it was indeed Eudora's sky-ship. "They must have regained control from their spin!"

The sky-ship slowed smoothly to a stop, hovering above the spot where the earth-bear and Eudora stood.

Smethwyck and most of Eudora's crew were on deck, peering down the tip of something like a large harpoon angled over the side. It was aimed at Gaia, who seemed to be frozen in shock, just as everyone else was on the ground.

"No!"Arthur shouted as a shot echoed through the valley. Frantically, he looked back to the earth-bear. With one last, mighty roar, Gaia jolted backward. The ground shook.

Eudora squealed in delight.

The earth-bear swayed.

"Maybe they missed," said Arthur, hoping the words might make it true. Gaia looked to them, her obsidian eyes large and full of sadness.

The bear stumbled. *The beat of the earth is strong, strong . . .* " The earth-bear's voice faded to silence.

"No!" the children cried out as Gaia thudded to the ground. Arthur wanted to rush over to help her, but the still-flowing lava had them all trapped in place.

A hatch opened in the bottom of Eudora's sky-ship. Crew members shimmied down to the ground on ropes and swiftly attached a hoist to the earth-bear.

Arthur could barely watch, but Maudie grabbed his hand. "Look, her chest is still heaving! She's alive! Smethwyck hit her with some sort of dart, not a bullet. See the feather sticking out where it hit?"

Within minutes, the earth-bear's great body was lifted up into the air and disappeared into the sky-ship along with the crew members. Eudora brushed herself down with a smile and moved beneath the hatch, grabbing a rope. As she was hauled upward, she twisted to face the Brightstorms and give them a wave before she disappeared into the hatch and her sky-ship sped away.

Arthur pointed to the volcano, where the roar

had set off another cascade of lava spewing from the top.

They all knew this was the end of the valley. It was likely to be entirely filled with lava within the next chime, if not sooner.

And the lava encircling them inched closer with every moment.

"Has anyone got a plan D?" asked Gan.

But it was hopeless. Their only chance of escape had just been captured.

Arthur, Maudie, and Gan huddled together on the last piece of land. Strange cracking and splitting sounds were coming from the volcano, which unnerved the panicked children even more. The clouds had settled, but the winds had severely picked up, throwing sickening waves of heat and burning flecks their way.

All they could do was hold each other and hope for a miracle.

It came with a rhythmic whirr and chug, and a great squawk from Parthena. The *Aurora*'s prow speared above the valley edge, the moon-bright hawk leading the way. Arthur, Maudie, and Gan cried out in joy and relief, then began waving and calling. Hugo and Felicity cried out to them from the distant deck as the *Aurora* headed their way. Hugo tried to throw down the ladder, but the *Aurora* couldn't get near enough; the wind was too fierce, and the sky-ship was being blown all over the place.

Harriet called out, "I'm going to have to bring her down! Even if I could get you the rope, you might be thrown into the lava lake in this wind! It's the only way to keep her steady! Climb onto that rock and, whatever you do, *don't fall in!* I'm going to have to descend suddenly, or we risk being blown into the lava!"

The patch of land left was barely big enough to fit the *Aurora*, so they carefully climbed onto the rock beside the creeping lake of lava and clung on for their lives. The heat was becoming unbearable, scorching their throats and stinging their eyes.

"Ready?" Harriet called as the sky-ship shuddered and swayed over their small piece of remaining land.

As the wind broke for a moment and the *Aurora* hovered just above the small landing patch, Harriet dropped the sky-ship at breath-catching speed, and it *thudded* into the ground with an ominous splinter.

"Quick, get on board!" Harriet shouted. "You'll have to use the rope ladder as there's no room to lower the gangplank."

Hugo swiftly lowered the ladder and Arthur urged Gan upward.

The lava edged closer to the hull. They didn't have much time left.

Maudie pushed Arthur ahead of her. He grabbed the rope on one side, swiftly sliding his hand up with every step to hold him steady. The heat was so intense that sweat poured down his back.

Felicity pulled him up onto the deck, her eyes a picture of worry. "Oh my, oh my, you poor things. Don't you worry, though, Harriet will get us out."

"Hurry up, Maud!" Arthur called. But Maudie was already being pulled up and over the side by Hugo.

Harriet ran back to the wheel, but as she grasped it there was a terrible jolt and a *boom* from below. "The heat shields should hold it! If we can just . . ." Harriet tried to fire the engines. But there was another awful vibration, and the aft end of the *Aurora* dropped a few inches.

Hugo ran to look over the side. "The lava's reached the hull!"

Harriet's breath heaved in her chest as she tried to fire the engines again. A chug sounded as they fired and Harriet swiftly pulled levers. The front end began lifting.

They were going to make it.

Just then, another enormous ripping sound split

the air and the *Aurora* dropped back down. The heat shields cracked.

"Keep trying!" Arthur cried, rushing to her side.

Harriet went through the procedures again, but this time the engine sounded worse. It coughed and spluttered as it tried to fire up, as though being choked. Water hissed violently out of the engine room and the terrible scent of burning wood filled the air. Billows of smoke rose from the end of the sky-ship.

Harriet looked at Arthur, then at the others. Her hands relaxed on the wheel and she said, "There's not much time. We have to take the sky-aks." There was absolute resignation in her voice.

Arthur and Maudie felt as though their hearts had been pulled from their chests.

"Maudie, Felicity, Hugo, take that sky-ak. Arthur, Gan, we'll take this one. And hurry!"

They rushed to the sky-aks as the *Aurora* shook and dropped as more of the hull was consumed by lava.

"What about our belongings?" Arthur called in despair. This was all his fault—if he hadn't been pigheaded, if he hadn't decided to lie and run off—

Harriet shook her head. "There's no time."

But there was one thing Arthur could do. He rushed to the prow, leaned over, and pulled at the

Aurora's name plate. Then Maudie was there, whipping a screwdriver from her belt to help. In moments, she'd handed him the plate and they rushed back to the sky-aks. As the sky-ship groaned and shuddered again, they started the small engines of the two vessels and took flight, rising swiftly upward.

The air grew cooler, and the wind changed direction slightly, blowing the smoke toward the east. The sight of what they were leaving behind broke everyone's hearts. The *Aurora*, faithful to the last, was now completely surrounded by lava and collapsing rapidly as fire took hold. Arthur grabbed Harriet's hand and squeezed it tightly.

CHAPTER 22

THE RETURN

THE ERUPTION RELENTED and the two lone sky-aks chugged beyond the valley edge back toward the black beach on the southern coast. The shoreline had remained untouched, out of reach of the lava rivers. It was a safe haven, for now.

Numb, the small crew made a makeshift camp on the beach. Harriet and Hugo made a fire, and they washed as best they could in the ocean to remove the dust and ash from their hair and faces, then sat together, shivering.

"We're so sorry about the *Aurora*," Arthur blurted out to Harriet, but how could words ever be enough? His heart tightened. Nothing would bring it back. And Gaia was captured. How could everything have gone so wrong? An expression of sad resolution was on Harriet's face. They'd lied about going to find the earth-bear, and now look what had happened. "And we're sorry about sneaking off to find the earth-bear."

She gave a sad smile and pulled Arthur closer, into a hug. "I just wish you could have trusted me to help. To help you make better choices." She sighed. "I'm glad you're all safe."

"It was your home," said Maudie, her lip trembling. "Everything you have . . ."

"A home is more than wood and metal. Sky-ships can be rebuilt; humans, not so easily."

"But she was unique!" said Arthur.

"The *Aurora* saw us through some tough times," said Felicity. "And at the end of it, she saved our lives."

"And . . . and . . ." Loss and anger engulfed Arthur in a stomach-churning wave. "They took the earth-bear."

"Wait, who's they? And—" Harriet gasped in surprise, "—and you saw the bear?"

Nodding, Maudie said, "And we spoke to her."

"Oh, Harrie, she's the most incredible creature!" said Arthur. "She can talk, she can read your soul, your intentions, just with her roar. She *did* call us here with the Firesong. We had to hear the full song to know why she needed us. It was a call for help. Pitch mines are undermining the stability of the land."

"They're encroaching farther up and deeper in, ruining habitats and upsetting the balance," said Maudie.

"The thought-wolves told her we would help, so she called out for us, and we came up with a plan to help, only then everything went wrong and . . ." The words were cascading out of Arthur.

Felicity put a hand on his shoulder and passed him a cup of warm water. "It's not much, but it's warm."

"Tell me exactly what happened before we arrived," said Harriet. "I *thought* I saw another sky-ship!"

Arthur nodded. "It was Eudora Vane."

"But the *Victorious* perished in Erythea," said Felicity. "I hadn't heard she'd rebuilt it, or that she'd hired another! Although it's not beyond her to keep a big secret."

"The sky-ship could have been her fiancé's, Carinthius Catmole's," suggested Maudie.

"I think it was," replied Arthur.

"But he doesn't explore," said Hugo.

Maudie shrugged, but it was more of a shiver, and Arthur knew she was feeling as tormented over the *Aurora* and the earth-bear as he was. Her voice was strained. "Maybe he was below deck. She must have persuaded him into taking her, or borrowed it, or something. I don't remember seeing him on the deck. He seemed nice, I'm sure he wouldn't have been aware of her intentions. We all know how convincing she can be."

Frosty clouds swept in from the west and a chill wind washed over them, making them shiver even more.

"The eruption only happened when Eudora arrived," said Arthur. "The bear is bound to the deep earth in an ancient, mystical way. It wasn't the natural movement of the earth that caused it; I think it was the earth-bear's emotions!"

"We couldn't protect the earth-bear from her," said Gan. "They shot it with something, but we think it might still be alive."

"Can the sky-aks catch them?" Arthur asked futilely, for he knew all too well that the sky-aks were only for short journeys. And they had no supplies. It was hopeless, but he felt that they had to try something, anything . . .

"You saw the speed of that sky-ship. Even the *Aurora* wouldn't have caught it," said Maudie.

"We'll send Parthena to Snae Strond to fetch Batzorig," said Harriet. "That's if she's not too exhausted by events?"

Parthena butted her head into Arthur's cheek, telling him of course she would, as fast as she could. "Thank you, girl," Arthur whispered into her feathers.

Retrieving a pencil and her pocket journal from her jacket, Harriet scribbled a note and passed it to Arthur, who rolled it up and attached it to Parthena. She gave a soft nod of her head, then took flight.

"Where do you think they've taken the earth-bear? What will they do?" asked Maudie.

Harriet frowned. "If their sky-ship is as fast as you say, they will be long gone. But if we can find out where they're heading . . ."

Stoking the fire, Hugo shuffled his feet in the black sand. His shoulders were tense.

"Hugo?" Harriet asked.

He heaved a deep breath. "When I came to Lontown on other business, I was investigating the appearance of a facility in the mountains in the north-west of Vornatania."

"The place we flew over?" asked Arthur, remembering the strange clinical straight lines, like some sort of great factory.

Hugo nodded solemnly. "I wanted to tell you at the time, but I was still getting to know you and working out what your allegiances were. My suspicion is that it's a testing facility run by a wealthy family in Lontown."

"Testing? What are they testing?" asked Arthur. But a cold thought had entered his brain. "Sapients?"

Hugo nodded. "It's not confirmed. No one can get in, and no information comes out. But that's my hunch."

"The Vanes?" Harriet asked.

The thought of a facility created to test sapients made Arthur's stomach churn.

"But Eudora loves Miptera!" said Maudie with a frown.

Harriet poked the fire with a stick, sending a blaze of sparks flittering into the sky. "But she also believes humans are far superior, and that sapients are something to be controlled. And her father, Thaddeus, has long been known to have a particular disdain for animals of any kind."

Exchanging a glance, Arthur suspected that both Maudie and he were remembering the time they'd been outside Vane Manor and Thaddeus had lashed out at Miptera.

Harriet's frown deepened. "I knew the HAC was surfacing again, but I didn't know things had gone this far."

"HAC?" asked Felicity.

"The Human Authority Collective. A vile group who believes humans to be wholly superior. They feel threatened by sapients."

"Poor Gaia! What will they do to her?" said Arthur, feeling his heart twist again.

"Gaia?" asked Harriet.

"That's the earth-bear's name."

"Try not to think about it. There is no sense fretting over what we can't control; it will only distract us from the actions we need to take."

As always, Harriet was wise and pragmatic in her words. It didn't stop the fury and worry churning in Arthur's belly, but it helped focus him. They needed a plan.

Harriet took out her journal again and started sketching. "Twins, tell me everything you can remember about what you saw when we flew over the building. Arthur, I know your maps of the area were on the *Aurora*, but you've got a good memory for detail. Maudie, get thinking on the equipment we might need. I know you had a look at the tools on board the *Altan* in Snae Strond, so think about what we've got to work with, what might make a sufficient weapon; and Hugo, tell us everything you might have heard about the facility." Harriet sat forward, pencil poised.

Sorrow and rage were channeled into action as they planned long into the night, until hunger gouged at their bellies and they drifted into sleep, heads slumped on each others' shoulders. Snow fell around them and the muted embers of the fire became a small dot of warmth under the starlight of the vast black night.

✦ ✦ ✦

Batzorig arrived with his crew and sky-ship two days later. Harriet and the others had survived by makeshift fishing and upturning the sky-aks to make shelters.

"My, look at the state of you! Like pallid ghosts! Let's get you on board and warmed properly!"

They boarded the sky-ship and went to Batzorig's quarters to tell him the details of what had happened.

"Eudora Vane left you there to perish?" Batzorig blurted, his cheeks red and incredulous. "My princess and the twins left like scraps of jetsam to fend for themselves in a sea of lava? Some Lontonians need to cleanse their foul minds with the ways of the Citadel.

When you catch her, send her my way and I shall show her a lesson or two about respect and care for your kin."

"Starting with scrubbing the sewers, no doubt," winked Gan. "It was always his favorite threat."

"A hard day's work is not above any king, nor any Lontonian. I scrubbed them myself as a boy."

Harriet smiled. "Before we can arrange any sort of retribution for that woman, who let me tell you, Batzorig, has an uncanny way of slipping beyond any responsibility for her actions, we need some help."

"I am at your service," said Batzorig with a reverent nod. "My crew too, although they have not been with me for long. Should we keep the details of what's happened to ourselves?"

"Indeed, it would be wise to mask the truth. Perhaps tell them we were saved from an unexpected volcanic eruption."

They set sail for the facility straight away. Batzorig insisted they all rest properly and that his crew had everything under control. The wind was with them and they made good progress with few stops. Every day stretched painfully, knowing that Eudora was so far ahead and there was nothing they could do to catch up.

Half a moon cycle later, the crew were a day's flight from the facility when they made a fuel stop not far from the Hawk Isles. Parthena had been disappearing for hours at a time and Arthur was growing concerned about her.

Arthur, Maudie, and Harriet were in Batzorig's quarters going over their plan for the hundredth time.

"Parthena's not herself," said Arthur. "Perhaps she can sense that we're close to the earth-bear."

Maudie nodded. "And there was definitely some telepathic communication between us and Gaia with the Firesong. Why can't we hear it anymore? She reached out to us before; surely she would call for help again?"

"Unless she thinks we're dead, or she's given up on us. We did lead Eudora to her. It's our fault."

"Don't think the worst, Arty."

"Or what if . . . what if it's too late for her?"

"I said don't think the worst."

Harriet looked up from her journal. "Maudie is right, you know."

Silence hung for a moment.

A thought struck Arthur. "Maybe we could try Tuyok? Maybe he'll know if the earth-bear is all right?" They'd had communication from Tuyok in

Erythea on the last expedition, even though he was a great distance away. Arthur had no idea how it worked but it might be worth a try.

Maudie nodded and Arthur closed his eyes, trying to reach out with his mind. *Tuyok*, he thought, *are you there?* But there was only the stream of his panicked thoughts and he huffed in exasperation. "I've no idea how it works!"

Softly, Harriet closed her journal and laid it to one side. She clasped her hands and leaned forward. "What does your gut tell you?"

Arthur's gut instinct had sometimes gotten him into dangerous scrapes, but he had learned that it wasn't often wrong. "That Gaia is alive. For the moment." He tried not to think of the animal heads displayed like prizes at Vane Manor.

Hugo hurried into the room. "Eudora's sky-ship was seen heading for the mountains by a trade ship in the northern marshes four days ago. I said we were asking after it for supplies, just in case any suspicion was aroused. Pigeon messenger is faster than the *Altan* and it's better to be cautious. Batzorig says we're taking flight immediately."

"Good. Then it looks like our plan is on track," said Harriet. "Have you found the best place to land near the facility, Arthur?"

He pointed to his map. "If we fly low through the valley here, we should keep out of sight long enough so they don't sound the alarm. But we'll get close enough to proceed on foot."

Harriet nodded. "We need to avoid the front entrance. We're all certain we saw a ventilation shaft when we passed over. That's our way in."

"We decided the sky-aks are too risky, right?" asked Arthur. "So unless anyone's grown wings, how's that going to work?"

"Hey, these aren't just for mountains, you know." Maudie waved several pairs of the gloves she'd been creating since they'd left Hyrrholm. "Luckily Batzorig had some adaptable materials on board. Here, I've sewn socks too, to make it easier for you."

"Genius, Maud." Her inventive talents never ceased to amaze him.

Felicity entered the room with Gan, holding a platter of jam tarts. It was the second batch she'd made that day to keep herself busy.

Batzorig followed close behind. "I thought I smelled something good," he said.

"The gloves haven't been thoroughly tested yet, but there's no time like the present. Fancy extending our wing walks to a hull walk?" asked Maudie, wiggling her eyebrows at Arthur.

"Oh, my diddling dumplings!" said Felicity, clutching her lucky spoon. "You're not thinking what I think you are?"

A wry grin edged Harriet's lips. "With harnesses, please."

Gan jumped to her feet. "Can I do it too?"

"Not on your belly!" said Batzorig.

"Nelly," corrected Arthur with a smile.

"Sorry, I haven't got enough pairs yet," said Maudie. She lowered her voice. "But I'll make you some, I promise. You can try them back in the Citadel."

"It'll just be the three of us going in," said Harriet. "Hugo suspects the facility is being run by a core team. There won't be many employees, because the Vanes won't have wanted to arouse suspicion about what they're doing. It's highly controversial, after all. But the fewer of us that go in, the lower the chance of being seen. The rest of you will be waiting in the tree line for our signal. Once we've released the earth-bear, we'll need to get her back out the front entrance to the sky-ship, and we'll need you to cause some sort of disturbance, Gan."

"Now, *that* I can handle." Gan smiled.

"I would like to disagree, but she is right," shrugged Batzorig.

CHAPTER 23

THE RESCUE

THE *ALTAN* SET down in the valley in the afternoon, but Harriet insisted they wait until sunset before setting off. Hopefully by then the workers would have finished for the day and they would be able to sneak in unnoticed.

As twilight fell, Arthur, Maudie, and Harriet set off with the gloves and ropes, hurrying silently through the woods. As the trees thinned, the facility came into view. A large area of the mountainside had been blasted away to make room for its fierce gray angles and jutting corners.

They crept like insects around the back of the building, hurrying past the opaque glass walls and cement blocks until they reached the ventilation shaft, where they put on their special gear. The gloves were softly padded, and the tips were covered with lines of raised material running across the palms and the lengths of the fingers.

Standing before Arthur and Harriet, Maudie gave a swift demonstration. "They're buttoned tightly at the wrist to avoid slippage, and your sock is too, Arty. It goes on the right foot so it can work diagonally with your hand. When you place them on the wall, press firmly like so." She reached high above with one hand, her feet dangling below. "Then to release draw back palm first, retracting the fingers, almost as though you're trying to pull sticky gum from the surface. Arty, your sock works similarly but the grip is focused on the toe area."

They all practiced on the wall before them. When they'd first tried on the hull with harnesses, Arthur had fallen several times, but with the sock he had two limbs working together and he soon got the hang of it.

"Ready?" asked Harriet. The twins nodded. "Remember, there are no harnesses."

They moved slowly at first, but as they found their rhythm they began speeding up. It was freeing for Arthur not to have to search hard for the best hand or foot hold, which was his main concern of climbing, and he was soon scurrying as quick as a lizard up the cold gray vent.

Reaching the top, the three of them sat with legs dangling into the central cavity of the shaft. The distant yip and yowl of creatures drifted from below, making Arthur's stomach turn. As much as he hoped that they would be able to rescue the earth-bear, he had also hoped that the stories of it being a sapient testing facility had been wrong. But hearing the sounds made his muscles tense. What were they doing in there?

"I'll go down first with the rope and make sure we can get through," said Harriet. "Once I'm down, I'll give it one tug for follow, two if it's wait, and three if—"

"—Harrie, let's not think about three," said Arthur with a shudder.

"Just know that if it's three you go back to the sky-ship and wait. I can handle myself." She gave a nod, then secured the rope around the top of the shaft, lowered it down, and, with one last look to the twins, she disappeared inside.

Soon the rope slackened as Harriet reached the bottom. After ten seconds or so it tugged once. They waited without breathing, hoping there wouldn't be another signal. There wasn't.

"You go next and I'll follow," said Maudie.

Arthur took a breath, then wrapped his feet around the rope and slid down. It was difficult to control his momentum with his single hand, but the climbing glove helped slow him. At the bottom, the shaft turned at a right angle and dim light shone. "Arthur, is that you?" whispered Harriet.

"Yes."

"Hurry, it's some sort of boiler room. There's no one about."

He shuffled into the room where a grate lay on the floor, which Harriet had removed from the shaft opening. He tugged the rope, letting Maudie know it was clear.

Soon, she joined him. Harriet peered through the small glass window in the door and gave the all-clear. "Judging by the distance we came down and the height of the shaft, I'd say we're underground."

They hurried along the corridor to a large door at the end. There was no window, so Harriet pressed her ear to the door. "I can't hear any people."

The animal cries still sounded, louder now.

They were at the end of another long corridor, bright white and clinical. Many doors with small windows lined the walls, evenly spaced apart, presumably leading to different rooms.

"They could be laboratories," said Maudie.

Arthur knew the earth-bear would have to be kept in a big room, and these rooms were too small.

"There's something on the wall along there," said Arthur, noticing some sort of chart by the door at the opposite end. "Come on, it might be a floor plan or fire notice that can help us."

He led the way but paused by the first door they happened across. He peeked inside the window, and saw small cages labeled with numbers: one with a sleeping cat, another with an owl. They barely had enough room to move. Charts were hung on the outside, and there were drawers and glass cabinets filled with bottles, gloves, syringes, and the like. The scene turned his stomach. The owl looked at him with eyes half terrified, half pleading.

"How can they keep them cooped up like this?" he asked almost silently.

"We have to save them too," said Maudie.

Harriet nodded. "And we will. But we need to find the earth-bear first. We may need her help to save the rest."

Tearing his eyes from the poor owl, Arthur hurried to the sign, which, it turned out, was some sort of building plan. He'd glanced in the other laboratories as he'd passed them: a rabbit, an otter, a hedgehog, a squirrel, and was that a small deer? All in horribly small cages.

Taming the fury he felt for the Vanes at that moment, he stood before the plan.

Maudie jabbed a finger at it. "That's where we are: the east-wing labs. All these rooms are too small for the earth-bear, where could it—"

Distant voices sounded from the other side of the door. Footsteps.

Exchanging wide-eyed glances with the twins, Harriet gently opened the door of the nearest lab room and pulled them inside. Crouching low, they clicked the door shut just as the door they'd been standing beside swung open.

"I tell you, they sound agitated tonight."

"More so than usual?"

"Well . . ."

"You're just jittery because of that bear."

Arthur's heart leaped at the word.

The voices, a man's and a woman's, paused just outside their door. Harriet beckoned them to crawl behind a long cabinet of drawers, in case the speakers were heading into their hiding place. They were now close to a cage where a small dog, a terrier of sorts, thought Arthur, stared at them with knowing brown eyes. It had been yipping before they had entered the room, but now it observed them silently. Slowly it tilted its head. Arthur put a finger to his lips. "It's OK. We're on your side," he whispered.

There was a cringingly loud clunk as the handle turned. A sliver of light shone across the white floor, hovering but not growing.

"Of course I'm jittery," one of the voices continued, the man. "And don't pretend you're not too. Have you ever seen anything like that bear?"

There was a pause, then the woman said, "The HAC has warned everyone that this could happen, ever since those thinking-wolf things. Although I have to say, I always presumed that story was made up by those Brightstorm twins."

Arthur clenched and unclenched his fist . . . and noticed Maudie had done the same with hers.

The woman's voice continued, "Well, now we've seen the danger."

"In fact, aren't you meant to be in Storage A now, Ebba?"

"I was going to check on Fra—I mean, the terrier, but you're right. If the boss comes back unexpectedly, I don't want to be late with my duties!"

The door shut again.

They all exhaled heavily.

"At least we know where to head," whispered Maudie. "It sounds like Storage A is where they have the bear."

The sound of footsteps faded, and finally another door distantly banged shut.

"They've probably adapted a large storage room for the earth-bear, as these lab cages wouldn't be big enough," said Harriet, standing. "We'll give it a moment, then make our move."

Arthur crouched so that he was eye level with the dog. "I take it you're Fra—something? We'll be back for you. I promise."

The dog blinked.

Soundlessly, Arthur, Maudie, and Harriet made their way back into the hallway and approached the door. Arthur pointed to Storage A, which looked to be along a different corridor at the far end of the building. Cautiously, they left the laboratory wing and found themselves in another clinical corridor, only wider and with a higher ceiling. The closest door read Storage E, and, farther to the right, was Storage D.

"This way." Arthur pointed.

Harriet tugged his arm to a stop. "Hold on," she whispered. "We need to be ready. I have a knife in my belt in case we need to threaten whoever is in there.

But this place doesn't seem heavily guarded, so it's likely just the scientist we heard. I have rope to tie her, and we'll gag her, so she can't call for help."

The twins nodded.

They approached the huge double doors of Storage A, nervous anticipation twisting Arthur's stomach.

"On three," whispered Harriet.

We're coming, he said in his thoughts, hoping beyond hope that, whatever state poor Gaia was in, she would be able to hear.

"One . . . two . . ."

On three, they burst through the doors.

Their forward charge became a stumble at the sight before them.

The three stood gaping.

The vast room was empty apart from a woman in a long white coat who stood staring back at them with a broom in her hand.

Her features were blank with ignorance for a moment. "Are you part of the transport crew?" Then her eyes darted to the knife tucked into Harriet's belt and the rope in her hand. Her features hardened and she drew her shoulders back. "Who are you?"

"Where's the bear?" said Arthur, scowling.

"Wait, how do you know—?"

"It doesn't matter how we know," said Maudie. "Where is it?"

"It's gone."

Grief twisted inside of Arthur. Were they too late? Had they tested on her, then killed her? "Gone?" The word came out like gravel.

"To Lontown, to the Geographical Society. But why they took it without one of us, I don't know." Her voice drifted for a moment. "Look, if you were hoping to get a look at the beast before the display, this is a pretty extreme way of going about it. Now, if you'll excuse me, I'll be calling security."

"Not so fast," said Harriet, stepping in front of her.

The woman moved to grab some sort of phono-portal, but Harriet lunged, deftly dislodging the woman's legs from beneath her. Then she pinned her to the floor.

Harriet glanced at the twins and winked. "Welby taught me a few tricks. Bind her hands for me and cut the rope so we can tie any others we come across."

"What do you think she meant by display?" asked Arthur, but as the words left his lips he already knew. Eudora wasn't the sort to keep such a prize quiet. She would want the acclaim of discovery paraded for all to see.

"It means we need to get back there as soon as possible." Harriet turned to the woman, who was still struggling beneath her. "How many other workers are at this facility this evening?"

"If you think I'm going to tell you—"

Maudie tied her hands behind her back with a stiff knot.

"We can do this the easy way or the hard way," said Harriet matter-of-factly.

Sweat beaded on the woman's forehead. "Me, another scientist, and the security guard in the entrance. How did you get in?"

But Harriet bound her mouth so she couldn't talk anymore, and the three ran back to the corridor.

Arthur led the way, rushing toward the laboratory rooms.

"You liberate the animals from their cages, and I'll deal with the other scientist!" said Harriet.

Without another word they split up and hurried about their tasks. Arthur went straight back into the room with the small dog. "There, I told you we'd be back." He unhitched the lock. "There you go, you're free now."

The dog tilted its head and then leaped from the cage. Arthur and Maudie made their way up the corridor, releasing the captives, and they were soon joined by Harriet, who had located and detained the other scientist. Soon the corridor was filled with dogs, cats, badgers, squirrels, the deer, and all manner of other sapients, looking at Arthur, Maudie, and Harriet curiously.

"Is that all of them?" asked Harriet.

The twins nodded.

"Well, this should baffle the security guard," she said with a wink. After a quick glance at the building plan, she pushed open the door and charged along the corridor to a large flight of stairs, swiftly followed by the Brightstorm twins and a train of animals.

They emerged into a large foyer, where a young security guard jumped to her feet. "What the—?"

Before she could say any more, or reach for her gun, Harriet had swept her to the floor and disarmed her.

Spying the button to release the large set of glass entrance doors, Arthur slammed it with the palm of his hand, and the animals began rushing toward freedom. The deer sniffed the air and shut her eyes before bolting toward the trees; several squirrels hopped off, tails entwined; a rabbit leaped and clapped its back feet together. One after another, they ran for their freedom. The last out was the terrier, who paused by the security guard's desk.

"Come on," urged Arthur. "The world is your oyster now."

The dog jumped over the guard, leaped onto the desk, grabbed what appeared to be the latest copy of the *Lontown Chronicle* in his mouth, then bolted for the door with what Arthur was certain was a wry grin.

Parthena swooped gleefully above as the sapients sprang, scurried, and trotted away. The calls of creatures rang down the valley as Arthur and Maudie jogged out after them into the open.

Gan ran toward them from the tree line. She had some sort of flare tied to an arrow in her hand, her bow at the ready. "What happened? I guess you won't be needing that distraction anymore?"

"The earth-bear's in Lontown!" said Arthur. "There's some sort of display going on at the Geographical Society. We're heading there now."

"Eudora's probably selling tickets," said Maudie, scowling.

Arthur set his teeth. "Well, she didn't bank on us making it away from Hyrrholm alive, so let's surprise her and reveal what she's really like and that she left us there for dead. We'll persuade the Geographical Society that the earth-bear isn't a specimen, or a danger."

"Come on," said Harriet. "Let's get back to the

Altan. We should arrive by sunrise, and I suggest you all get some sleep on the way."

"I can take the first shift at the wheel," said Arthur, whose thoughts were still too active to even consider sleep. It seemed as though every time they were on the verge of something positive, another rug was whipped from beneath their feet.

Maudie grasped his arm. "Don't worry. We *will* free Gaia."

CHAPTER 24

THE GEOGRAPHICAL SOCIETY

THE AUDITORIUM OF the Lontown Geographical Society was brimming with explorers. They were fidgeting in their seats, all in their best finery, and their expressions were gleeful, full of unrestrained curiosity about what was going to unfold. They had been told in no uncertain terms that Eudora Vane would be unveiling an extraordinary discovery from the Volcanic North, and that it was not a presentation anyone would want to miss.

The stage was dominated by an enormous wooden crate, twice the height of a person, far larger than anything anyone had ever seen on this stage before. It had been challenging to get the crate inside the building, but grand statues and paintings were commonplace at the Geographical Society, so the doors backstage opened wide. Eudora stood backstage now, taking in the moment. Her name would surely go down in history, and at the same time she would be bringing down the Brightstorm name once and for all.

It was a good day.

No, it was a *historic* day, and her name would be written in bold type in the history books, her legacy cemented for generations to come.

The last of the board members filed into the reserved seats at the front of the auditorium.

Eudora couldn't wait to parade the bear through the streets. She had already commissioned a collar to be designed for it, but first she had to get permission from the board for the parade. However, for her, the red tape of Lontown was merely a box-ticking exercise; she had friends in all the right places, and at least sixty percent of the board could be counted on.

Eudora approached Smethwyck, who was standing sentry at the back of the stage. "Did you relax the sedation as I instructed? I want to give them a little something to talk about, rather than just staring at dead weight on the stage."

Smethwyck nodded.

"Excellent. Then let us begin."

She walked around the massive crate over to the

lectern at the front of the stage. The crowd hushed and settled, leaning forward in anticipation.

"Esteemed members of the Geographical Society." To Eudora, the crowd's attention was like oxygen. "As you know, the existence of so-called super-sapients has long been rumored. But what do we really know about such creatures? About the threat they may pose? Sapient creatures have long been the pets of explorers, kept in their natural place." She avoided eye contact with her father, who had frequently argued with her on this point. "But these super-sapients are different from our pets. Their intentions toward humans are uncertain. And what if they intend to have humans as their pets?"

The audience fidgeted uncomfortably, nervous at the thought. Eudora hid a smile.

"I have captured such a creature."

To this, the audience gasped as one.

"I did it to show you that human's superior power is unassailable, uncontroversial." She felt like a pitch engine when it was reaching full flight, leaving a glorious trail in its path. And the best was yet to come.

She looked to the crate, and all eyes in the auditorium followed hers. Nodding to Smethwyck, she stepped back. "Members of the board, fellow explorers, I give you . . . the great bear!"

❋ 292 ❋

The sides of the crate crashed to the floor simultaneously, kicking up a cloud of dust.

Silence thick as glue united the room as all staring eyes and boggled minds took in the sight of the sleeping great earth-bear, every bit as wide as the crate that had contained it. Its head was slumped on its front paws. Its markings were dull, barely visible, so that it looked as though its fur was merely matted and bald in places.

Then the chatter started as each audience member began sharing their thoughts with the person beside them.

Eudora would allow it for a moment; it all added to the spectacle that would be described in the next morning's *Lontown Chronicle* and in future books.

She nodded to a photographer who had been waiting in the shadows at the side of the room. He scurried forward, and Eudora smiled sweetly beside the bear as the blinding flash of his camera bathed them in glorious, white light.

Madame Gainsford, elected head of the Geographical Society board, who had been sitting front and center, stood up. Draped around her neck, her sapient stoat looked at Eudora with wide eyes, and anyone close enough would have noticed the tremble in its fur. Madame Gainsford stroked it as she said in a haughty voice, "Madame Vane. When you sent a note requesting an audience for a new sapient discovery, you somehow failed to mention the enormity of your find!"

"Magnificent, isn't it?" Eudora smiled.

"Perhaps it would have been prudent to at least have given the board a little information. Look at the size of that thing!"

Eudora approached the small, stocky woman and leaned in to whisper, "Oh, Gertie, stop working yourself up and enjoy the spectacle. It's well sedated." She had always found Gertrude Gainsford a little too much in the middle of matters, too cautious and indecisive. Gertrude could often be swayed to the Vanes' side and wasn't beyond a persuasive gift or two, but Eudora was looking forward to the day when her father would be elected.

She glanced to Thaddeus now, who was sitting to the right of Madame Gainsford. He gave her a single nod of approval . . . or was it a sign that she should proceed with the next step in her plan?

Elegantly, she raised a pink-gloved hand and in moments the audience fell silent.

"This great beast was captured by me in the Volcanic North. The creature attacked me, but I was able to restrain it. As many of you know, the Culpepper crew and the Brightstorm twins were heading that way on a so-called heritage expedition." She took a breath and put a hand on her heart. "Arthur and Maudie Brightstorm are my niece and nephew by blood, children of my beloved sister Violetta Vane. It pains me more than you can know to say what I need to tell you now. I've tried to welcome them, to help them even, but . . . It is time to reveal the true nature of these children."

The audience exchanged perplexed glances.

"I can report, with evidence, their severe violation of the Explorer's Code!"

Incredulous huffs and outraged sneers surged in the auditorium. The code was the highest law of Lontown. Eudora had almost successfully convicted Ernest Brightstorm of it and destroyed his family name once before, but those wretched twins and the crew of the *Aurora* had managed to find proof against it. But not this time.

Pulling the letter from her pocket, she waved it at the crowd. "Here! In his own hand. Ernest Brightstorm knew that a dangerous super-sapient existed in the Volcanic North, yet he took it upon himself to hide it from the rest of us, thinking he knew better than the very bedrock of Lontown, the board of the Geographical Society. And his children knew too!"

✳ ✳ ✳

The earth-bear felt the strange, smooth wood beneath her and the stifling, warm air all around.

She wasn't in the North. She was far away. The sinews that connected her to the earth were strained, stretched over a thousand miles.

Her head swam and she felt dizzy and sick, and it wasn't just inside of her, the sickness was all around her in this place where she lay.

Where was she?

She stirred and lifted a sleepy eyelid.

Humans. So many of them, their faces twisted in expressions of . . . what was it? Anger, outrage, wrath.

And where was it directed? At her?

She had always protected humans, not directly, but in upholding the gentle balance, the beat of the earth. And was this how they repay her? By tearing her from her homeland and dragging her thousands of miles away?

And where were the children? Those she had called for help? She had last seen them at her heart-home.

Then that woman had arrived, and her intentions were dark and full of malice, and the woman had fired the death shard at her, and she'd tried to escape and to help them, but she was angry and the earth became angry with her.

What had she done?

They were going to help her stop the earth ravaging that had gripped the North, the great gouging and obliteration of the green.

Instead, had she now been the cause of their deaths?

Straining to keep her eyelids open, she noticed the woman in pink before her, addressing the crowd. She knew by her foul stink that it was her. The woman could try to mask it with that sickly sweet elixir, but Gaia was the earth-bear. She could read the truth.

The emulsion of sorrow and fury churned deep in her fiery core, awakening her, bringing strength to her limbs, sharpening her mind.

She had to stop these humans, she had to protect the earth, she had to get back to her heart-home.

Straining, she stumbled to her feet.

She could read the soul of an individual, but could she read a collective soul? Could she summon the deep earth to her aid, so far from her heart-home? The connection was frayed, but it was still there. She would show the humans, with the might of the earth.

From deep in her belly, she called out to the earth-soul.

Fury became fuel to her fire.

She was the earth-bear.

She would show them.

The audience, seeing the earth-bear slowly rise, stood up from their seats and gaped open-mouthed as the bear's jaw opened wide and fury-red firelight ignited in its markings and throat. The force of its roar blasted them like a storm, hurtling them off their feet, sending them sprawling backward over the chairs, the sound shattering the windows and blowing open the hall doors.

For a moment, Eudora lay in shock. How could it be? The bear was meant to still be mostly sedated!

Smethwyck appeared before her, windswept and stunned, attempting to pull her up, but she shoved him away.

"You must have gotten the dose wrong, you utter fool!"

The restraining chains attached to the earth-bear's limbs snapped like dead wood. Screams and hollers of utter horror filled the room as everyone burst into action. Bodies clambered over each other in a blind panic to escape.

Then, a sound like the fracturing of glacial ice sliced the air, and above, the great domed roof cracked like a brittle shell.

CHAPTER 25

FIRES OF LONTOWN

S THE *ALTAN* sailed toward Lontown, the sky remained overcast, with only the faintest tinge of red on the horizon to indicate sunrise.

By nine chimes, they'd set down the sky-ship in the western docks, the closest area to the Geographical Society. Hurriedly, they secured the ship, leaving the majority of the crew to finish up, and raced to the esteemed building, its great dome visible above all others. They traveled a few blocks before they caught sight of the *Lontown Chronicle*, an impressive building in its own right, with a tower to rival, though not quite reach, the Geographical Society's dome.

"Nearly there," said Maudie.

"Is it me, or are there an unusual number of

animals in the streets?" asked Arthur, brushing past a large dark-furred fox that stood perfectly still in the street, staring toward the Geographical Society square.

A thunderous, bone-shaking roar halted them in their tracks.

Felicity clutched her lucky spoon. "Oh, no."

"I fear we're too late," said Harriet, wide-eyed.

Suddenly, the doors of the Geographical Society burst open and people flooded from the entrance into the square in a river of panic. Arthur glanced back, instinctively worried about the beautiful fox being trampled, but it had disappeared.

"Come, on, we need to get in there!" Arthur dove into the crowd, but it was like swimming against the tide, and he was jostled and pushed to the ground. Harriet pulled him to his feet and yanked him to the side, to take cover at the *Lontown Chronicle* building's entrance beside Maudie, Gan, and Felicity.

"Look!" Harriet pointed to an enormous crack fracturing the great dome ahead of them.

The earth rumbled, shaking the cobblestones beneath them and vibrating every cell in their bodies so that they had to clutch each other just to stay on their feet. A bellow like a deathly thunderclap came from somewhere deep beneath them.

"Clanking cogs, we're all in trouble," breathed Felicity.

Then, an ear-splitting crack echoed in the square as the earth ripped apart.

Just a couple of feet at first.

The last of the fleeing Geographical Society crowd ran down the marble staircase, rushing into the shadows. Arthur caught sight of Eudora running away too. Seconds later, another mighty shatter sounded as the dome of the great Geographical Society began crashing in on itself. Everything growled as the building shook and the structure beneath the dome buckled. Chunks of marble and boulder-sized sections of pillars came tumbling down.

The magnificent dome collapsed, along with most of the building, engulfing the entire square and several streets beyond in a wave of choking smoke. They squeezed their eyes shut and pulled their sweaters over their mouths as the dark, acrid wind blasted them.

In debilitating shock, they watched as the dust cloud slowly settled.

Among the fallen pillars and cracked marble ruins of the Geographical Society stood the earth-bear.

Arthur could feel her fury and her fear as though they were his own. He called out to her—*we are here, it's all right, we will help you*—but she had already unleashed another colossal roar and his plea was drowned out.

She reared back onto her hind legs. The markings in her fur illuminated with a vicious glow, and her eyes seemed different, crazed with red light as though she was in a deep fog of pure anger.

The clouds above swirled and darkened further, becoming charcoal-hued, and bursts of lightning rippled in the gloom.

With a thunderous smack, the earth-bear's forepaws bore into what was left of the Geographical Society steps. The marble ignited with firelight, and

the ground shook. The crack in the cobbles in the square splintered further, forking in a blaze of red. Lava spilled up from the earth, oozing from the cracks.

A hot wind assaulted them, and Arthur called out again. He had to try and stop Gaia, to calm her down. Somewhere beneath the roar of thunder, he was aware of Maudie crying out too, but it was futile: the bear was in a frenzy. She thundered down the remaining steps and galloped northward along Montgolfiere Parade, the great split in the earth expanding in her wake.

Vents exploded in the street, sending grates flying upward. Screams of terror filled the air.

"Watch out!" called Gan, pulling Arthur back.

A hunk of metal smashed to the ground and clattered on the cobbles inches away from where Arthur had just stood.

"We need to get to safety in the residential areas, and swiftly," said Harriet.

"The rip is blocking our way," said Maudie, her voice tight with alarm.

Felicity wiped the sweat from her brow. "Where can we go? Four Archangel Street doesn't exactly have a house anymore."

"Welby House?" suggested Arthur. It was the one safe place he could think of.

"Good call," said Harriet. "It's far enough away

from the split but near enough that we can reassess our next steps and act."

"Will the docks be all right?" asked Gan.

"Batzorig is far enough away from this chaos and the crew should be safe, for now. And at least they can take off. Come on, let's go before we run out of options. We work as a team: Maudie and Gan will look to the sky for incoming danger, while Arthur, Felicity, and I will keep our eyes on the streets. Hold hands, no one is to get left behind."

They were on the opposite side of the square from where they needed to be to reach Welby House. Their only hope was to head across and try to make it before the lava river reached them. They charged forward as the lava rip zigzagged down the length of the square.

"Hurry!" Harriet urged.

But the fracturing earth was faster, and the ground tore in front of them.

"Jump!" yelled Harriet, and, without thinking, for fear it would stop them, they leaped across the expanding lava split, crashing and rolling on the other side.

The earth groaned.

Hauling themselves to their feet, they kept going, and Harriet pointed to Sovereign Street, which led to Eastside Uptown.

The smoke and heat were overwhelming as they forged on. Lontonians scattered and darted like ants away from the square, heading toward the residential areas.

As they entered Sovereign Street, Maudie lunged at Arthur and started patting him: an ember had landed on him and set his jacket on fire, and he hadn't even realized.

The clouds were now so dark it was like nightfall. Nearby, a vent had exploded and a plume of fire spewed into the sky. They sprinted along the opposite side, then were forced to cross again to avoid a blazing tree. Harriet swiftly darted to help up a young lady who had tripped inches from the fire. The quality of the flames was different from anything Arthur had ever seen, as though they had life of their own, the very soul of the Wide angered into being.

They made it to Periwhistle Grove. Somewhere in the distance came another roar from the earthbear, then an earth-quaking tremor hit, knocking them off their feet. The building walls shook around them, and then a terrible crash sounded as a chunk of masonry fell only feet away.

And still they ran on, the stink of singed clothes and burning all around. They ran down an alley and onto Ashbury Terrace; they were close to Welby

House now. The streets were becoming devoid of people as everyone made it back to their homes. The mayhem became less fierce as they put more distance between themselves and the center of town. They slowed to a jog, turning onto Fontaine Row before finally finding themselves in the square before Welby House.

Hastily they knocked on the door. Madame Mills, who was in charge of the orphanage, opened the door.

"What in all of the Wide is going on out there? Hurry, come inside, all of you!"

They tumbled into the entrance hall and lay gasping and coughing.

Felicity retched. "I'm not built for such heat," she spluttered, her curls now a chaotic mass of matted black.

"Come into the parlor, I'll fetch you some water and something to clean you all up with," urged Madame Mills.

Wide eyes peered at them from over the staircase banister and from the doors of the rooms feeding off the hall. The children of the orphanage couldn't believe what they were seeing.

The five of them slumped on chairs in the parlor, still panting.

"We must be a sight," said Maudie.

Their faces were smudged with ash and their clothes were torn and singed.

"I'll update Madame Mills," said Harriet, pushing herself to her feet and rubbing her side before walking unsteadily toward the kitchen.

As they sat there, stunned and spent from their exertion, silence fell. The muted roars of thunder and fire faded.

Arthur looked around as though he'd suddenly fallen into a dream. They were here, in Brightstorm House! Well, that's what it had been called, before it had been sold from under them after their father had died in South Polaris. Welby had managed to repurchase it for them at the time of their previous expedition to the Stella Oceanus, and they'd repurposed the building into a safe and warm haven for the homeless children of the Slumps, named in his honor: Welby House.

The fireplace was exactly the same as before, the black slate surrounded with rich copper and russet marbleized panels, the ornate decoration of silvered ivy with seven rivets along the mantle seam. He could almost see his father sitting beside it in his chair, head resting in the indentation on the cushion, his sunblushed, freckled face smiling down at them, and his large hands placed on the frayed arms. When they had lived here it had been full of books and tools.

"Maud, this used to be the library," he said softly. "Remember?"

Felicity exhaled a sad sigh, put a hand on Arthur's knee, then stood up. "Come on, Gan. What do you say we join Harrie and Madame Mills, and see if we can comfort all the scared little eyes out there with something yummy from the pantry?"

"I'd rather—" started Gan.

But Felicity pulled her gently into the hall and clicked the door shut behind them, leaving Arthur and Maudie alone.

CHAPTER 26

WELBY HOUSE

"**D**O YOU REMEMBER how it felt," said Arthur, "when Dad used to disappear for whole moon cycles exploring?"

Maudie stoked the embers in the fire. "When we were really young it felt like he might never come back."

"But then he made those charts and we'd count down the days."

"And he'd always be delayed for some reason, so we'd climb on the roof and wait for him."

"It hurt, didn't it?"

"But we never said it. To each other, or him."

He paused. "Perhaps we should have."

"Perhaps. But it wouldn't have changed anything.

And he always made sure we were well looked after while he was away. And we had each other."

All the hurt he had felt on the expedition when she'd revealed her plans rushed back to him. Dad was an explorer at his core. Just like them. "He would want us to continue his work."

"Are you forgetting that Mum was an engineer too?" She raised her palms quickly. "They would want us to do whatever makes us happy! Just like they did. Yes, Dad left us here to go exploring, and that must have been a hard choice for him, but he did it."

"He left us because he knew how dangerous exploring was! We were going to explore *together*, when we were old enough."

"No, he did it because he wanted to do the thing that made him happiest, even if it meant sacrificing time with us!"

"Or because it was *all* of our destinies! Maud, how could you even consider not coming on another expedition? Why would you do this to us, to me? Why are you insisting on tearing us apart?"

Maudie raised her eyebrows, incredulous. "Me? You're the one insisting on carrying on exploring!"

"It's in our blood! That's why Dad left—"

"So are other things!"

They glared at each other, livid.

Silence hung like a wall between them. Arthur stood, then shuffled to the window, pushing the curtain back to look up at the menacing sky. Although it was still early afternoon, the opaque cloud cover cast an ominous shadow over the city, turning day to night. Red reflected on the underside of the rumbling clouds to the west in the direction of the city center. The pitch lamp on the wall flickered.

He could hear Maudie breathing and sighing behind him.

Time stretched.

After a while she said, "Look, it's Welby's old banjo on the wall! Harriet must have given it to the orphanage."

He wanted to turn around and have a look, but for some reason it just made him feel *more* cross. They'd lost Welby—yet another reason why they should stick together. His shoulders stiffened and he set his jaw.

"Arthur, you do realize it's not distance that will separate us, it's arguing . . . or silence."

Her words were like an arrow to his heart. She was right. Suddenly, a tear streamed down his cheek. Deep down he knew the truth. It had been there all along. Arguing about who Dad was or what he represented was pointless. It wasn't that they had their own paths to follow that made him feel so full of sorrow. It was only when the idea of separation struck that the real depth of his feelings gripped him.

He turned around. "Oh, Maud. I'm sorry."

Tears glistened on her cheek too.

"I know."

"I've just been so scared of what the future means for us."

"Me too. But remember when Dad would come back? How we appreciated every moment with him, treasuring it like stardust? He would have been miserable if he'd stayed here in Lontown all the time. The smile on his face when we were reunited, the stories he told us, the fun days we had together. He could make toasting marshmallows on the fire the most glorious event."

She was right. There was something in the act of being apart that made them appreciate how precious their time was together. They knew to make the most of every moment. In some way, even though it had been hard and painful at times to be separated, especially as they'd never known their mother, their love was unbreakable. Time and distance away from their dad was difficult, but when they were back together none of that mattered.

They sat beside each other, taking in the room: the details of the fireplace, the same cracked chips of paint on the skirting, the slightly wonky shelf, the soft dent in the door where Maudie had been experimenting with a new invention that backfired. Some things changed, but some things would always be the same.

"Love from a distance is still love. It's distance, not an ending," she said.

The pitch lamp flickered once more, then went out. The children upstairs let out worried cries.

Arthur leaped up and looked out the window as lights in the streets and houses extinguished. "The central pitch lamp system has gone down! Things don't seem to be calming down." He turned back to Maudie, now shrouded in darkness. "We can't lose sight of what we need to do. We're the only ones who can stop it."

Harriet hurried into the room with a candle. "Power's out across the city. I've been on the roof, and from what I can see with my binoscope, the earth-bear is in the northwest of the city."

"And is the lava stream still active along Montgolfiere?" asked Arthur.

"Parthena flew over the area. From what I can interpret from her, it's still there and as dangerous as ever, and fires are still burning in the streets. The core around the Geographical Society, or what's left of it, is a no-go zone. People have retreated to the residential outskirts, and . . ."

"And?" asked Arthur, concerned by her tone.

"Hugo sent a pigeon from the docks. The authorities are preparing a sky-ship with cannons and artillery. All other sky-ships are forbidden to fly into the danger zone, but most have fled."

He glanced at Maudie. "We have to go out and find Gaia. We could calm her down if we could get close enough in time. Then we could lead her to the North, get her to safety."

"Just the small matter of a huge fracture in the earth, raging fires in the streets, and a river of lava between us," said Maudie with a nervous laugh.

Felicity and Gan entered with trays of biscuits and water, and the others gratefully accepted them. They hadn't realized how hungry and thirsty they were.

Arthur gulped down a glass of water. His thoughts became clearer. They needed a plan, and he had an idea. "We need to get to the docks; they're not many blocks away."

"Why the docks?" asked Maudie curiously.

"Then we can get a sky-ak and head to the northwest where the earth-bear is. Sky-ships may be grounded, but a sky-ak can get away unnoticed. It'll keep us safe from the dangers below, and we can approach Gaia from the sky without alarming her. Once she sees it's us, we can calm her down and show her a safe route out of the city. We'll hide her in the forest until we can get a sky-ship to take her back home."

"It's not a bad plan," said Gan, taking an arrow from her quiver and thoughtfully twirling it in her hair. "But you've overlooked one big thing: the fact that there's a huge lava river in the street!"

Maudie narrowed her eyes. "What are you thinking, Arty?"

He grinned. "It's been a while since we've done it."

Maudie joined him in a grin. "We go up."

"Up?" asked Gan.

Maudie gave her a wry smile. "We're not going *through* the streets, we're going over."

"I always thought you two were a bit daring, but that sounds impossible."

"Says the girl with a bow—this should be right up your alley, so to speak," said Arthur with a smile. "Anyway, the houses are closer than you think. The terraces are quite tight, if you know the right way to go and where the buildings are closest. We can leap the roofs until Sovereign Street."

"But again, you can't jump over a lava river," said Gan.

"Could we get a rope across, Maud? Between the corner of Sovereign Street and the *Lontown Chronicle* tower?"

"Maybe, but we'd need some sort of grappling hook to secure it, and I'm not sure we could throw one that far."

Gan cleared her throat. "Er, *I* can," she said, tapping her bow as if it were a faithful pet.

"Have you ever shot a grappling hook?" asked Maudie.

"I was scaling the walls of the Citadel when I was three."

Arthur raised his eyebrows disbelievingly.

"All right, I was seven." She smiled.

"So we use the rope as a zip line, make it across the lava river to the *Chronicle* tower, then we pray to the Wide that we make it past any other smaller fires and obstacles to the docks."

"Anyone happen to have a long piece of rope and a grappling hook?" asked Arthur doubtfully.

"There should be rope in the pantry to hang washing, will that do?" asked Felicity.

"Excellent," said Maudie.

"An orphanage probably doesn't have much use for grappling hooks, though. I don't suppose you have one hidden in your tool belt, Maud?"

"I'm not magic, Arty." After a frown of deep thought, Maudie added, "But I am resourceful." She smiled. "I expect there are some large nails in the house somewhere. I'll need a pipe and a fire wand to bend them into shape, and something to twine them together."

Arthur thought for a moment. "We always used to keep spare tools in that cupboard under the stairs. I'll have a look. Maud, you get the rope and I'll meet you back here." Arthur took a candle from Felicity and hurried along the corridor to the stairs.

As he opened the door to the cupboard, something flinched inside. A pair of eyes glinted in the dark.

"Oh, sorry! I didn't mean to make you jump. I'm just after some tools, to sort out the problems outside." The figure shrank into the corner. He thought perhaps it was a young girl. "Are you scared?" he asked.

She nodded. "It's dark."

"Don't worry, we're all scared, but it'll be all right.

We'll all look after each other." He put the candle down between them and knelt just inside the door.

"I'm always scared," she said, her voice hushed as a snowflake.

He gave her a soft smile. "I used to live here once."

"Are you an orphan?"

"Yes. Not when I lived here, but I became one. Although I've never really felt like one, not for long, anyway." He thought about how terrible it was living with the Begginses, which felt like a lifetime ago, and how the crew of the *Aurora* had quickly become a real family to him. "If you don't like the dark, a cupboard is a strange place to hide."

Reaching forward a little, she opened her hands and revealed a small white mouse. "I'm not alone. Mousey finds me. He knows when I'm feeling sad, or scared."

"May I?" He reached his hand out gently and stroked the mouse's head. *Definitely sapient,* he thought. They were always adept at reading human emotion.

"He's been worried too. He keeps trying to run."

"I'm Arthur Brightstorm. What's your name?"

After a pause she said, "Brea."

"Well, Brea, do you know what I think?"

She shook her head.

"I think Brea is a fine name. It sounds like the name of a warrior."

The girl leaned forward in the candlelight. Large eyes open with curiosity, nervous, yet bright as buttons, stared up at him. Her cheeks were round with youth and brown hair tickled her chin, one side held back by a metal barrette, something like a twisted key with a couple of blue gems. There were some gaps in the metal where gems had perhaps been lost over time. Arthur wondered if it was a memory of a family that once was, just as he treasured Dad's journal and Maudie did Mum's toolbelt.

"But how can a warrior be someone who hides in the dark?" she asked.

"I want you to remember something, Brea." She leaned closer. "My dad used to say that it's only in the darkness that you can see the stars."

Her eyes became even wider as she tried to work out what he was saying. Arthur hadn't remembered Dad saying that until that moment, and it wasn't until now that he'd really understood the meaning. They were all stars in the night: him, Maudie, Harrie, Felicity, even Gan.

"Now, Brea, I have a job to do, and I need your help. I'm looking for large nails and some wire, for a start."

The young girl crawled out of the cupboard and pointed to the toolbox she'd been sitting on. The mouse hopped onto her shoulder.

"And hopefully there's a fire wand in there too?"

The tiny mouse nodded.

CHAPTER 27

PURSUING THE BEAR

"**H**ERE," SAID MAUDIE, putting one of her gloves on Arthur's hand. "It'll help you climb to the upper roof."

"Thanks," he said, swinging his legs out of their former bedroom window. "Ah, just like old times!"

"With added lava."

"Be careful!" called Harriet. "Send Parthena if you need backup!" Harriet had wanted to go with them, but she needed to check that Octavie and Valiant were safe, so they'd decided it was best if she went to find them.

The twins scurried up to the roof, followed by Gan. She was an incredibly confident climber, so Arthur knew that she hadn't been joking about scaling the walls of the Citadel.

They balanced their way along the roof ridge, around the chimney, and on to the adjoining house. The city skyline of arches and spires so familiar to them was now broken in the distance, a great gap where the Geographical Society dome had been. It was difficult to know what time of day it was, as the clouds were still so angry and black, but Arthur guessed it was midafternoon by now. He looked northwest, toward their destination, where the underbelly of the clouds reflected the glowing hues of fires below. Far off roars traveled the distance, but the streets below were all eerily devoid of people. Instead, there were calls from creatures: the yowl of dogs, the screech of bats, the bellow of deer, the squeak of rabbits and squirrels. It was as though sapients in the city were rising to answer the roar of the earth-bear, rampaging the streets with cries of mutiny. Even Parthena kept leaving them to swoop through the streets, cawing loudly with the other creatures.

They made it to the next block but had to head north a short distance where they could leap across a narrow alley rather than the larger street on the more direct route.

"I'll go first," said Maudie. "There's a strong lip on the gutter, Gan. You can get a good grip, and I'll grab you if you look unsteady on landing."

Rocking her body back to gain momentum, Maudie took a few steps then jumped, landing deftly on the other side as though she'd leaped a small puddle, not a forty-foot drop.

Gan went next, followed by Arthur. As his feet left the roof, he became suddenly distracted by chatter and squeaks below. He glanced down to see a small group of rats gathered in the alley beneath them. They seemed to pause and look up as he flew through the air above. Just in time, Arthur looked to his landing spot, but his balance was off and he wobbled as he landed.

Maudie grabbed his jacket.

"Did you see those rats?" he asked her, breathless with excitement. "It was like they were having a meeting."

"Arthur, keep your eyes ahead! You know how you have a knack for falling into things," she snapped.

"Yes, but I have your super glove." He wiggled his fingers playfully at her. But she was right, he did tend to fall into situations. He remembered the quicksand in Nadvaaryn, and the great frozen lake in the South, and the jungle depths of Erythea . . . He shouldn't keep pressing his luck.

On they went, across Ashbury Terrace, then to Periwhistle Grove, where they had to leap a slightly bigger alley that made even Gan turn a little pale. Then they were on Sovereign Street, where the buildings were taller still. They had to use Maudie's gloves to navigate the height and traverse several nerve-shakingly high ridges, which slowed them down, but at last they made it to the final building on the corner of Sovereign Street and faced the great square of the Geographical Society.

The clouds that blanketed Lontown seemed to spiral around the dark central point above the square. They crackled with lightning and growled a constant roar.

Below looked like a scene from the end of the world. The lava river ran like an angry slash through the center of the city, surging from north to south as far as they could see. The sky was a livid mix of mauve and red. Flames had devoured the trees, and great chunks of buildings had fallen. With the collapse of the Geographical Society building, the skyline seemed unrecognizable. By a stroke of good luck, the tower of the *Lontown Chronicle* was intact. Arthur strained to see beyond the trails of smoke for any sign of the artillery sky-ship, but to his relief there was nothing.

"It's farther than I remembered," said Gan, swallowing hard.

Maudie began unhitching the bag of equipment from her shoulders. She took out her binoscope and scoured the tower, then she passed it to Gan. "There, see the ridge beneath the clock? That's where I want you to aim."

"We've only got one shot. If we miss and it falls into the fire, we're done for."

"Thanks for the positive pep talk, Arthur," Gan said, hoisting up her bow.

"Sorry, I meant good luck."

But with barely any hesitation, Gan shot the grapple-hook arrow.

It whizzed through the sky like a firework, the rope flying behind it, uncoiling from the tiles beside Gan. But the trajectory of the arrow seemed way off; it was heading too far north of the building.

Arthur's stomach clenched in disappointment. Then the hot wind gusted and the arrow shifted from northwest to west.

"Come on, come on," willed Maudie.

Gan's grip on her bow tightened.

At that moment the arrow struck the tower. "Yes!" exclaimed Gan, just as the last of the rope flew into the air!

"No!" Arthur lunged for the rope and grabbed the

end of it with his hand just in time. But he was too far off balance and suddenly gravity was tugging him downward. He couldn't let go of the rope, and yet he was going to fall—

He heard a cry behind him as Maudie grabbed his jacket, yanking him back before he lost his footing. They collapsed, panting on the roof, Arthur's grip still like a vise on the end of the rope.

"That was close," said Gan.

"Again, please stop falling!" Maudie begged.

After catching their breath, Arthur and Maudie pulled the rope taut and secured it around the chimney.

The heat from below was relentless and sweat beaded on their faces.

"What are we going to use as the sling?" asked Arthur.

Maudie took a metal clasp from her tool belt. "OK, well, I guess I should tell you now that I could only find one suitable clamp. Only one of us can go across."

"Maud! Why didn't you say?"

"Because I knew it would stress you out and there wasn't anything I could do about it!"

"Then who goes?" asked Gan.

"You should go, Maud. You're the best at flying the sky-ak, and . . . well, it could be your last big adventure, after all."

Their eyes locked. She gave a sad nod.

"Go on, we're wasting time!" said Arthur, swallowing hard.

After a swift hug and a word of good luck, he watched her slide across the expanse, his heart in his mouth as she passed over the lava river. She seemed to thwack into the tower with some force, but she swiftly turned to wave, indicating she was all right.

It felt as though an ocean now existed between them.

"Stay safe!" Arthur called.

Gan gave a small cough. "You could use my bow."

"Pardon?"

"My bow. You could use it to get across. It's well balanced, and the wood is the toughest on Nadvaaryn, and the string and joints are engineered by the top engineers in the Citadel. There's not a stronger bow in the Wide."

He couldn't believe what he was hearing. "Me go across there, with your bow?"

"Arthur, you're always repeating what I say, and it's very annoying. Yes, but the only question is: are you strong enough?"

He fell silent, thinking he absolutely would be pushing the limits of his strength.

"Felicity told me you once hung from a rope over the edge of the *Aurora* while it took flight."

He blushed. "Well, yes."

"And that was ages ago. You're bigger and stronger now, so this should be a walk in the park."

He *was* bigger . . . which also meant he was *heavier*.

But before he could question any further, Gan had unhitched her bow, detached the string from one end, then reattached it over the rope. "Get your hand in the middle so the balance is right."

He nodded, then sat on the edge of the building, clasped the string of the bow with his glove, and took the longest inhale of his life.

"Now hurry before Maudie gets too far ahead!"

And with that, as he saw Maudie disappear into the tower, Arthur leaped and hurtled into the unknown.

Warm air rushed at him, and his hand clutched the bowstring with all he had. He was glad of the glove, as the bowstring would surely have cut through his hand. He couldn't help but glance below as another wave of heat enveloped him: he was directly above the lava. He set his teeth as his shoulder strained and his muscles began to burn. The thought that he was just a movement away from death entered his mind, but he pushed it away and gripped tighter, flying across the lava, over great piles of fallen debris from what was once the Geographical Society, and then . . . he realized he was approaching the tower at great speed. There was no brake, and no Maudie at the other end to help him. Bracing his muscles, he smashed into the wall. The bow jolted, and it took all of his strength for the string not to be yanked from his hand.

He attempted to swing his legs up, but he couldn't gain momentum enough. Panic threatened to rise within him, but he realized there was only one thing for it: he'd have to leap and hope that the glove would save him.

Before he could question his decision, he leaped, propelling his palm toward the brickwork. By all good fortune it worked!

Except now he was stuck, his hand on the building and his legs dangling like string beans below.

His left foot found a tiny jut, and he used it to push himself upward, then released his hand briefly and grasped the target edge, and somehow hauled his body over to safety. He looked back across the square to Gan, who was fist-pumping the air and whooping.

Then she jabbed her finger at him and hollered, "Don't forget my bow, I want it back!"

After unclasping the bow from the rope, he waved goodbye to Gan and found the clock maintenance passage where he presumed Maudie had gone.

The stairs spiraled downward, and deep below he could hear the echo of Maudie's steps. He called out to her.

"Arthur?" Her voice echoed back at him. "How the clanking cogs did you make it across?"

Hurrying to join her, they embraced, then he tapped the bow slung across his body.

She smiled and her shoulders relaxed. "I'm so pleased to see you. I wasn't keen on facing this alone, to tell you the truth."

"Come on," he said.

She nodded. "Together."

Stumbling and staggering out of the tower and over fallen masonry, they coughed through the drifts of black smoke and inched past flaming vents toward the west dock. As they neared the water's edge, the damage lessened, and they pelted, heads down, through the remaining streets.

"Hugo!" Arthur called, seeing him pacing the deck of the *Altan*.

"Arthur? Maudie? Oh, thank the Wide you made it! I've been worried sick since Harriet sent a pigeon alerting me to your plan."

They hurried up the gangplank. Batzorig rushed across. He looked with alarm at the sight of Gan's bow around Arthur. "Is Gan all right?"

"She's fine," said Arthur. "She just lent this to me. She's gone back to Welby House to wait with Felicity."

"The sky-ak is ready for you. There's drinking water and something to eat."

"Thanks," said Maudie, hopping inside.

"The guards are by the artillery ship farther down. They're currently experiencing a little engine trouble," said Batzorig with a wry smile, holding what looked to be a small but vital engine component. "If you fly straight north, they won't even notice you."

In moments, the balloon was fully inflated, and they ascended above the rooftops and headed northwest.

A grim haze hung over the city. Arthur was sure

it must be dinnertime by now because his stomach complained in a loud grumble. Maudie thrust him a chunk of bread and cheese. "Here, eat this while you navigate." She held the steering wheel with one hand and stuffed a piece of bread in her mouth with the other. When they had gotten a little higher, the full danger around the city came into view: great paths of lava cut a glowing swath through various neighborhoods, leading to the great shape of the earth-bear, who galloped between buildings in the distance.

"I think Gaia is trying to keep safe from the people," said Arthur. "And if you think about it, the lava patterns seem remarkably controlled: I don't think she wants to harm people, she just wants to keep them away!"

"Look at her!" Maudie called. "She's frantic, trying to find a way out!"

They sped toward the northwest trading area of Lontown, stalls abandoned and burning.

"Gaia! It's us! Arthur and Maudie."

The earth-bear raised her great snout. She seemed to hear them, but her eyes were still fiery red with rage.

"Up here!" called Maudie. "It's us, the Brightstorms!"

"Take us lower, Maud."

"I don't think we should be within jumping distance."

"But she's not hearing us."

Maudie exhaled, her hands tightening on the small steering wheel. "OK . . . just a little."

"Gaia!" Arthur called, leaning over the edge of the sky-ak.

The earth-bear looked up at him. She reared back, her hackles raised, her markings illuminating with fiery power.

"Gaia!" He shouted again, pleading.

Gaia opened her mouth, readying to roar, and Arthur took in the white-hot heat of the anger building inside her. She wasn't listening! She wasn't seeing them!

"Arthur!" Maudie's cry was full of anguish.

Somewhere nearby, Parthena squawked desperately.

And then, it was as though time slowed and a strange stillness overtook Arthur. Several thoughts converged in his mind: meeting Tuyok, the leader of the thought-wolves in the Everlasting Forest, when he had been pinned down and Tuyok was trying to communicate; the terrifying encounter with the darkwhispers in Erythea, when one of them had transferred Welby's memories to him; the long-distance reassurance from

Tuyok on the lake at Tempestra after Welby had died; the way Parthena could so often anticipate his moves before he could; the Firesong that found them from thousands of miles away, a song only they could hear.

It was all done through the mind. Shouting at the bear to listen was futile; he had to call out in thought.

He closed his eyes. *"Gaia, it's Arthur and Maudie, your friends."*

Gaia paused. She sniffed the air.

"Please, we know how scared and angry you must be with the humans that took you, with how you've been treated. But we're not all like that."

"Whatever you're doing, keep it up. I'll hold the sky-ak steady," said Maudie, as the earth-bear's features softened.

"We're going to get you out of here. We can show you the way out of the city and hide you in the forest, then get our sky-ship to fly you home."

The earth-bear went from two legs to four, her markings darkened, and the red rage slowly faded in her eyes.

"Set the sky-ak down, Maud." Arthur smiled.

As soon as they were on the ground, they jumped out and sprinted to the earth-bear.

She mumbled and groaned, as though awakening from a deep dream.

"Oh, Gaia, we're so sorry we led them to you!" Arthur cried, running up to her. "If we'd known . . ." He flung his arm around the earth-bear and pressed into her warm fur, taking in the scent, which was sweet like meadows and as rich as earth.

Maudie joined him. "Arthur, we should lead Gaia out of the city as soon as possible. Look at the fire!"

Around them, anything that had been burning began receding, as if a giant stove dial were being turned down.

"Arthur, Maudie!" said Gaia, blinking. "I believed you had perished! I didn't think to reach out."

"Our crew saved us. We went to that awful facility and looked for you, but we were too late. We came as fast as we could."

"There is so much malevolence in this place," said Gaia, more with disappointment than disbelief. "And souls that look in, never out. I understand why the land destruction has become so easy for them."

"We're still going to stop that, Gaia," Arthur reassured her.

Around them, the lava had disappeared back below the cobbles like blood into sand. Any lava that remained above the surface began cooling and solidi- fying, the thunder-growl of the earth ceased, and the clouds turned from angry mauve to gray. Ash drifted like snowflakes, settling gently on their shoulders and coating their hair.

"Come on, just follow us. We'll lead you to safety with this," said Maudie.

Gaia nodded, and Arthur and Maudie leaped back into the sky-ak. Relief and elation filled Arthur's veins, and he looked at Maudie and smiled, knowing that perhaps this was the last of their great Wide adventures as a team, and that it was strange how it was ending where it all started, in Lontown. Quelling the sadness, he focused on Gaia and the route out of the city.

A whistling noise flew by his ear, soft as an insect rushing past. Then another.

For the briefest moment he remained oblivious to what was happening, then the shadow of a sky-ship swallowed them. Arthur looked up to see a shower of darts heading for Gaia.

"No!" he shouted.

Then something hit him too, and Maudie cried out. The great earth-bear was falling. There was a mighty thud, and Arthur was helpless as an intense cold spread through his veins. Darkness swaddled him. He could do nothing but submit to an endless night.

CHAPTER 28

GAIA

MOONLIGHT GLEAMING through a window woke Arthur. His head felt heavy, as though his blood had been replaced with lead. He glanced across to see Maudie blinking slowly. She groaned.

"Maud, where are we?" he rasped.

A hand stroked back his hair. "Now, now, take it easy." It was the affectionate voice of Felicity Wiggety. "You're safe, back at Welby House."

"Gaia?" he groaned.

"Just you worry about yourself for the moment. Here, see if you can have a sip of water. Gan, help Maudie."

His lips were dry as the deserts of Nadvaaryn. The water cleared his mind, and he remembered the whistling sound, and feeling something hit his rear.

"What chime is it? Where's Harrie?"

"Hush now. I dare say she'll be in soon. I heard her return not long ago."

"How did we get back here?"

Felicity propped him up on more pillows. "Here, you'll need something sweet to get your strength back." She passed him a piece of buttered berry loaf. "Harriet and Hugo found you. Parthena led them to you."

Parthena, who was perched on the edge of the bed, gave Arthur a gentle nod.

"Thank you, girl."

Maudie swung her feet around. "But Gaia! We were so close, we have to . . ." Her voice faded.

"Steady now," said Felicity, hurrying over to her. "You twinnies need to learn when the off switch needs applying. I'm sure Harrie will—"

At that moment, the door opened and Harriet's face peered inside. "You're awake!" Her shoulders relaxed and she closed her eyes in a moment of relief. She entered the room, still covered in soot, followed by Hugo, who turned up the lights. She kissed Maudie and Arthur lightly on their heads, then sat on the end of Arthur's bed, and Hugo sat on a chair beside Maudie. Queenie followed Harriet and jumped on her lap. She exchanged a "Prwwt" with Parthena.

Harriet looked drawn and exhausted.

"Dr. Quirke checked you over and assured me you would be fine. Fortunately, they hit you with a very low dose."

"So they were clearly aiming for you, weren't they?" Felicity tutted.

"The earth-bear has been taken back to the Geographical Society square."

"Is she . . . is she . . . ?" The words choked him. It was as though if he said it, it would somehow make the thought real.

"I don't know," Harriet said sadly. "I couldn't get close enough. There are so many guards."

A great lump formed in his chest.

Hugo shifted uncomfortably. "We didn't know the Vanes were preparing a second sky-ship in the east. They suspected you would try something, so they followed you, and by the time we knew it was too late."

"I managed to speak to Madame Gainsford. There's going to be an emergency trial at eight chimes in the morning, if the bear survives the night."

It was all so terrible. Arthur's tears were only held back by blind fury at Eudora Vane. She was responsible for all of this. Again.

"It's not far past one chime. I suggest we all get

some sleep and prepare to defend the earth-bear at first light." Harriet stood and gave a resolute nod, then led the others out of the room, turning out the lights.

Although his body felt heavy, his thoughts raced. Nearly a chime passed, but he felt no closer to sleep.

Parthena looked across at him in the moonlight, and he smiled. "I do appreciate all you've done," he whispered. "You don't need to do any of this, to help our family and be so loyal, but you do it without question, without wanting anything in return." He stroked the soft white feathers of her head. "I guess that's the difference between you and most humans." Sighing, he looked to the moon and watched a pale cloud block it from view. The window was iced at the edges outside, and his breath misted the glass. It was such a strange contrast to the previous day, when heat and fire had raged. Something drifted past the window, and at first Arthur thought it was falling ash still, but when he opened the window and reached out, he felt the sweet sting of cold on his hand and realized it was snow.

"It's early for snow," said Maudie.

He glanced back. "Sorry, did the draft wake you?" It was just like old times when they'd shared a room and would often have whispered conversations in the night.

"It's almost as though the Wide is trying to cleanse Lontown." He watched as the snow became thicker, resting on the railings and pitch lamps below.

When he turned, he realized Maudie had dressed in her pants and put on her tool belt and jacket.

He didn't need to ask her intentions because he was having the same thoughts and was pulling on his own pants and jacket. They were going to be with Gaia, to make sure she was all right, and stay with her even if she wasn't.

Knowing every creaking spot to avoid on the stairs and the exact motion to make the front door close soundlessly, the twins left a note for Harriet and Felicity and stole into the night. Somewhere in the distance a clock struck five chimes, and they hurried, without need for words, arm in arm toward the Geographical Society square. The snowflakes fell steadily, an inch or so of white already coating the city. They trudged onward.

They slowed as they reached the edge of Sovereign Street, both scared of what they might find and of what the guards might do. But such was their need to see Gaia, whatever state she was in. They turned the corner.

The once-magnificent creature lay at the top of the white steps, with her chest to the floor, great limbs splayed, paws shackled by thick iron bands, her body restrained by chains with each loop as big as a hand. Her head lolled to the side, and an enormous metal muzzle bound her jaw. Rubble and debris had been pushed to the sides, and two guards were perched on fallen masonry. One was sleeping and one was monitoring the square. Both were clutching guns. The twins watched for a moment, then the awake guard yawned and took a quick look around. He nudged the sleeping guard, saying something before hurrying off down an alley. The sleeping guard let out a snore.

Without thinking, Arthur and Maudie ran toward the bear, their feet swooshing through the increasingly heavy snow.

They fell to their knees and flung their arms around her.

"Gaia! Oh, Gaia!"

Ice crusted her fur, and Arthur tried desperately to feel the rise of her chest, the exhale of her warm, earthy breath. Sobs heaved his chest as the hideous sadness of the scene gripped him like nothing before.

"How could they?" Maudie wept beside him.

Arthur dug his fingers into the soft pelt, feeling the weight of responsibility like a ton on his chest. "If we'd only stayed in Lontown, maybe she would have been safe."

And there they remained, two tiny figures entwined in the body of the greatest bear the Wide had ever seen, snow softly blanketing them as the moonlight lent the city its soft, sorrowful blue hue.

✧ ✲ ✧

"What are you doing here?"

Something hard jabbed Arthur in the ribs. Bleary-eyed, he looked up. Sunrise bloomed in the east and thick snow lay all around. His clothes creaked, stiff with ice, and the snowfall had lessened to occasional elegant crystals of white.

A miserable daze hung in Arthur's heart as he pushed away from the earth-bear, but as he did so, his fingers felt warmth; somewhere deep inside Gaia there was still life!

The guard yanked him to his feet.

"Maud, she's alive!" Arthur said, ecstatic, as another guard pried Maudie from the bear's body.

"Not for long," sneered the guard, her breath hot in Arthur's ear.

Arthur became aware that a crowd of people had gathered in the square, and chairs were being laid out on the cracked marble behind the bear.

Amid the hubbub of the crowd, a stern voice called out, "Unhand those children, you've caused quite enough harm!" It was Harriet.

Such was the force and intention in her words that the guards loosened their grip. She ran to the twins and pulled them close. "You're like icicles!"

She sat them on the steps at the edge, close to the main seats, as more members of Lontown society began filtering in and taking their positions: Madame Gainsford, the Blarthingtons, Evelyn Acquafreeda, Hilda Hilbury.

Felicity joined them with Hugo, Gan, and Batzorig, who all began fussing over the twins, throwing blankets around their shoulders and shoving warm flasks of hot liquid into their hands.

There was a collective look of ghostliness to the citizens of Lontown. Everyone seemed to be in a state of dishevelment, ragged at the edges and smudged with ash and dirt. The clock of the *Lontown Chronicle* chimed eight with a solemn knell. The tower still stood, but chunks were missing from the masonry and the bell at the top was visibly dented.

Eudora and Thaddeus Vane strolled in. They were both utterly pristine: Thaddeus in a pressed black suit, Eudora in a long, light-pink coat with fur-trimmed edges at the cuffs and ankles. Her hair was styled elaborately, pinned high on her head in loops with soft curls cascading over one shoulder. The venom Arthur felt toward her churned his stomach and made him clench his teeth.

Carinthius Catmole followed a short distance behind. His face looked pale and strained. Arthur hoped that Carinthius was now having doubts, that he was starting to see who Eudora really was.

Smethwyck dragged a chair close to the board for Eudora to sit in. Thaddeus was the tenth member to make up the board, so he joined them in the center. They sat in a semicircle of chairs around the bear, the crowd gathered silently in anticipation. Guards surrounded the scene, their guns trained on Gaia.

Madame Gainsford cleared her throat and pushed a stray strand of hair away from her forehead. Her sapient stoat companion was nowhere to be seen.

"It has been a night of extraordinary events in Lontown," she began, frowning. "One that none of us will forget for a long time." Her gaze drifted to the earth-bear. She half-sighed, then stiffened. "We find ourselves in an unthinkable situation. Yet here we are. The creature, this bear, unleashed havoc the likes of which we have never seen in Lontown before. Utter devastation of our homes and most beloved building! Fires in the streets! The very foundation of Lontown split, spilling the earth's flames."

Arthur opened his mouth to say something, anything, in defense of the earth-bear. Yes, the earth-bear had done that, but she wasn't the cause!

Harriet gently touched his arm. "Don't interrupt her," she whispered. "It won't help our case. Your moment will come soon enough. We have to tread carefully if we're to save the earth-bear now."

Arthur scanned the faces of the crowd. Harriet was right. The silence was strained, the mood baleful. Some remained in a state of shock, pale as mist; some looked confused, as though they'd stepped into a bad dream; and many clenched their fists angrily, their jaws tight, hungry for retribution.

"But we are a fair city, a civilized city, and we must uphold the values we were built upon even in the very grimmest of times," Madame Gainsford continued. "We will hear the cases *for* this sapient bear, and *against*. If we decide in the creature's favor, it will be taken back from whence it came, and if not . . . well, there are only two options, then. Confinement or . . ."

"Termination," finished Thaddeus, who sat to the right of her.

She threw him a glare.

"Madame, I am merely speaking the voice of the people!" Thaddeus huffed. "Everyone is thinking it. It's a miracle we didn't lose any lives as it is. The moment that thing wakes, *if* that thing wakes, none of us are safe. What further proof do you need than the events of yesterday? I can't believe we are even having this discussion!"

Miptera scurried underneath Eudora's collar.

"Thaddeus—Mr. Vane—I implore you to hold your tongue, by the order of the Explorer's Code, until such time as I may call on you." She was small but mightily fierce, and even though Arthur was unsure on which side her allegiance might fall, he felt glad that it was she who was at the helm and not Thaddeus.

"Maybe the board needs a new head," Thaddeus said, tersely.

"Then that would be decided in a separate democratic election," Madame Gainsford said firmly. "And until such a time, I will carry about my duties and *you* will carry out your role as one tenth of the board." She pulled the bottom edge of her ragged tweed jacket. "Do we have anyone at all who could speak in defense of the bear?"

CHAPTER 29

THE TRIAL

ARTHUR GLANCED AT Harriet, who gave him the nod. He stumbled to his feet, his muscles like rusted hinges from the cold. Maudie and Gan joined him. Side by side, they took a shaky step forward. All eyes were suddenly trained on them like arrows.

"Please, Madame Gainsford. We were in the Volcanic North when the earth-bear was taken," said Arthur.

"Ah, yes. Arthur Brightstorm, isn't it? You were on a heritage mission on the *Aurora* with Captain Culpepper." She glanced at Harriet. "Perhaps it would be better if she spoke."

Harriet stepped beside Arthur. "I was the captain of the expedition, but it was Arthur, Maudie, and Gan, Princess of Nadvaaryn, who spoke with the bear. I believe them perfectly capable and best positioned to defend it."

"Children!" scoffed Hilda Hilbury beside Thaddeus. Some in the crowd laughed.

"Yes, children. Who see things with clarity and sense, unlike many others," said Harriet calmly.

"I see no reason why they shouldn't be heard." Madame Gainsford nodded.

Arthur noticed Madame Gainsford's sapient stoat peering cagily from behind a fallen pillar. He could feel how torn Madame Gainsford was between the safety of the city and the sapients. If he could make her see, as the leader of the board, that it was Eudora who had caused this, then perhaps the board would swing in their favor. He became aware of other sapients in the shadows, observing the scene quietly from hiding places: Parthena on a rooftop in Sovereign Street, a squirrel peering out from atop a charred tree, a squirrel behind a broken table, the midnight-dark fox in an alley behind the crowd.

"The bear is not a threat," said Arthur.

Several members of the board and many in the crowd let out incredulous laughter.

"Let the boy speak," said Madame Gainsford, exasperated.

Arthur continued, feeling his voice grow in

strength. "The bear was terrified. That's why she behaved the way she did. She's a sapient with power unlike anything we've seen before. She called us to the North to protect her, and look how she was repaid! If you took the time to understand her rather than capture and mistreat her, you would see that she's good, kind, and more intelligent than . . ." Arthur took a breath—he felt desperate to explain, but his words were starting to spill angrily from his mouth.

"He's right," said Maudie, her shoulder brushing his. "The earth-bear is a super-sapient, like the thought-wolves of the South, but different. She has an ancient connection with the land and the power of the North. In her homeland, if left unthreatened, she is peaceful. She maintains the balance of the earth."

Arthur took over. "Imagine if you were hoisted violently from your homeland, taken to strange lands, and treated terribly! How would you feel?" He now noticed nods of acknowledgment in the crowd. Not many, but it showed that some were warming to their point.

Gan picked up the baton. "When creatures are threatened and afraid, they protect themselves in the best way they can. It's nature. Even humans do it."

"And the earth-bear has a name," said Arthur.

"Creatures shouldn't have names," spat Thaddeus.

Arthur ignored him as best he could. "It's Gaia. Not that Eudora Vane thought to ask when she ripped the earth-bear from her homeland to parade her around Lontown like some great prize!" He shot an accusing finger at her.

Eudora Vane's features remained soft, unfazed.

"Perhaps it's an apt moment to let Madame Vane speak." Madame Gainsford frowned.

As Eudora stood, a smile edged her lips. She was up to something, Arthur knew her too well.

"It seems the right moment to remind the board and to reveal to the citizens of Lontown the revelations made in the moments before this beast attempted to destroy our great city."

Arthur and Maudie exchanged a glance.

"I never wanted it to come to this. As many of you know, the Brightstorm twins are my niece and nephew by blood and . . ." She took a breath and put a hand on her heart. "It pains me more than you can know to tell you this. I've tried to accept them, to embrace them, even, but . . ."

Carinthius Catmole looked on, frowning in the crowd.

"I wish they had been like my sister, to have inherited Vane courage and honesty, but alas, they appear to have been corrupted by their father early on. The twins lied! The Brightstorms knew about this super-sapient for many years. They have been breaking the Explorer's Code by not reporting it to the Geographical Society."

"To protect it!" Arthur blurted.

Eudora shook her head in a patronizing manner. "To exploit it for their own means. The bear is a clear threat to Lontown. It should have been declared long ago so that we may have had at least a chance to contain it. Indeed, if they had made us aware of how dangerous it was, we would have never brought it to the heart of our city! We would have employed far greater security measures."

Behind her, Thaddeus Vane grinned silently.

"I suspected they were up to something when they set off for the North, and in my role as concerned aunt, knowing by instinct that something was up but without proof, I followed them. Seeing the danger they were in, despite their foolish choices, I had to save them and bring the bear back here as proof. I thought they had perished in the North, and I was devastated by it. We searched and searched, but they must have hidden from me, scared or embarrassed by the consequences. Meanwhile, none of us realized what this animal was capable of. If only we'd been told years ago." She looked to the floor and shook her head sadly.

"I can't believe anyone's buying this," Maudie said under her breath, but there were many nods of agreement coming from the crowd.

"It's all lies! Well, most of it," blurted Arthur. "She left us there on purpose! She planned this all along."

"And break the sacred Explorer's Code? I would rather die myself." Eudora took a step back in a display of indignation.

Arthur looked out at the people of Lontown. He remembered those stares when their father was accused of stealing fuel from another sky-ship in South Polaris: they carried the weight of a sentence, and it was guilty.

Eudora waited a moment for the glares to build weight on the Brightstorms. "We need to take more control over *all* the sapients, ensure they realize who is in charge, and install a clear system of hierarchy not only here in Lontown, but across the Great Wide."

The crowd murmured in agreement.

Arthur let out an exasperated gasp.

"But what if this earth-bear is as intelligent as the Brightstorms say?" asked Madame Gainsford.

"It is!" said Arthur. "You just haven't treated her in a way that would encourage her to trust you."

"She can talk in words, just like we do," said Maudie. "Eudora knows it's true!"

There appeared to be several from the group of Wolf-Listeners in the crowd, and they gasped in amazement and began talking among themselves.

Eudora gave a pitying laugh and shook her head sadly. She gestured with her pink gloved hand. "Do you see the extent of their delusions now?"

Unease stirred the crowd: some started to laugh at the idea of a talking bear; some frowned, utterly perplexed by the idea; some eyes were wide, perhaps open to the possibility. Arthur recognized the young woman from the markets, from the Wolf-Listeners. She was gesturing excitedly with the group around her. Perhaps there were more people in favor of the sapients than he'd realized? He looked to the board. Perhaps there was a chance.

"Order!" called Madame Gainsford, banging her gavel on a boulder close by.

The crowd eventually fell silent.

"Well, perhaps the board should deliberate and vote."

Eudora gave a little cough.

"You have more to add, Madame Vane?"

She smiled, and Thaddeus continued to glare at the twins with his baleful stare. "I'm afraid so. If the revelations about the secrets the Brightstorms kept in the North weren't enough, I'm sorry to say, I have more."

Arthur's stomach twisted in a tight knot. Surely she wasn't about to do what he thought? But of course she would use every card she had to get the result she wanted.

"When the Brightstorms were part of the armada searching for Ermitage Wrigglesworth in the reaches of the Eastern Isles, they found a new continent."

As one, the crowd gasped. Madame Gainsford looked at them in disbelief.

"An inhabited continent!" continued Eudora, raising her voice to a crescendo. "A state known as Erythea. You may ask what evidence I have. As you know, I lost my memory in an incident during that expedition. However, lately it has slowly returned, and the details have become clear. They thought they could hide the knowledge from the Geographical Society, from you good people, no doubt to steal resources for themselves! Yes, ladies and gentlemen of Lontown, the Brightstorms have broken the Explorer's Code in the most heinous of ways!"

The crowd burst with shouts of outrage.

Arthur and Maudie looked to each other, to Harriet and Felicity, the four of them feeling utter despair. It was hopeless. They would fail Gaia, and they would fail the Erytheans too.

Arthur felt dizzy. He looked to the sky, trying desperately to blink back the tears that were forming. His vision speckled with dots; was he going to faint? The speckles grew larger, hundreds of them, thousands, closing in.

Maudie grabbed his arm and pointed to the sky. "Are you seeing that too?"

The dots were forming in a great cloud, heading toward the square.

CHAPTER 30

THE MOTHS

THE SCENE ABOVE began catching the attention of the crowd below. At first, people assumed it was more bad weather sweeping in, and some took out umbrellas or put up their hoods. But as the cloud neared, it became clearer that it was no ordinary cloud.

Soon the sky was alive with fluttering wings.

"It can't be," Arthur said, squinting at the sight. "How could they come all this way?"

"Well, they don't need sky-ships," said Hugo, who had walked forward in amazement.

Hundreds of thousands of moths filled the space above.

"What is the meaning of this intrusion?" demanded Eudora.

"They're perfectly safe!" Arthur called, fearing the crowd might start to panic, but they looked more mesmerized by the spectacle.

One moth flew down, making a straight line for Arthur and Maudie. Maudie stretched out an arm and the moth landed on it. "Urania? What are you up to?" Maudie breathed.

Urania looked at her with her huge, black eyes, and her great feathery antennae quivered. She appeared to blink at Maudie, then her head tilted slightly toward Arthur and she did the same. The markings on her wings illuminated, rippling with orange and ruby, before she took flight and fluttered up and up to join the others. Tingles ran the length of Arthur's spine. He had no idea what was happening, but a spark seemed to have ignited in his flesh and every cell felt alive and connected to something . . . He just wasn't sure what yet.

The moths flew high above the square and began swirling and swooping together in what appeared to be coordinated patterns across the sky.

"Phenomenal! I've seen birds perform like this in

the east of Nadvaaryn but nothing like this," Harriet marveled.

"It's like they're dancing!" said Arthur.

"It's a sort of murmuration," replied Harriet.

"A moth murmuration!" said Felicity. "I swear I felt a tingling in my toes before they arrived, and no mistaking."

The moths continued swirling, turning, and twisting in the sky.

As they grew in numbers the patterns began changing.

"It's as though they're making a picture, a dancing picture!" said Arthur, because somehow the Brightstorm moths were working together to form an image.

The moth murmuration became great ocean waves, islands rising from beneath the water, trees growing and flowers blooming. But Arthur was transfixed by the moth dance because it was becoming something new.

"Are they . . ." Arthur couldn't believe he was about to say it. " . . . are they forming . . . a *sky-ship*?"

"I do believe they are," said Harriet.

The moths became a different moving picture. A sky-ship sailing over a great forest landscape.

"That looks like Dad's sky-ship, the *Violetta*!"

"And is that the *Victorious*, Eudora's old sky-ship?"

The images were a little tricky to make out, but the moths seemed to know how to create the right features to let the audience fill in the gaps, and their sheer numbers allowed them to forge details.

The moth sky-ship murmuration dissolved and then re-formed to become two figures.

Blinking, Arthur said, "Is that . . . is that . . . Eudora?" Chameleon-like, the moths were changing the colors of their wings to form Eudora Vane's signature shade of pink.

"What is the meaning of this?" Eudora shouted, futilely flapping her hands in the air.

"I do believe that's you," said Madame Gainsford, a growing suspicion in her voice.

Then the moths dispersed and re-formed once more. This time they became a huge bottle shape with a skull and two crossed bones.

"Poison!" said Arthur.

The moths re-formed into a pink figure walking toward the *Violetta*. Hushed conversations and gasps came from the crowd as they began working out what the moths were showing them.

"It's the frozen lake, and she's holding a bottle!"

"That's Madame Vane, and she's heading for the *Violetta*," people called from the crowd, who now seemed to be enjoying unraveling the puzzle above.

Then the moths seemed to zoom into the *Violetta*: a crew member eating a cake, then putting their hands to their neck and falling.

"They've died!" someone called.

"Poisoned!"

"By the hand of Madame Vane!"

Then, as though a gust of wind blew through the scene, the moths scattered, flying to land on the rooftops surrounding the square.

A moment of utter stillness followed where neither Arthur nor Maudie dared to breathe or move, as though the quiet would somehow help them to absorb what they'd just witnessed.

Could it be happening? The moths had re-created what had happened in the frozen South. How Eudora had killed Ernest Brightstorm's crew. Eudora had destroyed all evidence they'd had, so they'd never been able to reveal the truth, but now . . . was this the evidence they needed? Would people listen to them now?

Arthur had stopped believing that justice for their father's death would ever be possible. And now, the long-forgotten hope flared to life within him.

Maudie turned to Hugo. "Did you know the moths could do that?"

Hugo shook his head. "That I didn't know!"

"I suspect your mother's sapient moth, Urania, orchestrated it," said Harriet. "Sapients have been known to communicate with non-sapients and lead them into action. There's been some research on it published in the Geographical Society papers. Nothing on this scale or so sophisticated, but it would point to a reason for what we just witnessed."

"They can't tell the truth in words, but they can in images!" said Arthur.

"But how did Urania know? This happened long after our mother's death."

Parthena flew to land before Arthur and nodded her head in a bow. "You!" he breathed. "You told her!"

The entire square was looking at Eudora, who had turned a shade of pink darker than her outfit.

Arthur noticed Carinthius Catmole looking on from the sidelines, eyes wide. Perhaps at last he too was realizing who the real Eudora was, and how he had been taken in with the pretense of her memory loss.

"This is preposterous!" Eudora said, her voice losing its soft control and growing high and forced. She pointed a flapping hand at Maudie. "You all saw how the girl communicated with one of the moths before it flew!"

Rumpole Blarthington stood up behind her,

pointing an accusing finger through the flounces of his lace cuffs. "It's true, I saw her whispering, instructing it to fool you all."

"Now we truly see the extent to which the Brightstorms will go with their lies and trickery!" Eudora's face was returning to its usual composed mask. She'd found a way to discredit what everyone had just witnessed, and she was going to make sure they believed her.

Thaddeus stood and leaned on his cane. "Surely this is yet another example of the fact that the intentions of all sapients are in question. None of them are to be trusted! Who knows what plans they have to overthrow us?"

Like a turning tide, Arthur could see that the anti-sapient forces within the city were shifting the mood, and he became aware of a few people moving through the crowd distributing leaflets. One passed not far away, and he caught a flash of the HAC symbol on the back of a leaflet. The sapient animals in the square retreated farther into the shadows. A tussle broke out in one corner of the square between a boy in a wolf hat and one of the leaflet distributers.

Harriet shook her head and muttered, "Social control can always be managed by fear. The Human

Authority Collective knows that, and they're playing that card now."

People began shouting:

"Sapient lies!"

"The sapients want to take Lontown!"

"We should kill the lot of them!"

Eudora looked to her father, who gave a small nod. Things were going their way. "And yet another reason why the Brightstorms and their ally Harriet Culpepper need to be thrown out of the Geographical Society membership with immediate effect!" she shouted. She may have been able to contain her smile of glee, but Arthur could see it in the lights of her eyes. "And why this bear should be terminated once and for all!"

Arthur turned to Harriet. "What do we do?"

"I'll speak with the board. We need to stop this spectacle."

Just then, two figures in long green cloaks stepped forward from the increasingly agitated crowd, climbing the marble steps before the earth-bear and the board. The shorter of the two held a leather briefcase.

They unhitched their hoods in front of Madame Gainsford.

One of the figures had short, wavy, gray hair. She carried the Culpepper swallow tattoo on her inner wrist and the triangles of the Votary of Four, who had believed in the existence of a fourth continent, and a ring on her finger, the concealed symbol that she was an agent protecting the secret of Erythea.

"Octavie?" said Arthur. It was Harriet's great-aunt.

A small furry face peered from the bag across Octavie's shoulders. "Valiant!" Maudie cried. The small water-bear jumped out and skittered across to Maudie, jumping into her arms. "Oh, Valiant, you're all right! I've missed you," she whispered.

Beside Octavie Culpepper stood a young man with bottle-green eyes. He glanced over at them and flashed a wide smile.

"It's Florian!" Maudie called.

CHAPTER 31

AGENTS

MAUDIE HAD MET Florian in Erythea, when she'd been lost in the jungle and he'd helped the twins to overcome Eudora there. Her eyes lit up when she saw him and her heart leaped. It was like a nightmare turning into a brilliant dream.

"What are you doing here?" She hadn't realized how much she'd missed him, and seeing him now filled her with hope. She wanted to run over, but this wasn't the moment.

He smiled again, then he and Octavie began talking in hushed whispers with Madame Gainsford. Eudora Vane looked on, unsure what to make of the interruption.

"I think I know what they're up to," whispered Harriet. "They're revealing themselves and verifying the existence of Erythea."

"But why?" asked Arthur.

Maudie had an idea. Eudora had revealed the secret of the fourth continent, but she had failed to disclose how events had unfolded out there. She stroked Valiant, his fur feeling soft and familiar, like home.

Unable to contain herself, Eudora approached Madame Gainsford. "What's going on? More lies, I expect?"

"Perhaps it's a matter for the board to discuss," said Madame Gainsford tersely.

"And pull the wool over the eyes of the good people yet again?" Eudora said in a loud voice, playing to the crowd. "My father is right: it's time for a new leader of the board!"

Madame Gainsford heaved a long sigh. "Again, Eudora, that is for the board to decide, not you. But . . . perhaps this new matter should be addressed here, as you yourself have brought the issue onto the agenda." She indicated to Octavie and Florian to address the crowd.

"My name is Octavie Culpepper. Many of you have long known me, but what you don't know is that I am also closely linked to the continent of Erythea. Yes, it does exist, and some of us have known about it for many years. Do you see this ring? It has the fire-bird symbol of Erythea upon it, and I carry other documents proving my connection. This is Florian, a native-born citizen of Erythea, and he has an identical ring."

Florian nodded, and the crowd seemed frozen in stunned silence.

Octavie continued. "While in Erythea, Madame Vane learned of a rare pink jewel found in the crystal caves and collected by a species previously unknown to Lontown, the water-bear." She indicated toward Maudie and Valiant on her shoulder.

Valiant gave the crowd a little wave.

Several in the crowd gave a small "Aw" of delight.

Florian took over. "There used to be hundreds of water-bears, peace-loving creatures equally at home in the trees and the sea, who collected the jewels to illuminate their nests at night."

Maudie knew it must have been daunting, addressing such an enormous city crowd so far from the familiarity of his own city of Tempestra, but Florian didn't show it.

"But upon discovering their location, this woman," Florian pointed to Eudora, "slaughtered the water-bears, all for the jewels!"

The crowd gave a collective sound, a cross between "Urgh!" and "Oh!"

Eudora hastily tucked a pink jewel necklace strung around her neck into her jacket. Miptera scurried and hid under Eudora's fur collar.

Octavie raised her chin. She had a captivating and commanding aura, similar to Harriet, who looked on proudly. "This massacre, of which we can produce incontrovertible proof, is exactly why Erythea has had to protect itself, and was right to keep itself safe and secret from the likes of explorers such as Madame Vane. That woman is a monster, someone who has caused premeditated and remorseless harm and death to competitors and to creatures of the Wide. And all for what?"

The crowd were leaning in, hungry for more.

"For acclaim. For sovereigns. And because she has a particular penchant for *pink*." Octavie emphasized the last word.

Eudora laughed. "This is ridiculous! I don't have to stay and listen while my good name is sullied by these ludicrous claims. Erytheans living among us? No. They are liars and fantasists."

"But Madame Vane, you yourself have testified to the existence of this continent. And they say they are carrying documents and other proof," said Madame Gainsford, exasperated. "So, are you saying they knew about your claim and produced all these things fraudulently, in advance?"

Eudora's mouth opened to respond, but nothing came out.

Madame Gainsford turned to Octavie and Florian. "And you are prepared to give sworn statements to the board to show what Madame Vane did?" she asked.

Octavie and Florian both nodded, and Octavia lifted the briefcase she held.

"We have brought with us full documentation of her crimes in Erythea, assiduously compiled by our colleagues there."

"Then I declare this trial over. The board will deliberate and come to a decision on the validity of the claims and the actions to be taken. Thaddeus, under the circumstances, you should abstain."

"You will find no clause within the Code that makes a family connection void from a board vote," he said, narrowing his eyes. "Unless you want to petition for an amendment and delay the trial vote?"

She shook her head, clearly exhausted and exasperated. "I'm not waiting for an amendment to be passed . . . Very well. The full board will vote now. And for goodness sake, will someone check whether this bear is all right?"

Eudora slumped into a chair, fuming, while the board formed a group and began talking animatedly. She looked across at Carinthius, but he had turned away and was talking with someone else.

Arthur and Harriet rushed over to Gaia as she stirred gently, whispering that everything was going to be all right soon. Felicity came up behind them with her warm flask of milk.

Maudie dashed over to Florian. "I can't believe you're here!"

"Surprise," he said, smiling, his eyes twinkling like emeralds.

They formed a tight embrace, both wanting to hold on longer than they thought they should. Eventually they parted awkwardly, and Maudie looked to the floor, feeling a surprising burn in her cheeks.

"Thanks for doing what you did just then." She glanced up to see that he too was looking at the floor, a soft grin on his lips.

"It was nothing."

She shrugged. "Oh, just the small matter of revealing a secret that's been kept for many decades!"

"Times are changing," he said.

"Have you become an agent? Well, I guess that job is pretty redundant now."

"Not exactly. I've been allowed to travel here

to study engineering at your universitas, with the understanding that I will report back on how things are done. Harriet has helped me to do the applications, but I wanted to surprise you . . . and Arthur, of course."

"So, we'll be going together!" Maudie gasped and grabbed his forearms excitedly.

"Yes, I hope so."

Maudie caught sight of Arthur stroking the earth-bear, speaking gently to her, and her soaring spirits leveled a bit. "How do you think this is going to go?" She tilted her head in the direction of the board. They still needed to come to a conclusion, even as she dared hope that the odds would fall in their favor.

"I feel most people are with you and the sapients, so I think the board will be too."

Arthur approached them and gave Florian a hug. "Well, this is a surprise!"

"How's Gaia?" asked Maudie. "Is she going to be all right?"

"Dr. Quirke's tending to her now. She says she's not a vet, but she thinks that, with care, Gaia will be fine, once she gets back to the North."

They glanced at Eudora, who stood alone, her scowl deepening.

"She knows she's lost," said Arthur.

"The board could find in her favor," said Maudie. "You know how many of them she has in her pocket."

It was the sad truth. "But the people have seen and heard enough for themselves now. She's going to have a hard time coming back from that. Carinthius has distanced himself, and even Smethwyck appears to have gone missing."

The board reconvened in their places and the chattering crowd grew silent once more. Madame Gainsford took her position again at the center of the cracked marble steps. Her face was deadly serious and she drew a long breath in, a controlled breath out, and began speaking: "The board finds the moths' murmuration evidence inconclusive . . ."

Arthur's heart sank.

"We expected that," whispered Maudie.

" . . . but the board finds Madame Vane's crimes in Erythea corroborated."

Eudora Vane stood, her face a mixture of disbelief and fury. A couple of guards moved in behind her and many in the crowd gasped.

"As for the earth-bear and the Brightstorms' crimes against the Explorer's Code . . ."

Eudora's eyes widened in hope.

"The board found that their membership to the Geographical Society should be suspended—"

"What?" exclaimed Arthur, interrupting Madame Gainsford. "That's outrageous!" He felt anger welling up within himself. "Well, if kindness, empathy, and learning have no place in your Society, I don't want to be a part of it anyway!" His voice grew louder, and he couldn't stop the words spilling from his mouth. "If this is what it means, then I don't want to be an explorer!"

"Mr. Brightstorm!" said Madame Gainsford forcefully. It stopped Arthur in his tracks. He had never been called Mr. Brightstorm before; to him, that was his father's name.

"Mr. Brightstorm, if you would let me finish, I was about to say that the board found that your membership to the Geographical Society should be suspended *on a split vote*, five versus five, and in such situations, the leader of the Geographical Society carries the casting vote. As such, it is my decision that you should remain members."

The crowd erupted once more into excited discussion.

"Oh!" said Arthur, his heart leaping with glee . . . and a large dash of embarrassment at jumping the gun.

"The earth-bear is to be returned to its natural home in the North under the strict conditions that a neutral party of explorers be put together, by the board, and the board only, to reintroduce it to its remote island habitat." She glanced warningly at Arthur and Maudie. "And there will be a new post established near Hyrrholm so that we may keep a close eye on this super-sapient." She turned to Eudora. "Madame Vane, you, on the other hand, will return your membership stamp with immediate effect and are to be placed in custody where you can cause no further harm."

"What? You can't do this!" Eudora called. "Father? Do something!" She turned to Thaddeus.

"I have no daughter now," he said solemnly, and turned away.

"Carinthius?" Eudora called over to Carinthius Catmole, who had shrunk into the crowd and faced the other way.

"Hilda!" Eudora fell to her knees and tugged at the towering woman's cape. "We've long been allies!"

Hilda Hilbury pulled her cape from Eudora's hands and walked away.

Then Eudora began yelling, thumping the ground and pulling at her clothes in blind fury. Some in the crowd began laughing at her. Miptera scurried onto Eudora's shoulder and stroked her cheek.

Guards marched toward her and enclosed her from behind.

"Smethwyck!" she called, scouring the crowds for her so-called trusted friend, who was nowhere to be seen.

"I almost feel sorry for her," said Gan.

"We really don't," said Arthur and Maudie as one. Finally, at last the truth was out.

They looked at each other and nodded. They were free of her.

A commotion erupted and they looked back to see that Eudora had pulled out a gun from her sleeve and was pointing it at the approaching guards. "Stay back! I've done it before, and I *will* do it again!" She backed toward the edge of the stage. Miptera hovered above, clacking her mandibles.

"Eudora!" said Madame Gainsford. But Eudora shot at the sky, making everyone freeze and plunging the crowd into silence. She waved the gun in the direction of the twins. "I have nothing more to lose," she said coldly. Her mask of perfection had cracked like glass and the hatred in her eyes burned for all to see.

Instinctively, the twins lunged to protect each other as Eudora's finger tightened on the trigger.

With a whoosh of air and a cry of resolve, Parthena swooped in from nowhere and grasped the gun in her talons as the shot fired. A boom split the air and the bullet hit a fallen pillar beside them.

Eudora bolted behind the remains of the Geographical Society building, running through the fallen snow, hotly pursued by the guards.

Harriet hurried over to Arthur and Maudie. "Are you both OK?"

They nodded, still trembling.

"I guess she had one last thing up her sleeve, literally," said Felicity, rushing to check them over. "If there was any justice, that woman would be wiped from the face of the Wide forever."

"I dare say, for her, a social death is a far worse experience than losing her life," said Harriet.

"Do you think they'll catch her?" asked Maudie anxiously.

"I doubt she'll get far, and even if she made it out of the city, Eudora was never one to blend in and hide. She wouldn't last long out there." Harriet put a reassuring hand to both their shoulders.

Parthena dropped the gun in the snow and Madame Gainsford's stoat hurried over and passed it to her.

"I think we'd better get rid of that before any more harm is done!" Madame Gainsford said with a nod.

Arthur and Maudie crouched before Parthena. "Thank you."

Parthena bowed her head and Arthur realized that's what sapient birds were adept at: protecting, just like the fire-bird of Erythea.

Soon, calls came from a short distance away. "We've apprehended her!"

The twins exchanged a nod.

Harriet exhaled in relief. "You're safe now. Truly."

CHAPTER 32

ONCE UPON A CHIME

FELICITY CALLED TO Arthur and Maudie. "The earth-bear is waking up! Dr. Quirke says she's asking for you."

The twins hurried over.

"Oh, dear Gaia, we're so pleased you're all right!" said Arthur.

The bear was sitting up on her haunches now, observing the crowd that had gathered to marvel at her.

"And I you," she said, in her deep, layered tones.

"We promise you'll get home," said Maudie.

"Everything will be all right," said Arthur. "You won't be threatened again—not by guns, and not by mining."

They explained to Gaia about what had happened

in the trial and about their plans for organizing the paperwork to stop the mining, while Felicity massaged the earth-bear's great paws.

"Thank you, Brightstorms. The thought-wolves were right about you." Gaia turned to Felicity. "You have a talent for that," said Gaia, nodding her head at her paws.

"It's a gift." Felicity smiled, wiggling her toes. "Here, have another marsh cake," she said, tossing one from her pocket, which Gaia caught deftly and swallowed in one gulp. "I daresay, I could get my cousin Bernie to get you some fresh salmon from the rivers of Chesterford. He owes me a few favors."

"Perhaps you could eat fewer of the moths when you get back? They did come and save us, after all . . ." Arthur tried.

Gaia smiled. "Maybe. I can give berries a try, at least."

Arthur became aware that, close by, a young man and woman in wolf hats were in a heated discussion about whether they should now get bear hats, and whether calling their group the Wolf-Listeners and Bear-Orators was catchy enough. He smiled to himself. At least there seemed to be some people fiercely on their side, no matter how they expressed their allegiance.

Hugo approached. "I've submitted my request to be a part of the party to return you to Hyrrholm, Gaia. Madame Gainsford wants to return you as soon as possible. Perhaps as early as the morning."

"So this might be the last time we see you both, at least for a while," said Arthur, sadly.

Hugo put a hand on the twins' shoulders. "We know each other now. Distance needs not be as big a barrier as you think. And I *will* be back." Arthur noticed Hugo's eyes flit to Harriet, and he and Maudie exchanged a small grin.

"I wish we had more time with you too, Gaia," said Arthur. "I have so many questions about how sapients communicate. And the song . . ." He desperately wanted to ask about the eight mentioned in the words, but he was aware that prying ears were close by in the crowds.

Gaia's eyes, which seemed to contain the knowledge of all the Wide, observed him, and Arthur was certain she gave the slightest dip of her head in answer to the question he couldn't speak. "Everything has its moment, and the Firesong speaks truth. Our paths may yet cross again." She bowed her head and the twins did the same in return before officials appeared to take the earth-bear back to the docks.

After swift hugs goodbye, Arthur noticed Thaddeus Vane walking away from the square. He nudged Maudie. "With all the drama in Lontown, he probably doesn't know that we liberated the sapients at their facility," said Arthur.

The twins only needed to exchange the briefest of glances before they both strode over to him.

"Mr. Vane, may we have a word?" asked Arthur.

As always, Thaddeus Vane looked at them as though they were vermin.

Maudie narrowed her eyes and matched Thaddeus's disdain. "It's been quite the past few days for the Vanes. Did you hear the rumor about the release of the animals at your testing facility in the mountains?"

Thaddeus observed them with a pin-sharp glare. "Facility?"

"Of course, it's just hearsay because such a facility doesn't exist on the Lontown records, does it?" added Arthur, planting his hand on his hip.

Thaddeus leaned in, hands atop his cane so that his face was inches from Arthur's. "Why should I care? The facility doesn't belong to the Vanes, boy." He gave a malevolent smile and turned away, leaving Arthur and Maudie perplexed.

"Do you think he was lying?" asked Maudie as they watched him walk away.

"I don't know . . . Probably." Arthur frowned. He

was sure the look of truth *had* been in Thaddeus's eye. "But if he was telling the truth, who could possibly be running the facility?"

Harriet approached from where she had been speaking with Octavie and Florian a short distance away. "Is everything all right?"

"Thaddeus said the Vanes aren't responsible for the facility we liberated," said Arthur.

Harriet paused and drew a thoughtful breath. "The thing with monsters is that, even if you defeat one, there will always be another one waiting in the shadows. All we can do is keep fighting them."

It was something Arthur and Maudie would remember for the rest of their days. Some said monsters were the likes of the earth-bear and the thought-wolves, while others knew the truth: that real monsters often masqueraded as something harmless. But for now, at least, the stage in their life dominated by Eudora Vane was over.

"Come on, let's get out of this square," said Harriet.

"Where will we stay?"Arthur said, remembering they didn't actually have a house anymore.

"For now, at least, Madame Mills has already agreed about you staying at Welby House," said Harriet. "There are some spare rooms, and she is only too pleased to help. That's if it won't be too odd for you to stay at your former home; I know being there must have brought up many memories."

"Well, I suppose we qualify, at least; we are technically homeless orphans again . . ." Arthur frowned.

"Oh, dear me, no!" Harriet blurted. "I didn't mean on your own!" And for once her cheeks were rosy with embarrassment. "I'll be with you, and it's only temporary while we build a replacement for the *Aurora* at Archangel Street. We have Octavie's home as an option too, but I didn't want to overload her, so I thought Felicity and Florian could go there, and Batzorig and Gan will stay on the *Altan* until they head back to the Citadel. So, we have some time now to work out what your next steps might be after that. You have your grandparents in the North, after all, and Hugo . . ." Her sentence trailed off.

It was true, they did have grandparents now. But Arthur couldn't think about the future at that moment, so the thought of being back at Welby House for a moon cycle or two warmed him, and, looking across at Maudie as she nodded keenly, he knew she felt the same.

"That would be great," they both said.

"That's settled, then. Madame Mills will be pleased. She said the children can't wait to have some real-life explorers staying with them!"

After an expedition, returning to Lontown usually felt as though nothing had changed, like slipping back into huge, comfortable slippers, as Felicity would say. But this time, as the twins slowly walked with Harriet and Felicity back from the Geographical Society square to Welby House, through the ravaged, soot-stained streets of the city, everything was different. The skyline of Lontown wasn't the same without the Geographical Society's great dome, and they noticed more leaflets among the debris promoting the HAC. Graffiti on alley walls read "sapients are friends" crossed with "watch your back; sapients are coming." It felt like the city was more divided than ever. And coming back without the *Aurora* was like they'd lost a crew member as well as their home.

But a warm welcome awaited Arthur and Maudie at Welby House.

"Madame Mills said you stopped the bang bangs!" cried a boy of around three, hanging on to Madame Mills's apron when she opened the door.

"She said you're heroes," called an older boy.

They were barely in the hallway when a small girl grabbed Arthur's arm. "Tell us a story about your explorditions!"

"Our expeditions, you mean?" Arthur smiled. "Which would you like? Riding on the back of giant wolves, or the one where we escaped some particularly fearsome creatures who wanted to steal our memories?"

"Oooh!" the children all exclaimed. "Wolves!" "Fearsome creatures!" they called as they tugged Arthur and Maudie into the parlor.

"Or the one where your arm was ripped off by a giant crocodile!" called one child.

"Have you been up to your old stories again, Maud?" said Arthur, glancing across with a smile.

"That one wasn't from me, promise." She winked and linked her arm in his as they sat together on the sofa surrounded by tiny people.

"Gather round, then," Arthur said, as the children planted themselves around their feet and looked up at them with wide, keen eyes. He noticed Brea sitting among them, her little mouse's head sticking out of her petticoat pocket. He smiled at her.

"I suddenly feel rather old," whispered Maudie.

She was right. They'd been through so much in the past few years and had become young adults without having the time to realize it.

"Me too," he said. Squeezing her hand, he looked

at the eager faces before him. "Right, if you're sitting comfortably, then I'll begin."

"That's what Dad used to say!" Maudie said quietly.

Warmth filled Arthur. He leaned forward. "Once upon a time, there was a frozen forest that stretched for a hundred miles in all directions . . ."

CHAPTER 33

THE ALLIANCE OF EIGHT

A COUPLE OF DAYS LATER, Harriet called a meeting at Octavie's house with Arthur, Maudie, Batzorig, Gan, Felicity, Octavie, and Florian. The white-stone houses on Montague Street were symmetrical in their arched windows and pillars, but inside, Octavie's was a jumble of interesting oddments of machinery, old books, and tools. The group congregated in the study around the large oak table.

"The Geographical Society board is still split," said Harriet. "And I'm sure it comes as no surprise that those in the anti-sapient camp are heavily aligned with Thaddeus and what is now firmly established as an official organization, the HAC—the Human Authority Collective."

"Things are a-changing in the Wide," said Felicity. "I feel it in my toes."

"But we're not going to let it get us down," said Harriet. "My lawyer is also looking into the legalities of the pitch mines in the North. As you know, the earth-bear's call to Arthur and Maudie was a cry for help due to the destabilization of the area caused by aggressive pitch mining. The good news is that while there is some legal uncertainty due to the independent status of the islands, thanks to Arthur's astute reading we have invoked a petition of assumed guardianship over the domain for the city of Fellsandur. As such, all mining must stop immediately in the area."

"That's brilliant, Harrie," said Arthur.

"Rumors of other super-sapients are spreading," Harriet continued. "And as far as we can gather, the Geographical Society board will plan an expedition and a meeting with the leaders of Erythea as soon as possible."

Octavie narrowed her eyes. "We'll have to keep an eye on who is chosen to go."

"Indeed," Harriet agreed. "And there's one other thing: Arthur has a theory."

All eyes fell on him. "It's to do with the super-sapients and the Firesong," he said. "When Gaia, the earth-bear, sang the complete song, I noticed that the first verse and the last mirrored each other, except in the last it mentions the 'eight.' It's been bothering me for a while, and I didn't have a chance to ask Gaia, but I think it might mean there are eight super-sapients in the Wide."

Octavie nodded thoughtfully. "That could make sense."

Arthur leaned forward. "We know the thought-wolves and the earth-bear can communicate telepathically, so it's likely that the earth-bear would know about the existence of other super-sapients. She as much hinted that to me. We know of the thought-wolves, the fire-bird, the darkwhispers, and now the earth-bear. That means there are possibly four more out there somewhere."

"A creature that speaks through thought? There is a myth that such a creature exists in Nadvaaryn!" said Gan. "All children know the story of the serpent of the sands."

"There is no evidence that it is based in fact," warned Batzorig.

"A sand serpent, wow! I wonder what the others might be, and where they'll be," Maudie mused.

Arthur frowned. "The difficulty is that, if we're wondering about more beings like this, you can bet the HAC is too."

"I have a proposal, something I mentioned to Hugo before he left for the North with the earth-bear," said Harriet. "We form a counter-group to the HAC."

"Like that cult of wolf-listeners?" asked Felicity. "Bit of a weird bunch, if you ask me. I've been accosted by them several times at the market."

"Sort of, but something more serious. An organization that will be kept secret to combat the movement that's targeting sapients."

"That's an excellent idea, Harrie," said Arthur. "What should we call ourselves?"

"Well, I was thinking, with your theory of eight super-sapients, perhaps we should call ourselves the Alliance of Eight?"

"It'd certainly make a secret symbol easy," said Maudie, drawing an eight in the air with her finger.

"It's also like an infinity loop. Clever," said Florian, who sat on Maudie's other side.

Arthur noticed Maudie blush a little, and he looked at her suspiciously.

"What?" she whispered.

He gave a little shrug.

"Then I declare this to be the first meeting of the Alliance of Eight," said Harriet. "Perhaps we can talk about roles and what's next."

"Ooh, can we all get tattoos?" asked Gan.

"No," Batzorig said swiftly, and everyone laughed.

Arthur couldn't help but smile at how he had judged Gan when she'd arrived, but how now he thought that she suited being so brilliantly un-princesslike. And who was he to judge what made a princess anyway? If it was bravery, guts, and standing by your friends, she had it in spades.

The doorbell rang.

"I'll go," said Octavie.

Muffled voices were heard in the hallway, then the door creaked open. Evelyn Acquafreeda and a young girl and boy around Gan's age entered the room. They were all dressed in shades of aqua blue—Evelyn in the iridescent coat she often wore, which shimmered like waves.

"I am just beside myself about this vile HAC group that Vane, Rumpole, and Hilbury are so entwined in!" Evelyn exclaimed, eyes wide with indignation. "Ondine here suggested I find like-minded friends to vent my frustrations with, and well, I hope you don't mind too terribly."

Harriet laughed heartily. "Evelyn, as always, you are a step ahead. Do sit down. If you can believe it, we are forming our own counter-group right at this very moment! And you're welcome to join us too, Ondine. And . . . ?"

"This is my grandson," said Evelyn.

"I'm Loch," said the boy, looking a little wary.

Arthur thought it must be intimidating to join a group like this when you didn't know anyone, so he smiled and offered his hand in introduction.

"I know they're young, but you can trust my family implicitly," Evelyn said, sitting down and rubbing her hands together in anticipation.

"Age has never been an issue within our walls." Harriet smiled. "They are, after all, the future."

Arthur couldn't help but glance around and smile at the range of generations in the room.

"I know the Joneses will be keen to join too," added Evelyn.

Harriet gave a nod. She had that twinkle in her eye that the twins had noticed the first time they'd met her. "Welcome to the Alliance of Eight."

At the end of the meeting, Batzorig and Gan announced they were heading back to Nadvaaryn in the morning, catching a lift on a trade sky-ship.

After everyone else had said their goodbyes, Arthur and Maudie were the last in Octavie's hallway with Batzorig and Gan. Batzorig put a hand to both the twins' cheeks as he had done back in the Citadel when they'd first met. "Ah, I think you are both exactly where you need to be." His eyes met Arthur's. "At last." He smiled.

"If you ever want to learn to shoot arrows properly and ride bareback across the desert . . ." said Gan, putting on her leather hat and goggles and straightening her quiver.

"That would be great," said Arthur.

"I was going to say, you'd better ask Batzorig or Temur because I'll be off adventuring somewhere!"

He nudged her and she thumped his arm playfully.

"Not until you've completed your royal duties," said Batzorig with a smile. He looked to Arthur and Maudie. "And she thinks I'm joking. Poor Temur will need a break when we're back!"

"It's been good to have another girl around," said Maudie, giving Gan a hug, then tucking a pair of her sticky gloves into Gan's quiver. "A parting gift."

On the way back to Welby House, Harriet asked if they might go back via Archangel Street to check if some timber materials she'd ordered had arrived. When they got there, there was no wood delivery yet, but the three of them sat for a while in the large space where the *Aurora* would have converted back into Number Four.

"I realize you may still decide to head north to

make a home with your Brightstorm grandparents," said Harriet. "And whatever you decide, you know I'm always here for you and behind you one hundred percent."

They nodded.

"There was one other piece of business I set in motion before we left for the North. My lawyer completed the paperwork and, well, here it is."

She took an envelope from her pocket. "I think of you both as my own blood. It's strange, but sometimes I feel as much a Brightstorm as a Culpepper! So, these are adoption papers, in case you might feel the same as me and want to make things feel more official and permanent at number four Archangel Street. When we've rebuilt it, of course. This piece of paper says that I'm approved to adopt you, and we can make our family official. But only if you want to, and with no pressure at all, because you have a home with me no matter what, and let's face it, you're almost grown adults anyway!"

"I don't know what to say," said Maudie.

"Why don't you both take your time to think about it." Harriet's expression was momentarily vulnerable, not something the twins were used to seeing. "Ah, there's the cart with my wood delivery; I'll go and sort it out."

Arthur and Maudie looked at each other as Harriet walked away.

"It feels right, doesn't it?" said Arthur. "Making our family official."

And with Harriet, who for some reason had taken a chance on them when their world had fallen apart and they'd had nothing. It would still be possible to visit their Brightstorm grandparents now, and they could write frequently.

But they knew that home was right here, in this moment, with Harriet.

Maudie nodded. "Let's go and tell her straight away."

CHAPTER 34

NEW BEGINNINGS

THE ALLIANCE OF EIGHT were focusing on their collective and individual missions. Hugo was keeping an eye on the earth-bear and the guards stationed on Hyrrholm, while ensuring that the pitch mines were closed down in the North. Octavie was getting word to Erythea that an envoy mission was heading their way and that they needed to make preparations to protect the fire-bird and the darkwhispers, just in case. Gan was investigating the rumors of the sand serpent super-sapient on her continent. The Acqua-freedas were charged with exploring the possibility of sea super-sapients. The Joneses were keeping an eye on the mountain facility. Harriet, Maudie, and Florian had been busy engineering and building the new *Aurora*. And Arthur? Well, Arthur had never felt more certain of his purpose and direction in life. It was clear to him that with the earth-bear having been captured, and the likes of Thaddeus and the HAC at large, there was a risk of the thought-wolves being the next target, so he'd begun planning their next expedition back to the Ice Continent. They would visit the thought-wolves to try to keep them safe and find out if there were clues to other super-sapients that might need protection.

It was now several moon cycles since they had returned from the Volcanic North, and Harriet, Arthur, Maudie, and Felicity were back on Archangel Street in the new house that contained the now public secret that it could convert into a sky-ship. Arthur and Maudie sat at the kitchen table, Arthur poring over maps and Maudie sketching a design for solar cobbles, which was an idea she and Florian were working on together.

"I'm pleased for you, Arty. You know what your place in the Wide finally is, beyond following in Dad's footsteps and being a sky-ship explorer."

Arthur smiled. No one knew him like Maudie. He could feel his place in the Wide with absolute certainty—to protect sapients, to educate Lontonians about their plight, and to fight the growing trend for the control and use of these creatures.

"I'm going to write books and document the wonders of the Wide so that it can be understood and protected, rather than controlled and feared."

She glanced up, smiling. "And you're going to do it brilliantly."

"I can't wait to see Tuyok again, Maud. Imagine what it'll feel like to ride through the Everlasting Forest on the back of a thought-wolf again!" But the picture he had in his mind was still of himself on pure white Tuyok and Maudie riding midnight black Slartok side by side, weaving through great pines heavy with snow. He still felt the prospect of their separation like a rip in the fabric of his heart, especially as that day was drawing ever closer, even though they had both made peace with it.

Maudie stood up abruptly and left the room, mumbling that she was going to do something to the boiler.

"What's that you're writing?" asked Harriet.

"A couple of things. I'm trying to work out a map from memory of the Everlasting Forest, and I thought I'd start a field guide of the Wide for the children of Welby House."

She squeezed his shoulder. "That's a lovely idea."

After studying Arthur's face for a moment, Harriet gave a nod to herself. "I think you're ready."

"Ready?"

"I've always thought that you have to live by your principles and be the change you wish to see in the Wide. Lead from the front and others will follow, and all that. So, it seems fitting that the maiden voyage of *Aurora II* should have a new captain."

Dropping his pencil, Arthur gaped.

"Yes, Arthur, I want you to captain the next expedition."

It was unbelievable, the last thing he'd expected. And the other surprising thing was that he felt ready for the challenge. "Wow, are you sure?"

"There's only one thing you need to promise."

"Anything!"

"That I can be your second-in-command."

✵　✵　✵

The day of the expedition arrived. Arthur and Maudie had both seemed to be avoiding each other over the past half a moon cycle. Felicity said they both had their defense mechanisms up for the looming change in their lives.

Florian had been granted his engineering scholarship at the universitas too, and Octavie was only too pleased to have them both stay while number four Archangel Street was away being a sky-ship.

The largest crowd ever gathered on Archangel Street for the inaugural launch of the *Aurora II*. Maudie had stayed until the last minute to help prepare the sky-ship, and with the transformation imminent, the last of Maudie's bags were packed and ready. She stood with Arthur by the front door, the excited chatter of the crowd muffled beyond.

"I suppose this is it, then," she said.

"I suppose it is."

"Take care out there, Arthur, and write lots, won't you?"

"Yeah, you take care with all that engineering equipment."

"I might not stay to watch the takeoff, because, well, you know."

Arthur wanted to say he did know why, because nothing had ever hurt this bad in his life and saying goodbye was ripping his heart from his chest.

They had a brisk hug and then Maudie turned, opened the door, and walked down the steps toward the crowd. Arthur quickly shut the door.

He stood there for a moment, staring, listening to the echo of the shut door, somehow louder than the crowd beyond, marking the end of something. He moved to turn away, then grabbed the handle and ran out toward Maudie, who was at the bottom of the path looking back.

"Wait! Your ribbon!" Tears rolled down his cheek. They drew stares from the crowd but he didn't care.

"I haven't worn it in ages," she sobbed.

He took it from his pocket. Together, they tied it in her hair.

"There."

They hugged again, this time so tightly that they felt as one.

"There's a new iron arm under your pillow. I know you don't need it but I fitted it with some cool gadgets for fun and there are some snacks and bits like that in

it and a thermo-heater blanket in case you fall in any ice lakes and stuff."

"That sounds brilliant. Thank you. I left a notebook you might like in your bag—it's called *How Maudie Brightstorm Invented the Sky-ak.*"

"Ha! That's brilliant, thank you."

"I've documented everything, and you can fill in the gaps and then perhaps get it published for real."

"That's really thoughtful. Thanks, Arty."

They smiled at each other and nodded, then began walking away.

After a few steps, Arthur called back to her.

"Hey, Maud. Remember when Batzorig called us siblings of the sun and moon when we first met him."

She nodded. "Yes, I do."

"I was thinking, even though we're going to be at opposite ends of the Wide, we're part of the same sky, and all we need do is look up at the stars at night or watch the sun rise and we'll be together."

"That's a nice thought," she said, eyes glistening. "Aren't we lucky to have each other to miss?"

His smile lit up Lontown. "Yes . . . we really are."

Inside, Harriet was waiting. "It's time to start the

transformation process." She smiled, but her eyes were asking if he was all right.

He nodded softly.

"You've been inseparable your whole lives, apart from the odd mishap, but every decision, every trial in your lives so far has been the two of you."

"I still don't want to go without her."

Putting a hand on his shoulder, Harriet said, "I know . . . I found it hard enough to say goodbye to her, but you *will* go without her because deep down you both know that although your lives might lead you in different directions, you are always in each other's hearts, no matter how far apart you are."

And as always, Harriet Culpepper spoke truth and reason. Because even now, although they weren't together, he could feel Maudie as though she was a part of him.

The roof began lifting backward. A thick beam of daylight illuminated the floorboards, which would soon become the deck, and as the roof folded in a huge accordion behind them, Arthur and the crew were bathed in warm sun. Balustrades took the place of the walls, and a panel slid back in the center of the floor. The great fabric balloon started to emerge.

Arthur released a lever and the huge steering

wheel rolled from beneath the deck into view. He clasped it.

The ground rumbled and the crowd gasped as the front of the building folded inward, great pistons and cogs whirring and crunching until the edges of the house and the door disappeared inside. Shutters opened beside the windows and propellers spiraled from the house, unfolding and turning.

They began lifting into the air as the final mechanisms slotted into place.

"Everyone to the cogs!" called Arthur. "Let's get the wings wide!"

The *Aurora II* was now above the houses, leaving the cheers of the people behind.

"Let Queenie take the wheel for a moment," called Harriet as the wings clunked into place. "Come and see the crowds."

Far below, the people waved and marveled as the sky-ship left Archangel Street behind, but two small dots, a young woman and a young man, ran through the streets beneath them, waving and waving, a small water-bear clinging to the young woman's neck.

"Fly safely!" called Florian.

"Give my love to the thought-wolves!" shouted Maudie.

Arthur was sure he saw the midnight fox running

somewhere behind them too, but it was getting hard to see as they rose higher.

"I will!" he called.

The string in his heart pulled, made of something pure that defied all description and explanation because his heart wasn't just the pumping organ made of cells in his chest; it was made of happiness and anguish, joy and despair, and most of all love. And now it hurt so badly that he feared it would crack like brittle glass if he dared take a breath. It was a pain he'd not experienced since losing his father, since losing Welby, but it was a different hurt, because it was a necessary part of growing up. Change couldn't be stopped. All he could do was make memories worth sharing and trust that he and Maudie would always find their way back to each other.

The rest of the crew joined Arthur at the side and waved back: Gilly, Meriwether, Barnes, Forbes, Cranken, Forsythe, Keene, Wordle, Hurley, Dr. Quirke, and, of course, Felicity, who waved her lucky spoon vigorously.

Then Harriet put a hand on his shoulder and Felicity took his hand. Arthur knew it was more than a reassuring hold. He glanced across to see Harriet's eyes shimmering and a tear rolling down Felicity's cheek.

Queenie meowed loudly from the steering wheel. Parthena gave a loud squawk from above.

"Oh, yikes, the new dome of the Geographical Society is going up and they've made it taller than ever!" said Arthur, rushing over to the wheel. He stroked Queenie's chin and thanked her, then grasped the wheel, feeling the rhythm of the *Aurora II* so that they felt as one, the breeze like silk against his skin. He banked right so that they would fly directly above the great dome, as was tradition at the start of all expeditions. Higher they rose until people became minuscule specks and Lontown a child's play set.

"Right—I'd say we deserve a nice cup of tea," called Felicity.

Harriet joined Arthur's side. "Here." She placed a new pair of flying goggles over his head. "Ready, Captain?"

"Someone once told me that titles have no place here. It's the strength of our ideas that will give us authority, not a title we bear." Arthur smiled.

Harriet shook her head. "Wow, I can't believe you remembered that from the first expedition! I guess you really are ready."

Arthur looked to the horizon. "Me? I'm a Brightstorm. I was born ready."

CARINTHIUS CATMOLE STOOD before the silver-framed mirror in his office tying his ink-blue tie. He ran a comb through his hair, then buttoned his impeccably tailored jacket. One thing he'd had in common with Eudora was an appreciation of fine tailoring. Unlike her, he preferred a narrow range of styles and nothing too flamboyant, favoring his double-breasted jacket and thin trousers. The purpose was twofold in that he could blend into the background when he wanted, but it also made his face the focal point. Glacial blue eyes and defined cheekbones made it easy for him to exude an air of stillness and control; his mother had told him at a young age that he had the potential to command a room without lifting a finger.

The events of the past moon cycles had certainly been interesting. He'd never really liked Eudora Vane that much. She'd been useful, for a while, but their time together had run its natural course and, with her name disgraced, Thaddeus would be easy to manage. He still marveled that she'd actually believed he might take the Vane name over Catmole. He smiled and shook his head.

He detested the way she was so attached to that disgusting sapient insect—the times he'd been tempted to squash it when she wasn't looking! The Brightstorms seemed convinced of his love for her, but did they really think he would have agreed to marry Eudora if he hadn't known that she had a secret that could lead to great power? She practically begged to tell him all the details of Erythea when he'd visited her in the hospital, and then she shared Ernest Brightstorm's letter about the secret in the North so readily and begged him to let her use his sky-ship. He'd agreed, as long as she let him carry on his important work and didn't involve him in the details of the expedition.

Carinthius understood the benefit of staying in the shadows; it was where the real power lay, not on show or on the front page of the *Lontown Chronicle*.

It was true: he couldn't abide expeditions, all the extremes away from Lontown comforts. He'd been dragged along as a boy, but even his parents could see that his talents lay elsewhere.

He'd planned to keep the earth-bear for himself at his mountain facility (to think of the tests he could have carried out!), but Eudora had insisted on taking it to Lontown. But then he'd realized it was an easy way to dispose of her; she didn't understand the true power the earth-bear had. She was too focused on bringing the Brightstorms down.

So, it was all too easy to ensure that the sedative doses he gave Eudora's crew to use were weak enough that the earth-bear would wake and cause chaos in Lontown. It had gone even better than he'd hoped: the Geographical Society collapse, the lava river. It had all been so useful in sowing fear and doubt into the heart of Lontown. And he would get the earth-bear back. All in good time.

Carefully, he pinned the emblem of the HAC on his lapel, the silver-winged man, a symbol of human identity and pride, but most of all, their power over all living things. He would only wear it at meetings; it was best to remain neutral in the public eye.

The Brightstorms had certainly been impressive: escaping Hyrrholm, their liberation stunt at his facility, saving the earth-bear in Lontown. It was perhaps their fire for what they believed in that he admired the most. It was a shame their allegiances were misplaced. He'd always respected Harriet

Culpepper too. He looked forward to converting them all to the new way soon, but the game along the way would be just as satisfying.

He grasped the handle and pushed open the door to the meeting room at the headquarters of the HAC.

"Good afternoon, my friends and colleagues. Welcome to the beginning."

AUTHOR'S NOTE

The world of Arthur and Maudie Brightstorm is one that may feel reminiscent of an alternative history, or that of a parallel world hidden within reach, or perhaps belonging to a galaxy some distance away. Wherever it exists, it has always been a place where emerging technology, the varied reasons for exploration, and anthropocentrism are important shaping forces, just as they are in our world today. It's my hope that readers take some time to think about how these themes are present everywhere around them, and what our responsibilities might be for each other, Earth, and its future. On another level, the series also wrestles with the question of what truly makes family, and I hope readers may have found answers for themselves in these pages.

Like the previous Brightstorm books, *Firesong* is set in the Wide, this time exploring the northern reaches, a place steeped in historical significance, myth and perhaps most importantly, truth. So while a map can show a place's geography and depict its features and contours, it takes a story to reveal the true nature of a place. And every location has its story—many stories, in fact. While *Firesong* may be the conclusion of the Brightstorm Trilogy and the twins' battle with Eudora Vane, by reaching the end you will now know there are more trials and adventures on the horizon for others within this world, and that within every end, there is a beginning . . .

ACKNOWLEDGMENTS

As ever, very special thanks to both Kate Shaw, my agent, and Linas Alsenas, UK and lead editor for the series. Both embraced the Brightstorm world from the beginning and have been pivotal in the trilogy's evolution. Eagle-eyed, inexhaustibly enthusiastic, supportive, and creatively sharp, they really are my own Harriet Culpeppers. Further extra special thanks to Kristin Allard, my North American editor, for embracing the crew as her first acquisition and for her wonderful support, creative input, and exemplary editorial eye, which always elevates the story to more than I could hope.

I'd like to thank Jamie Gregory, design manager at Scholastic UK, for his wondrous UK cover vision which oozes adventure, and George Ermos for illustrating the covers so wonderfully and making me want to dive into the image, and for his beautiful internal illustrations for North America. For the North American edition, huge thanks to Hana Nakamura, art director at Norton Young Readers, for all her amazing work and to Vivienne To for her extraordinarily beautiful, adventure-filled covers, which bring the sapient creatures—the beating heart of the Brightstorm world—front and center.

Extended thanks to the many departments who work on and support the books within my publishers near and far: copyediting, publicity, marketing, sales, and beyond, with a special mention to Sarah Dutton and Harriet Dunlea. I am incredibly fortunate that the series has been embraced around the globe by numerous publishers from France to China, and I would like to thank the foreign rights team in the UK and send my huge appreciation to my editors from afar and the translators who do such an incredible job.

For the audiobooks, it takes a special talent to bring the stories to life in such a captivating way. Special thanks to Samuel Roukin for Recorded Books and Ryan Ireland for Bolinda, whose talents blow me away!

Continued thanks to the many educators, librarians, booksellers, bloggers, and general reading enthusiasts who champion my stories. Teachers and booksellers have formed the bedrock of my crew and it's their enthusiasm and love for the story that has allowed it to flourish and reach so many readers, for which I am forever grateful.

And lastly, principally, to my loyal young readers. Having you on board really is the greatest privilege of all. When you need an adventure, or when things get tough, know that there is always a space and a home for you with the Brightstorm crew.